BLOODSTONE
Legend of the Last Engraving

.....blood shall stop flowing...
went the prophecy.
'It is only in the dead, Kuntal,
that blood stops flowing!' Bhairavi said.

An ancient, buried copper engraving is unearthed while tilling a virgin land by the ruins of a palace, threatening to alter prehistoric beliefs among both god and man.

Weaving through centuries in time and vastness in space, and embracing both the divine and the mortal, this is the tale of that copper engraving which the ill-fated, ill-begotten Princess Ambaa of Nepal etches as she mourns the death of her only friend Dakshyayani. It is this engraving, of Dakshyayani's yoni, that is destined to create havoc on earth and in heaven alike, but only if it is borne to where it belongs, by a virgin born out of humble seed in a fresh, hitherto unused and unstained womb and born a female..... neither a bastard nor born out of incest, nor conceived by divine, extraordinary or non-humanly simulated insemination, unscathed of skin and nail, undiseased of the mortal body, pure of soul, and black of hair and eyes....

Centuries later, would the dominated, silenced and barren Bhairavi eventually give birth and find her voice to raise it to confront even the Mother Goddess Durga? Will the Goddess at Kamakhya yield to her?

BLOODSTONE

Legend of the Last Engraving

RASHMI NARZARY

Published by Rashmi Narzary
Guwahati
Assam
India
E-mail: rashmi06narzary@gmail.com

Photo by: Jairaj Narzary

BLOODSTONE
Legend of the Last Engraving
First Published in 2021

ISBN 978-93-5457-571-6

Typeset and Design:
Bhaskar J Lahkar
E-mail: bhaskarlahkar@gmail.com

Be they truth, be they tale

Lores of the ancient past,

Never cease to bewilder...

Contents

PROLOGUE

The legend of the very ancient, 8th century temple of Kamakhya is one such lore. It is said that Dakshyayani renounced herself during the yagna at her father King Dakshya's place because he humiliated Shiva, calling him an untamed ascetic unfit and unworthy of being his son-in-law. Shattered with anguish and anger at the loss, Shiva carried the body of his beloved and wandered amok in grief and wrath, across mountain, forest, ocean and desert, refusing to let go of Dakshyayani's body. It was then that Vishnu began to disintegrate Dakshyayani's lifeless body with his disc, the Chakra, to end Shiva's ordeal. And as Vishnu's chakra went on disintegrating the body, the pieces kept falling all over the earth wherever Shiva went. And wherever the pieces fell, there arose a shrine. A Shakti Peeth. With time, one among the many forms of the Mother Goddess came to be worshipped in those shrines. So it was upon this spot on the Nilachal hills in Kamarupa that Dakshyayani's chopped off genital fell and the shrine of Kamakhya rose thereon as a Shakti Peeth. And yet, Kamakhya's mystique lay in the fact that no idol or form of the Mother Goddess is worshipped there even to this day. Instead, what is worshipped is what fell here of Dakshyayani's body, now turned to stone over hundreds of years.

The lore also goes that of the four chambers of this ancient temple dedicated to the Hindu goddess Durga, it is in the innermost, underground chamber referred to as the 'garbhagriha' that the entire mystic of ancient beliefs, tantric faith and powers of fertility unfold, in the stone fissure that is shaped like a vulva. This vulva, legends say, is that of Shiva's consort Dakshyayani, now turned into stone over the centuries. It is this stone yoni that is the centre of reverence at the sanctum sanctorum of the Kamakhya shrine. It is this stone yoni that bleeds once every year during the Hindu month of *Aashaar* which more or less coincides with the month of June, during the monsoons in Assam. And it is this menstruation of the goddess that the pious from across the globe celebrate as the three-day ambubasi fair, atop the Nilachal hills.

It is this **BLOODSTONE** that is celebrated.

But what if the Bloodstone someday ceases to bleed? Will the Kamakhya cease to be the legend bearer that it is? Will the ambubasi too cease to be the fair, the mela, that it is?

Only **BLOODSTONE** will tell.

CHAPTER 1

COPPER

It was a land never tilled.

Because it was a land rarely forayed into, except maybe by the occasional goatherd. And yet, that occasional goatherd who strayed into that clearing among the woods swore by the lush growth of wild bush, brambles and nettles there and the dark soil beneath, that it was a soil waiting to yield. And yet, it was a land never tilled.

Tucked into the mountainous forests, this clearing lay some distance away from the little hamlet of Tilibham in remote, rural Nepal, a hamlet of the Newar people. Land higher than this clearing upon the rugged slopes of the mountains was made into wide steps to grow corn and millet, on land lower in the valley they grew rice. But between these two lands, this clearing among the woods was left virgin, though the sun bathed the soil and the wind breathed through it, and though the monsoon rains soaked it and readied it like the womb. Dense, dark, woods stretched far from there, sheltering large noisy troops of small, swift, mountain monkeys and birds during the day. After nightfall, there were sounds of the forest, of boughs rubbing against one another, of cicadas in the shrubs and crawling insects rustling upon crisp, brown, fallen leaves upon the ground. While the nearest human and cattle retired early into huts and sheds in Tilibham.

Such was this clearing.

So standing in the middle of this clearing during the day, that occasional goatherd who strayed into that patch of land was also left in awe of the ancient, crumbling, stone walls upon the adjacent slope, by the little trickle of a mountain stream. Those were walls which stood majestic and alive with royals living within them upon a time when the Gods roamed the earth. But now these had fallen and lay in gloom and ruins. After dark, bats emerged from the crevices of the roof that had long caved in and rats scampered upon the debris on the floor, sometimes letting out piercing squeaks through the silence of the ruins. Ruins, through which once echoed beautiful music. Ruins, through which once also floated the laughter of young girls and the tinker of their ankle bells as they ran about those chambers which now lay dead for centuries. Skilfully and painstakingly sculpted pillars, large of girth, lay fallen on one another if not buried under more fallen wall. This, the villagers of Tilibham said, was the palace of princess Ambaa. Neither legend and mythology nor history ever caught up with princess Ambaa. Only the Newars of Tilibham knew of the princess and her palace just beyond that clearing in the woods. This perhaps was so only because the palace was in the vicinity of Tilibham. Were Tilibham farther away, were the goatherds never to stray into the ruins of the palace grounds, princess Ambaa would have remained unknown to the Newars of Tilibham as well. What someone wished to keep as a secret would have remained so. But for the palace's vicinity to Tilibham. For a friend, Ambaa had only Dakshyayani, the daughter of king Dakshya, son of Lord Brahma himself. In her Ambaa found her confidante. Sitting by the fire on chilly autumn evenings of the Himalayas, great grandparents in Tilibham narrated the lore of Princess Ambaa to their grandchildren.

Ambaa, so said the grand old folks, was pale of skin and small of stature but had straight and luscious black hair which, when left loose, fell down her back like a sheet of sky during the darkest hour of an eclipsed night. As if to hint upon the darkness in her life. And as if to hold back that darkness in restraint, her hair was most often made into a braid and the head was often covered with a scarf whose ends were tied into a little knot at the back of her head. She was one of Dakshyayani's dearest friends and as a young girl, Dakshyayani often came to visit Ambaa and stayed for days together in the palace. Like any other ten year old, Ambaa and Dakshyayani roamed the hills, chased mountain butterflies and imitated birdsong that echoed through the valley. In that palace, so the story of the old folks went, Ambaa was very lovingly looked after by the middle-aged couple Brajbhushan and Poorvi, who themselves were childless. Brajbhushan was a coppersmith of exceptional skill, a skill that he learned by himself. His first engraving, legend said, was that of a nude female figure sitting cross legged, which he etched out when he was still a young boy, with a piece of pointed stone on a small hexagonal piece of copper that was left over from the works of another coppersmith much older than him. Thereafter, the same coppersmith threw a small circular piece of copper sheet at him to try out something else. On this Brajbhushan etched out a pair of reptiles around a shivling inside a cave. With age and time, Brajbhushan became more and more skilled and soon became the most famous coppersmith in those parts of the Himalayan valleys. It was this skill that he wished to gift Ambaa. No one exactly knew which Nepalese mountain chieftain's clandestinely begotten child she was, thus hidden in the depths of the woods to keep her existence away from the world like a dark secret. But Poorvi and Brajbhushan never let even the breeze that blew in from the heartland of Nepal speak of it to their little princess. They doled out all the love their hearts could hold on Ambaa in that palace which formed the little princess's world. Ambaa didn't miss out on not having a mother or a father. She didn't know there was anything as such. Because for her, Poorvi mai and Braj baba were all she ever needed. And had. She didn't know anyone her age either to talk to her of what she didn't have. Except Dakshyayani. But when Dakshyayani visited, they didn't have time to talk about parents because in the hills, in the woods and along the stream there was so much more to seek and marvel at. When the girls were in each other's company, they never had a moment of idleness. And along with them, every maid and every servant in the palace were on their toes. The palace buzzed with life, of the happy sort. From morning to night, the large kitchen let out aroma of the choicest dishes that the girls loved. When laughter started in one corner of the palace, it didn't stop till it rolled over through every chamber and hallway, touching everyone as it passed by. Those days when Dakshyayani visited, the palace turned into a festival ground. Very early in the mornings maids went out to the garden to get fresh blooms for the little girls' hair. Little monkeys mocked them from tree tops and mimicked their action of plucking flowers by plucking off leaves from the branches as they swung from one tree to another. Sometimes in the morning, Poorvi took the little girls to the cow shed and taught them how to milk Garbha, the royal cow. Dakshyayani and Ambaa would fall back upon the ground, laughing, as the milk squirted all over their faces from Garbha's udder. Garbha too would moo away shaking her large head, taking part in the fun. In the late afternoons, when the trees cast long shadows upon the grounds outside the palace and when the monkeys quietened for a siesta, Poorvi sat with the girls and gave them lessons on dance and music. She taught them how to dance the Jyapu. And while Poorvi danced, one by one all the maids, the servants, the cooks and every other attendant in the palace came up and gathered round her to watch. As the Jyapu progressed, men and women who were all along just sitting and watching would begin to get carried away and from merely swaying their heads and tapping their feet, they stood up one by one to join Poorvi with absolute gusto. Such was the ambience in the palace those days. There was happy abandon in those moments of song and dance. There was an abundance that defiantly belied the impending doom upon the palace. And because Brajbhushan too wished to give the girls what he knew, he taught Dakshyayani and Ambaa to etch beautiful engravings on sheets of radiant red copper. Sometimes during the day when the aslant rays of the sun washed the mountain slopes around the palace, Brajbhushan and the girls sat on the ground outside under the shade of the wide canopy of some aged tree to learn Brajbhushan's art. And the *tap-tap-tonk* of little hammers beating on the copper sheets created almost a kind of music in itself that pervaded through the otherwise tranquil mountains. Dakshyayani and Ambaa engraved on these sheets of copper what they saw during their wanderings through the woods, the jewelleries upon their slender limbs, instruments of music which Poorvi taught them to play and also quails with which they amorously wrote about the soulmate they each would find, love and belong to someday. And as Poorvi sat with her little princess and Dakshyayani, she would run a loving hand through their hair and say, 'Hundreds of years from now, my dears, man will come to worship the innocence and divinity in little girls like you. They will worship the power of the pure in little, adorable girls. Like you. Because your purity is your power and yet, it is just this that makes you so vulnerable. Because you are the force of creation and yet, need to be sowed upon by another, to create. Man will worship you to atone for the sins of dishonouring you and to give you the honour you so deserve. You are the virgins that man will worship, my darlings, and they shall call it the Kumari Puja. They'll make goddesses out of adorable little girls like you.' The girls only giggled and hugged Poorvi and it is said that it is the sound of their giggles that flowed with the gush of the mountain brooks in Tilibham. This was how the old folks in Tilibham narrated the tale of Princess Ambaa and Dakshyayani.

Then as the snow fell and melted year after year and time rolled by, so the legend went, Dakshyayani's visits to the palace gradually became less frequent. For now her thoughts had started dwelling more and more on Shiva. She sought him out in her dreams in those hours that she slept and also in those hours that she tossed and turned to sleep but sleep evaded her. Back in the palace beyond Tilibham, Ambaa sometimes milked Garbha and sometimes took her dance lessons from Poorvi mai and yet at other times, tapped away upon sheets of copper, embossing strange images which even she herself had never really planned to etch. What was such fun doing together with Dakshyayani now merely helped to drag her through time. As she etched, her hands seemed to move on their own, as if they did their own thinking. Often, Ambaa made these engravings on sheets of copper all by herself, no longer waiting for Brajbhushan's guidance as she tapped and lightly hammered onto the sheets. She continued to look forward to Dakshyayani's visit.

The rare occasions when Dakshyayani now visited Ambaa were short periods. Ambaa then rejoiced and lost herself in Dakshyayani's company but deep in her heart sat a strange, anxious foreboding. Ambaa didn't understand what it might be. It nevertheless made her panic in a way she never understood. Soon, so the legends said, Dakshyayani visited Ambaa at the palace for the last time. For she was now preparing to become Shiva's consort. And when the visits stopped altogether, Ambaa started pouring out her loneliness through the little hammers onto the copper sheets which were in the shape of large banyan leaves.

And so the years came and went.

As time passed, Garbha's udders stopped squirting frothy milk. Poorvi still picked at the musical instruments but her ageing back no longer allowed her to dance the way she used to. Brajbhushan's hands too were no longer steady enough to stir up the life-like art in copper that he used to once upon a time. And in her solitude Ambaa often had the same foreboding, the same fear of the unseen and the unknown, the one that had earlier sat in her heart and stopped her joy from being whole during those last few visits from Dakshyayani. Just that, now that foreboding filled her entire being. It was this unforeseen fear, coupled with loneliness, that made Ambaa's hands move impulsively over the copper sheets, etching sometimes anklets, bracelets and earrings, at other times a neck and arms, a heart and a navel, and even a nose, a tongue and eyes. Most of the times, her hands seemed to move on their own, without following Ambaa's will or command. Ambaa just had to put the little brass hammer with the right head to the copper sheet and then on, her hands seemed to do the rest on their own. Sometimes Ambaa felt she knew what she was doing and at other times she was so lost in thoughts of Dakshyayani that the hands did their work all by themselves. Then when Ambaa came out of her reverie and looked at the images on the sheets, she thought they looked familiar and very dearly loved. She would then all of a sudden realize that she had actually, unawares, etched out parts that belonged to none other than her dearest and only friend Dakshyayani. To her disbelief, Ambaa found that she had etched out even the lips, the small of her waist and her knees. And to treasure all of these which reminded Ambaa of Dakshyayani, she had a small chamber built just outside her own room in the palace. Years later, the old Newar folks of Tilibham would call it the retreat chamber of the princess. Built of stone with a pagoda for a roof, this retreat chamber had just one door cut off on one wall. On the three other walls, there was one window each that brought in enough light for Ambaa to tap away on the copper sheets till late afternoon. Niches, the size of a large bull's head turned nostrils up, were grooved into each of the three walls to keep her engravings leaning against the wall. On each wall with a window, these niches were laid out in three neat rows with five niches in each row. And a row each of three such grooves, one groove below the other, were also cut into the wall on either side of the door. So it was here in this chamber that Ambaa started to spend more and more of her days. Even Ambaa didn't know that over time, these fifty one niches would fill in. All of them. So this was how the old people of Tilibham narrated the lore to their children and grandchildren, regaling them with as much of Dakshyayani's story as was related to Princess Ambaa's fate. And so the old in Tilibham wove into Ambaa and Dakshyayani's story about how Dakshyayani's father king Dakshya disapproved of Shiva but that Shiva and Dakshyayani's marriage yet took place. The great grand folks thus recounted that because king Dakshya thought Shiva the ascetic was wholly unfit to be his son-in-law, he let no opportunity go waste to humiliate Shiva. It was with such a purpose that king Dakshya performed a magnificent yajna, about which all time and space in Creation have since talked and to which every being of honour on Earth and in the Heavens was invited. Every being, except Shiva. And Dakshyayani. She yet went to the yajna at her father's house. Alone, without Shiva. But there, unable to bear the ridicule and the demeaning words which were said of Shiva by her father and so immense was the rage, anguish and hurt that befell her thereafter that the fire that all along singed her from within eventually erupted out of her being and engulfed her to take her life.

On one hand, when news of his beloved Dakshyayani reached Shiva, such profound grief and shock befell him that he went into a frenzy and set about creating havoc. The combined power of his fury and angst caused him to pull and tear at his own hair and out of this hair he created Virabhadra, whom he sent to raze king Dakshya's yajna. With this command and purpose Virabhadra stormed into the midst of the yajna, destroying everything and everyone that came in his way, even beheading king Dakshya himself. It was, as say the Epics and the Puranas, only when the gods pleaded with Shiva to calm Virabhadra that Shiva went to king Dakshya's palace and once again absorbed Virabhadra into himself. But his grief over the loss of Dakshyayani remained just the same. So he lovingly gathered Dakshyayani's lifeless body and holding her close to his heart, started wandering over mountains and across crags, sometimes howling and ranting to the high mountains and sometimes whimpering to the low seas, bringing all Creation to an entire disarray and panic.

On the other hand, when Ambaa heard that her only friend Dakshyayani was no more, she at once understood that the uncanny foreboding of some unknown fear that was gnawing at her was nothing else but this. However unlike Shiva, Ambaa retreated deep within herself, staying by herself in her retreat chamber and letting herself get more and more drowned into the embossing of images on sheets of copper. As if it had always been in her fate to remain thus alone and hidden from all time and existence. Sometimes to hide a covert relationship of some mountain chieftain and sometimes in her own grief over an irrevocable loss. While Shiva roamed the mountains and howled to the Heavens, Ambaa closed herself in her retreat chamber and doused in silence. The gods, meanwhile, trembled in fear out of an impending devastation of Creation because as long as Shiva held on to Dakshyayani, he would be filled over and over again with unimaginable pain at his loss. And so long as he was in pain, he would continue with his wild outbursts of fury and sorrow, which in turn would spell doom upon Creation. So it was then that Vishnu used his disc-like weapon with serrated edges, the one he called his sudarshan chakra, to disintegrate the lifeless body of Dakshyayani. Thus, while Shiva carried Dakshyayani's lifeless body around thinking it to still be whole, Ambaa carved images of that same lifeless body but in parts. Vishnu's disc cut the body into fifty one major parts and as Shiva wandered about, each of these fifty one parts fell scattered over different places on earth. And wherever one such part fell, a shrine emerged there. Meanwhile for Ambaa, day merged into night and night into day. Hunger and thirst abandoned her and she was slowly losing all sense of time, life and of self. Such was her grief over the loss of Dakshyayani. All she did was tap away onto the sheets of copper, putting in precious details as she embossed parts of Dakshyayani's body. And when one such part was done, with utmost care, almost like it had life in it and if held wrongly would cause pain to her friend, she placed it gently into one of the niches on the wall of her retreat chamber. As Ambaa thus went on carving organ after organ, part after part and sometimes pieces of jewellery from Dakshyayani's body, the fifty one niches started filling in. Just as the niches filled in, Ambaa's sanity emptied out. Lost in an existence that was almost a trance, when she wasn't tapping away at sheets of copper, she stared out of the three windows in turn for long periods as if searching the horizons for Dakshyayani's reappearance. And as the great grand folks in the hamlet of Tilibham said, each time Vishnu's disc detached a part of Dakshyayani and it fell away from the lifeless body Shiva was carrying, the copper sheet with the coinciding image of that part of Dakshyayani too fell from its groove on the wall of Ambaa's retreat chamber. As it fell with a *clang* on the stone floor of the chamber, it startled Ambaa out of her gaze into the horizon and at that very moment she knew, that part of her friend had fallen off from her lifeless body upon the ground, bleeding and soiled, left unattended where man and animal might carelessly tread upon. Still in a daze, she picked up that fallen embossed image of the detached part of Dakshyayani's body from the floor and having lovingly run a palm over it one last time, wailing and sobbing alternately, threw that copper sheet to the winds through the window. As she did so, she pleaded to the winds to take it to where that very part of Dakshyayani had fallen and to cover with this copper sheet that detached and fallen organ from dirt and humiliation, to shield it from pain, to stop it from bleeding. And the winds obeyed. They did not let the banyan-leaf-shaped sheet of copper touch the ground but instead took it to the nearest monkeys hanging around on the trees. And the monkeys sometimes swung from tree to tree, sometimes traversed steep, rocky mountain ridges and at other times ran on all fours to take the sheet to the fallen organ. And when the sea came in the way, the monkeys would stick to the shores forming a sort of relay. But never once did they let the sheet of copper touch the ground. It is said that because of this faithfulness of the monkeys of Tilibham, till this day, monkeys all over are allowed the privilege of scampering around temples of the gods. So said great grand folks at Tilibham that in this way, every detached and fallen organ from Dakshyayani's body got gently covered by the corresponding image carved by Ambaa on a copper sheet, which was why the organ stopped bleeding. And the shrine that rose thereupon became a Shakti Peeth. And from the stains of blood that dried underneath the copper sheet but yet revived because of the rejuvenating aura of the copper, a new image of Dakshyayani was formed and it was this image that came to be worshipped in the shrine that emerged at that very spot.

So while Shiva continued his frenzied wanderings and Vishnu continued his mission of disintegrating Dakshyayani's lifeless body, Ambaa stopped leaving her retreat chamber for fear that one of the embossed copper sheets may fall off its niche when she wasn't there and that part of Dakshyayani would hurt and bleed more. And so by then, Ambaa's pale skin got paler and her slim limbs wasted away. Neither cajoling nor persuading could make her take even a morsel of food. Fatigue pushed her to the brink of sleep upon the cold stone floor of the retreat chamber but anxiety and a rapidly beating heart often jolted her out of it. Then one day, the jolt that rudely woke her up was not that of a rapidly beating heart but the shattering noise of a copper sheet that fell from its niche on the wall. It sounded like silence was stabbed. Ambaa flung herself to reach the niche from where she was leaning against the wall near the window. It was the copper sheet with the image of Dakshyayani's yoni.

It had fallen.

Poorvi was approaching Ambaa with a small bowl of milk, though she knew she wouldn't be able to even make her look at it. She nevertheless persisted in her cajoling. In the hope that Ambaa might give in. But when she heard the sound of the copper sheet fall, she hurried into the retreat chamber and saw that what Ambaa was gingerly running her fingers over was an engraving of a yoni on the banyan-leaf shaped copper sheet. Ambaa and Poorvi looked at each other. For they knew at once that Dakshyayani's yoni had been detached from her lifeless body by Vishnu's disc and that it had fallen to the ground. Ambaa gingerly tossed it out of the window to the winds. But this time, however, the copper sheet with Dakshyayani's yoni engraved on it did not go away. Instead, it fell below the window inside the retreat chamber. It would have once again fallen on the stone floor had Ambaa not hurriedly placed her palms between the floor and the copper sheet. Legend went that the winds, so said the old in Tilibham, had shied away from carrying a yoni over mountains, crags and rivers, across valleys and fields, letting everyone see what they were carrying.

'But Dakshyayani's shame has to be covered, Poorvi mai, or else her yoni will continue to bleed...,' so said Ambaa, according to the very old in the hamlet of Tilibham.

'If her shame is to be covered, child, why do it by means of putting her to greater shame by sending the image of her yoni with monkeys who would swing through the winds in the forests, for all of Creation to see what they were carrying?' Poorvi had then answered.

Ambaa looked with sorrow and tenderness at the image of a part of her friend in her hands. Poorvi mai was right, she thought. She slowly looked up at Poorvi, asking without speaking a word, what was to be done. So Poorvi then gently led Ambaa by the hand to a small clearing of land beyond the palace and down the hillock, among the forests and hills. Ambaa was still holding the engraving of the yoni and Poorvi carried a small spade. And there, a few paces into the clearing, Poorvi helped Ambaa bury the copper image of the yoni into the earth. But before hiding away the image of Dakshyayani's yoni, Ambaa had sought a promise from Poorvi. And received it.

'Some faraway time, on a faraway land,

Unseen from where we now stand

Her yoni etched upon this sheet of copper

Shall Dakshyayani's shame surely cover

Ambaa, dear child, my word I give

This, for you, even in death shall I achieve...'

'But till then will her yoni remain in pain and bleed, Poorvi mai?'

'The hills and the earth upon which it had fallen will have turned it into stone so that it remains in pain no more. But bleed it yet will, though no more out of pain. It shall then be the bleeding of her youth and womanhood, of her power to create. Of a fertile womb.'

'Oh....!'

'And the yoni shall bleed not by the waning and waxing of the moon, but just once every monsoon.'

Ambaa had by now placed the banyan-leaf shaped copper sheet with the engraving of Dakshyayani's yoni into the hole Poorvi dug into the ground and was filling in the soil. With her hands still smoothening out the ground, so the very old folks said, Ambaa looked up at Poorvi questioningly.

'Then what, when the copper shield reaches there where it ought to?' She asked Poorvi.

'When the copper shield reaches there and at last covers the yoni from the view of mortals and from the onslaught of the elements, a hundred and two monsoons from that moment, the yoni which will have turned into stone and yet have life in it and also have the power of Creation, shall at last stop bleeding. And then shall befall doom upon the hills and valleys which will have turned Dakshyayani's yoni into stone.'

'A hundred and two monsoons from that moment?'

'A hundred and two monsoons from that moment! From that very moment when this sheet shall come to lie upon Dakshyayani's yoni.'

Poorvi knew Ambaa wished to ask why a hundred and two monsoons later. And Ambaa knew Poorvi did not wish to tell her why. But Poorvi would, upon her deathbed, tell Brajbhushan that fifty one of those hundred and two monsoons would be the grief the Heavens would shed as tears, one monsoon for each of the fifty one major parts that Vishnu's disc cut off from Dakshyayani's lifeless body. Dakshyayani, however, would then no more feel any pain upon the disc cutting her body, for there would be no life in it to feel the pain. Yet, the Heavens would shed their tears for her. And the remaining fifty one monsoons would be the grief the Heavens would shed for the pain Ambaa felt for those same fifty one parts in her own body because of the life in it. The Heavens would shed their tears for the pain Ambaa felt on the fifty one corresponding parts on her own self as if on behalf of the only friend she ever had. The Heavens would shed their tears because even in those moments of excruciating pain of the mind and the body, Ambaa would go unnoticed and unsympathized. Like it was in her fate to remain so always. And that's why a hundred and two monsoons from then, so Poorvi would tell Brajbhushan. But at that moment, standing there a few paces into the clearing beyond the palace, Poorvi did not make any of these revelations to Ambaa.

Ambaa looked up at the skies before languidly bringing her gaze to search far beyond the horizon. As if she would see the future there if she looked well.

'And because the image of the yoni of Shiva's consort cannot be defiled by being borne by anyone else, even the elements, it will only be a kumari, Ambaa, a little pre-pubescent virgin, to bear the image of the yoni on this copper sheet to the real organ wherever it had fallen.' Poorvi went on, 'So during that time, in another place and another age far from this, if the pre-pubescent virgin bearing this copper image of the yoni bequeaths her own youth and fertility at the shrine of Dakshyayani's yoni, then a new form of Dakshyayani will take shape in that shrine for man to worship. However, she will have to bequeath these even before they set upon her. And till such time, through hundreds of years, because there shall be no copper shield on that part of Dakshyayani's body, there shall thus be no blood stains rejuvenating on the insides of the shield. And hence, no new form or shape whatsoever of Dakshyayani will have appeared.'

'And just so, through time and space, among all the shrines that arose where the fifty one major parts of Dakshyayani's lifeless body fell, the one where her yoni fell will be without a whole and different form of Dakshyayani to be worshipped. There, the sanctum sanctorum of the shrine will have only a hardened yoni of stone. Because only at that place was there no copper shield to hold back the blood stains and revive them into a new figure. Through time and space, Ambaa, that shrine will come to be known as Kamakhya.'

'Poorvi mai, can you see into the future?' Ambaa asked, again taking her gaze to the horizon.

'I cannot.'

'Then how do you say all of this?'

'I don't say any of it.'

'Then who does?'

'Dakshyayani'

Elsewhere, Vishnu's disc continued to disintegrate the lifeless body slung across Shiva's shoulders and parts of it, organs, jewellery, clothing and drops of blood continued to fall on earth, creating big and small shrines wherever they fell. Only after the last such part fell away from Shiva did he begin to slowly calm down. And back in the palace near Tilibham, Ambaa, Poorvi and Brajbhushan embraced their deaths over time, one after the other, after the copper engraving of Dakshyayayni's yoni had been buried. By that time, all the other remaining copper engravings of Dakhyayani's body too had fallen out of their niches and had been sent through the winds and the monkeys to shield and protect the related parts that fell off from Dakshyayani's lifeless body. But during those last hours of life, Brajbhushan had placed his first engravings, the nude deity and the pair of reptiles coiled around the Shivling, on a banana leaf and left these in offering to the palace deities inside the palace temple. He placed red kurvak flowers, bananas and a handful of rice on that same leaf next to the engravings. And in his prayers that evening, he had said, '*What I had received from you, O Universe, I offer back to you. Accept, and do what you may of these. If, however, you make these get sucked and lost into the whirlpool of time and the elements, then so shall the truth of Ambaa's pitiful existence. And if you make these come to rest upon the core of another pious human's life, to keep these alive, then Ambaa's existence too shall relive, shall come to be spoken of, heard of and shall come to be known of! Do so then that what pleases you, O Universe, I offer these back to you!*' Brajbhushan had passed away in his sleep before the sun rose upon the next dawn. After dawn, when the death was discovered and while people at the palace fell into grief, shock, and disarray and got absorbed in funeral arrangements, birds and monkeys came into the door-less palace temple to pick and peck at the bananas and the grains of rice. Monkeys and birds came in and carried away Brajbhushan's offerings of his earliest engravings, thinking them to be food. But after having carried them far from the palace when they found out that those were not food, they dropped them among the trees in the mountains. When Brajbhushan, Ambaa and Poorvi were no more, all other maids, cooks, servants, gardeners and caretakers in the thriving palace too had gradually disappeared. Some passed away in grief, some out of old age and ailment. But most just left the palace, unable to bear memories haunting them from every stone in every wall and the shrieking solitude which was the only thing that remained there. Garbha too was set free so she and her calves wandered away into the hills. Even today the Newars believe that every cow and bullock which had since sustained them was a descendent of Garbha. Gradually, the palace too began to crumble and fall apart with no one staying in it and no one to care for it. Storms and earthquakes shook the pillars and made them collapse. Till it arrived at its present ruins.

And that was the tale of princess Ambaa and the palace in ruins that the old among the Newars in the remote hamlet of Tilibham in Nepal told. They even swore that the long dead Brajbhushan was heard tapping away on copper as he sat guard over the buried engraving of Dakshyayani's yoni. And so it was that the small clearing beyond the ruins of princess Ambaa's palace was a land never tilled.

~

Children in Tilibham grew up hearing the tales of princess Ambaa and Dakshyayani from their grand and great grandparents. Then when they had children, grandchildren and great grandchildren of their own, they passed down these tales to them. Thus the tale lived on, but only among the Newars in Tilibham.

Hundreds of years later, there would come a time when they would be telling the tale to other little children, sitting by the fire in the evenings after the year's Kumari Puja just got over.

....you are the force of Creation and yet, need to be sowed upon... you are the virgins that man will worship, my darlings, and they shall call it the Kumari Puja...

END OF CHAPTER 1

INTERLUDE

Since then......
           Eons have gone by, of time much has elapsed,
        Many a tide rose and fell, many an eclipse passed,
           Mountains rose from beneath the seas
        Civilizations birthed, grew, even came to cease!
              God and man, divine and human
              Treaded no more the same plane.
     And time moved on. Planets continued round the sun,
  When a hundred years ended, another hundred had begun.
                 For time is never stagnant
           Can even the gods the solstices prevent?
        So unhurried and un-slowed, time walked by
           Eons have gone, centuries passed by...
                  ...To arrive at Now...

CHAPTER 2

RED

Kamarupa, Assam, India.

Here stretches out the Nilachal Pahar, the Blue Hills, along the river Brahmaputra. Atop these hills is an ancient shrine which, till today, bears testimony to those fateful times hundreds and hundreds of years ago when Dakshyayani's lifeless body had to be disintegrated by Vishnu's disc, letting the pieces that happened fall all over and give rise to shrines wherever each such piece fell.

Since then, though, the Gods had stopped walking the earth.

And now upon the Nilachal hills it was that time of the year during the monsoons when a stone in the shape of a yoni inside that ancient shrine's deepest part, in what the people there called the '*garbha griha*', bled. The shrine, they called Kamakhya. The yoni, they said, was Dakshyayani's. It was that yoni which got cut off from Dakshayayani's lifeless body by Vishnu's disc and which fell upon the

Nilachal hills and caused the birth of the shrine they called Kamakhya. It was there that the yoni, now turned into stone, was resting. Resting, but not in peace. Turned into stone, but not yet dead. For deep in the womb of the blue hill itself the yoni never ceased to bleed the blood of life and womanhood, of youth and fertility. No limb and life, no head and heart, no wholeness in any form and yet, as if the lone stone yoni lay there in significance of the whole, of limb and life, head and heart. For it is that which led to Creation. For it bled the blood of fertility, of a womb that could yet create and give birth to the whole, despite its own self being only an organ of that whole. But she, like the mortal, did not bleed by the waning and waxing of the moon. She, because she was divine, bled by the falling of the year's rains upon the Nilachal hills. And every year for three days when the stone yoni bled inside the closed doors of the shrine, the monsoon rains cleansed her. So it was said. Incessant rains washed down the Nilachal hills those days and all over the valleys and plains of Kamarupa, people stayed away from ploughing and tilling the soil, lest it hurt the bleeding earth. For it was Dakshyayani's yoni that bled, as had said Poorvi, because the copper sheet on which Ambaa engraved an image of Dakshyayani's yoni had not yet reached it to cover the yoni and stop it from bleeding. Just so, because there had been no copper sheet under which the blood stains could dry and revive, there had been no image of Dakshyayani at all, of any form, in the Kamakhya shrine in Assam's Kamarupa. The Goddess here is perceived through the yoni, the most powerful of all organs in a woman, in Creation. It was the yoni and only that which formed the object of worship at the sanctum sanctorum. And outside the closed doors of the shrine, upon every stone step and every inch of gravelled courtyard, these blue hills now lay wrapped under a sea of a million shades of orange, saffron, red and even white, sometimes draped around and sometimes barely veiling, naked ashen limbs of fakirs. For now devotees, yogis and ascetics, men and women, even children have flocked to the temple grounds. Believers arrived by the hundreds because they believed in the power of the yoni, though the yoni itself had long turned into stone. Non believers too arrived by an equal number, if just to find out what it was that brought the believers there. At the Kamakhya, it was a time of congregation of the holy and those not so, the rich and the poor, those seeking ways to give and those seeking ways to derive, most offering wholehearted worship and few imposing themselves upon the worshipper as a link between man and divine, some looking at the temple as they would the Eiffel tower and others perceiving the goddess in that same stone structure. And the rains continued to lash while the river Brahmaputra continued to whip the foothills of the Nilachal range.

Maya had been brought there by her devout parents so that she might worship at the sanctum sanctorum and touch the waters that trickled out of the stone yoni, thereby assuring that she would get married soon. She was past her thirties and willing to marry but things were just not falling into place. Piyush was returning to the shrine after two years, to offer his gratitude for the job he acquired after his last visit. He promised he would return to offer a black goat at the shrine if he got a job. He did. And so he was returning with the black goat that year. And Naivedyaa was at the shrine to seek emotional solace after a divorce. Like Maya, Piyush and Naivedyaa, every devotee had a reason to come to the shrine. Some seeking, some thankful upon receiving and some just to collect merit at the court of the goddess. Because the belief went that he who ever came with a pure heart and sincere need to the shrine of the yoni at Kamakhya had never been disheartened. But besides many more Mayas, Piyush and Naivedyaas, there were those teeming devotees who arrived at the shrine at that time of the year to seek, and desperately so, a child of their own. They believed in the miracle of the blood from the stone yoni that brought life into barren wombs. They believed that the yoni stood as a symbol of fertility. And so it was this blood that prevailed as the soul of the Shrine.

And red prevailed, as the colour of this blood.

Red prevailed, in the vermillion upon the foreheads of the pilgrims and upon the black goats brought in for the sacrifice. Red also prevailed in the river Brahmaputra that caressed past the foot of the Nilachal hills and flowed muddy and red with mud swept down from the hills higher up during monsoon. There was flaming red again in the dupattas, some of silk, some of lattice and brocade, which hung inside tiny stalls that lined the steps to the temple on either side. All of these dupattas were destined to find their way to the sacred stone yoni as sartorial offerings. In Kamarupa, however, they never called it the sacred yoni. For it had always been the Mother Goddess there.

And so red prevailed. In silent compliance to the greater red which was the red blood that oozed from the divine yoni. Stone, but not dead. At rest, yet in the anguish of bleeding.

So while Dakshyayani bled in the cold dark solitude in the crevice of rocks inside the temple of the Mother Goddess Kamakhya, in the multitude outside, ash smeared fakirs blew clouds of smoke from their chillums, in praise of Dakshyayani's husband, Shiva. Leaving aside the walkway, every inch of the temple yard had mats and sheets spread upon them where fakirs and ascetics sat or slept or remained in incredible postures of yoga. Big and small sheets of tarpaulin hung like awnings to shelter people from the rains. Even mendicants and Aghoris from the charnal grounds, with their bowls of human skull and elbow rests of the thigh bone of some long dead human, occupied their fair share of the temple courtyard. Irrespective of what or who they were, these people formed into motley groups and sang, in high pitched voices, hymns and verses from the epics and the puranas. Their voices rose in accompaniment to those of crude stringed instruments, little drums and cymbals, giving birth to a live concert of combined efforts and religious zeal. And the sound of each such concert rose above the prevailing din, creating more din in the process.

Matted locks from the heads of both male fakirs and female saadhvis, in an unimaginable array of thickness, length and form, were on display. Some laid out their growths of matted hair upon the ground for the curious pilgrim to wonder and measure. And they found that these ran to lengths that would be more than double the heights of the entire frail, physical beings of the owners of those locks. Most of these matted crowns had strings of the rudraksh beads around them. Many among the sadhus and saadhvis had strings of these beads around their necks and arms as well. Kripababa was a regular at the shrine of Kamakhya every year at this time of the year. No one knew where he roamed before this time and thereafter but everyone remembered him as the fakir who came every year and whose matted beard was in an awesome disproportion to his head. And each year he came, the matted beard seemed to have grown greater than the previous year. Years back when the beard started getting all tangled and matted and fell upto his chest, Kripababa must have made two parts of it and let a part each to go over a shoulder to fall down his back. So now his beard ran not down his front but down his back. This year Kripababa's matted beard formed a round stool of about a foot and a half in height and about as much in diameter. And he remained vainly perched atop this stool, sitting with his legs crossed. Saadhvi Jayantimai, on the other hand, remained deliriously oblivious to the entire hubbub around her. For lying under a blue polythene sheet whose four corners were tied to the top of four short posts of bamboo, she was in an entirely different euphoria of her own. She, like many others there, had been only on cannabis for the past couple of days, since the stone yoni started bleeding. She didn't call it cannabis though. She, like others there, called it *bhang*. And just like so many other yogis and saadhvis there at this time, she too could otherwise make accurate predicaments about people's lives by reading their palms and feeling the bases of their fingers. But she preferred to stay in her delirium and not read palms. Sometimes she walked up to Kripababa, pulled her knee length red saree higher up her thighs and sat astride upon his lap, letting her naval touch his. Whenever she did this, Kripababa would later come and spend some time with her under her little blue polythene sheet. And because there was only crouching space for just one person under that sheet, the two had to lie entwined and wriggling, till finally he entered her. Their entwined meetings would have been more frequent had it not been for Kripababa's unwanted baggage of the matted beard. Meanwhile, all around the hum of chants and hymns, verses of prayer and the constant song of the motley groups of mendicants, fakirs and yogis filled the air. Just outside the main altar, people nudged and pushed to reach the long narrow rows of wrought iron rack lined with earthen lamps. Some of the lamps there were burning bright but the rain and the wind had blown out others. Yet others were flickering. People nudged and pushed around the rack to light their own earthen lamps in worship to the Goddess and place them on the rack. The lamps glowed, the cores of their flames a bright red. And red glowed. In reverence to the fertility of the stone yoni. Red prevailed.

There were also fakirs like Mounibaba who never spoke a word but intently listened to every word that was spoken to him, words which sought his intervention with the divine for favours of the material world. And Mounibaba would grant the favours in the form of little aluminium amulets which he blessed and which he strung through a red string and tied around the arm of the believer. This arm again, had to be sometimes the right arm and at other times the left. But the string always had to be red. For red prevailed. And after he was done tying the amulet, Mounibaba would stretch out his dented brass bowl for the favoured to drop in whatever they felt like. Some dropped a coin, some dropped bananas and apples and yet some folded currency notes and pressed them into the bowl. Mounibaba would then ask the person to move on with a wave of his hand. Because there were others waiting to prostrate at his feet for an amulet. And all along, there was never one moment of stagnation among the crowd. More and more bare feet stepped upon the temple grounds, undeterred by the merciless downpour, the heat and humidity and the near stampede like situation. Because each one there was driven by the awe in the divine power and miracle of the stone yoni. In and around the dry moat like area outside the main shrine, equally incredible were the feats of the large goats that feared neither fakir nor devotee. With beards almost competing with the ascetics and horns sometimes large enough to outwit a bull and sometimes stubbed, the goats often moved out of their area to wander among the crowd, feeling free to abide by neither method nor discipline that applied to the humans in that same crowd. Upon the ground, it was these goats that teased and bullied visitors and snatched at the long garlands of red hibiscus that hung from the arms of devotees and sometimes hung from the strings of the stalls that sold them. How they chewed and relished these flowers! And from the branches of trees above, the same nuisance was caused by monkeys. They, though, targeted not the garlands of hibiscus but the bananas in the baskets of offerings. And up on the temple dome, flocks of pigeons gurgled. They flew down to peck at grams and flew back to the dome, at times hopping close to humans without any fear. During this time at the Kamakhya shrine, there was a passionate and pious crowd that gave rise to some kind of a chaos. And yet, there was now order in that chaos in Kamakhya. And there was life in stone. Like order in chaos.

Also upon the temple grounds now, most among the fakirs and sadhus performed rare and at times bizarre feats, drawing to themselves men of media, paramedics and police. Yet others were drawn to them out of plain curiosity because there were times when few of these feats grazed the borders of titillation. Then there were vendors of every conceivable thing possibly linked to the tantric beliefs that the Kamakhya temple was associated with. Besides, conch shells, pictures of deities in frames of marble and plastic, strings of beads in all colours and sizes, trinkets of tin, plastic, ivory and animal bone, little round dots of bindis, small sachets of sugar coated grams and dry fruits, key-rings with images of gods and goddesses hanging from them, brass and copper stands to hold incense sticks, little pots made of metal to offer water to the gods and a whole array of this and that were spread out in stalls on either side of the steps that led to the temple, while stray dogs and goats stood their own uncontested ground in that throng. Nudging for space with these stalls were others which sold small and big earthen lamps, little bottles of ghee and mustard oil, wicks of yarn and cotton wool and also baskets of wicker to hold everything that would perhaps be offered at the sanctum at Dakshyayani's shrine. Long garlands of bright yellow and orange marigold and blood red hibiscus hung in abundance upon the stalls of the vendors. Because the colour of blood prevailed.

And dominated. There was also the odd stall that sold good-day biscuits and bottles of Sprite and Pepsi side by side with purses and belts of fake leather and *Pounds* fairness cream. Some spread out little sheets of plastic on the ground and spread a fare of *Luck-me* nail polish, lipstick, combs, mirrors, kohls and yes, vermillion too. Sindoor. And red reigned. These, the sellers convinced the pilgrim, were for Dakshyayani to adorn herself when she would have finished bleeding. But now, she bled.

And outside, incessant rains had brought a kind of gloss upon the stone, gravel and concrete courtyard of the temple. Every pair of feet that walked these grounds now was bare, for footwear had to be left way down the steps. The rains, sometimes a light spray and at other times a downpour, were cleansing Dakshyayani as she bled in solitude behind the closed doors of the Kamakhya temple perched on the Nilachal hills. These doors would be opened only on the fourth day since their closure. It is said that the rains ceased by then. And at the end of these three days of divine bleeding inside and human fanaticism outside, the waiting bevy of people thronged to the open doors of the temple to pay their obeisance to the stone yoni, to Dakshyayani and to Creation. But eventually, the ultimate object of yearning after these days of devotion were pieces of the cloth they called the *angodak,* which had been reddened with Dakshyayani's blood of the past three days. As a sign of life. And of creation.

And as the people and yogis, fakirs and saints, vendors and beggars, and pilgrims and tourists waited for those three days outside while Dakshyayani bled inside, the ambience at the Kamakhya temple grounds rose to that of a crowded fair. A mela. The Ambubasi mela.

END OF CHAPTER 2

CHAPTER 3

BARREN

Far away from Kamarupa and Kamakhya, away from the hustle and bustle of the ambubasi fair, the sleepy hamlet of Tilibham lay quiet as usual. Tucked away into a remote corner of Nepal, its handful of Newar households mostly stayed close to home. There it did not rain that day but the sky was yet cast with clouds thick, dark and heavy with rain in them, so much like the full and heavy belly of a demon. These clouds let out a roar every now and then like the burp of the demon. Despite the imminent fear of the thick clouds bursting open any moment to let out a downpour, Kuntal Newar headed for the clearing beyond the ruins of the ancient palace of princess Ambaa in the forests in the high hills. Because more than a satiated demon with a full belly, it was the insatiate, unseen demon dwelling in the words of a taunt that often drove man to do that which he never pushed himself to before. He did that only so that he might do away with that taunt. And just that was the reason why Kuntal Newar headed for the clearing with a hoe. To till that land with the force that he derived from scorn that had been hurting and haunting him.

When he reached the clearing, Kuntal Newar stopped and looked around for a while before putting the hoe down on the ground. He shifted a part of his body's weight from a leg onto the long wooden handle of the hoe and once again looked all around. This time he even looked skyward and down at the soil under his feet. To survey. And familiarize. Though the clearing was on even ground, it was never tilled, never sowed upon. Never with an opportunity to bear fruit but waiting to do so. The cool breeze of the night before had helped ebb a very small portion of the anguish and rancour that had accumulated in Kuntal over the years. But now, standing on that clearing and resting his weight on the hoe, all of that resentment suddenly rose to the brim once more. Because every hurtful word which stabbed at his heart and sliced through Bhairavi's womb and which brought him there that day came rushing back to his memory as if they were said just a moment ago.

'Barren land, Kuntal, is of no-one's use. Remember that!' Kuntal Newar's mother Kesari Devi had spewed those words at him, pointing a finger at his wife Bhairavi. And an eclipse was cast over Kuntal Newar.

There were times, years before his mother started taunting him, when there was never a festival or a celebration where Kuntal Newar didn't dance the Jyapu in happy abandon. He used to dance with his elder brothers Krishna and Kailash when they brought the harvest home from their field. Their field, though small, was fertile and gave good yield. Kesari Devi always observed how much snow fell and how long it lasted during the winter months. Then when the snow melted and the fields were ready to be ploughed and sowed, she looked hard at the sky, followed wind directions for a couple of days and watched changing patterns in the cloud before telling her sons what to sow. Corn, maize, rice or mustard. And the sons obeyed. They never knew that there could be any other way of doing things than doing as their mother told them to. They never tried any other way. For they never had the need to. And their small field continued to yield good harvest. 'Every good fortune can be made to occur and every person can be made to obey, if only your fields and your womb, or that of your wife's, yield abundantly,' Kesari Devi often said, likening her own field too to a fertile womb, not without a streak of pride. 'Praise Pashupatinath, barren lands and barren wombs have never afflicted this family,' she used to say thus during those days. More than praise for her God Pashupatinath, it was vanity and arrogance that oozed from her words. Not that anyone minded. For Kesari Devi herself bore six children and each of her daughters-in-law bore more than two so far. And their wombs were fertile to bear yet more. Krishna was her first born. Being so, he remained tied to puppet strings held by Kesari Devi. Then came two daughters in quick succession. The first eloped with a white skinned foreigner. So fearing a second such fiasco, she married off the second daughter at the age of twelve, a year after she stepped in to puberty. Kailash was Kesari's fourth. He did have a mind of his own, but had a greater fear to reveal that mind. So that mind of his stayed just there, suppressed within himself. The third daughter, a year younger, got decently sent away with a young man with a broad forehead, who sharpened sickles and khukri for a living. Kesari Devi took pride in how her daughters too bore children soon after they were sent to live with their husbands. Kuntal was the last. He might not have been, had Kesari Devi's husband lived for a few more years.   Now at twenty two, Kuntal was yet to bring in his bride. Not more than five feet when he stood at his tallest but sturdy to the bones, Kuntal Newar's mirth was contagious and his mind, sharp. His temper, though, was short and his heart, once bruised, could not be easily balmed. Few, however, saw this softness through his tough, carefree facade. Kuntal laughed when Kesari Devi used to announce among womenfolk while taking meal breaks during work in the fields, 'My kyeta Kuntal will give me at least three sons, eh, Kuntal?' she said, looking at Kuntal. The womenfolk laughed and teased Kuntal. Tara and Mohini would then stand up, wipe the grains of rice off their hands and dance an impromptu jyapu, celebrating in anticipation of Kuntal's first born. Both the women were already grandmothers themselves. But looking at their zest for life, it was hard to tell that they were old. 'Yes, Tara, keep the rehearsals on,' Kesari Devi would say in an equal zest, 'Just you wait and watch. I will bring home for him a bride who will put onto my lap a grandson in the very first year of her stepping into my threshold!'

Soon indeed the bride stepped into those thresholds. Her name was Bhairavi Devi. At fifteen, she had the innocence of a child, the vulnerability and fullness of an adolescent and the maturity that only a woman could have at fifteen. Never had a man such maturity at such an age. So Bhairavi Devi came with such innocence, vulnerability and maturity as Kuntal Newar's bride. The bride who was to give Kesari Devi three grandsons, with the first one within a year.

Bhairavi's skin was fair like the milk she milched and set in the fullness of her face, her eyes were small but glistening like that drop of dew about to fall off from the tip of a leaf. And when Kuntal held her in his arms and she raised her face to meet his, her eyes reached only upto his chin. The rings on her earlobes were slightly smaller than that on her nose but what she loved the most was to wear a string of bright, colourful beads around her neck. Pretending to marvel those beads and touch them, Kuntal would slowly let his hands fall down and caress her full breasts. Bhairavi knew what it was that Kuntal truly marvelled. She would blush and smile, feeling belonged. Rounded of buttocks and heavy of bosom, Kesari Devi saw in Bhairavi great promises of bearing a good brood.

'Raise those kids strong,' Kesari would tell her daughters-in-law, 'so that even when I am no more, their fathers and they can yet expand the field to a great size and till them well to make them yield harvests greater than as now. Raise those boys brave so that they can erect a large shed and fill it with bullocks strong enough to pull sturdy ploughs and with milch cows with udders that can drown the river Bagmati with the milk in them! Ah! Tilibham shall remember for all time to come what a home and hearth Kesari Devi raised. And reigned over. Ah! Let Tilibham remember!' That alone was Kesari Devi's dream. To reign over and live in a house with a roof of corrugated iron sheet instead of the present mildewed thatch roof which had moss-grown, leaking earthen tiles in places. She had dreams of someday living in a house with walls of brick and mortar instead of mountain reed smeared with a thick plaster of clay and cow dung. She dreamt of owning a house where she and their only cow would no longer share the same reed wall between them. But in the house Kesari Devi lived now, it was just like that. With Kesari Devi inside the wall and the cow outside it, under the hut's narrow eaves. When the chill winds from the north blew in during the cold months of winter, the cow and Kesari Devi were left sharing the same room, on the same side of the same wall. At times when Kesari Devi was in the house and the cow dropped dung outside, she could make out from the sound of the fall how thick or how much the dung was. And when the cow's urine fell splattered on the wall, the dampness seeped from the cow's side of the wall through to Kesari Devi's side. Even otherwise, the smell of dung always pervaded her hut of three rooms. And every whiff of it she breathed ignited in her the desire of someday owning and living in a house where she and the cow would not be sleeping on opposite sides of the same wall, sharing the dampness of the cow's dung and urine. Deservingly so, for she had given away the best part of her life raising her children and fending for herself. After her husband fell to his death into a deep ravine while out cutting mountain grass for their lone cow, Kesari Devi had gone through sufferings and lures of all kinds, including the temptation of a she goat in exchange for a night's sleep with her on her bed. She had been on her own since then. Brave and never giving up. Because there was no other way. The children were sent to school but only till the end of middle school at best. A few didn't reach even till there. Kuntal didn't. They instead reached the fields to lend a hand to their mother. During those helpless and harrowing days when she needed and sought compassion, no one showed her that. Just so, now she had none in her to show Bhairavi.

Three harvests had been brought in since Kuntal Newar wedded Bhairavi Devi. The fields continued to remain fertile. Kuntal's eldest sister-in-law Maili was once again with child. But Bhairavi was yet to show that she wasn't barren.

'My Kuntal, he is a man like his brothers, I know he is,' Kesari Devi often said these days, 'For hasn't Kesari Devi borne him and raised him like she did the rest of her sons? So will he in any way be different from them? Certainly not!' This was her way of pinning every fault on Bhairavi for being childless.

So on that particular day too Kesari Devi had started all over again, 'And when his brothers have sown fields and wombs, so must have Kuntal.' As she talked, she picked up Bhairavi's pet goat Shamlee's kid and took it to its mother. 'Hei Pashupatinath! But what can you do if the field itself is barren!' Soon, Maili's child was born. It was a son. Though the harvests continued to come in from their small field year after year, Kuntal Newar no more danced the jyapu. Music and dhimey abandoned his once happy soul, leaving it parched and wretched, longing for nothing but a child of his own from Bhairavi. A child not for his own sake or for his mother's but for the sake of a twinkle in the eyes of his Bhairavi. For the sake of those eyes to once more glisten like the drops of dew about to fall off from the tip of a leaf. And around the same time every month, Kesari Devi made it almost a habit to ask Bhairavi if she had bled for the month. When Bhairavi looked down and nodded, the malice began all over again. And after each of those periods when the malice resumed, it got more aggressive than the last. When the goat kid chewed on a black polythene bag and choked itself to death, the misfortune was attributed to Bhairavi. And her barren womb. Her sisters-in-law made attempts to show her some compassion but because those attempts were discreet, they were feeble. However, the second sister-in-law, Goma, did tell Bhairavi once to pray and invoke the blessings of Goddess Parvati, Pashupati's consort, and seek for a child. 'There is a shrine of the Goddess of fertility at Kamarupa. They call it Kamakhya,' she told Bhairavi, 'I've heard that no prayer goes unanswered at that shrine. And once you receive what you seek, visit the shrine with that what you sought and received. As paying your gratitude.' But because this was told just once and in whispers and to a mind that was unresponsive to all things else because of the spite that continually crippled it, Goma's words went unheeded and were soon forgotten. When Kuntal suggested that they sell the cow and buy a bullock to till the field, Kesari Devi vehemently disapproved. 'Bah!' she shot up fuming, 'So this whiff of a woman who does not even have the capacity to beget a mere child has but the capacity to influence my Kuntal to take decisions, eh? That too when I am yet alive and sane to take decisions in the family. Look! Just look at that audacity!' That allegation stunned Bhairavi because the decision came as a result of a discussion among all the brothers and Bhairavi knew nothing about it. The only thing that went against her was that it was her husband who happened to broach the matter to Kesari Devi. Had it been one of the other brothers, Kesari Devi might have even given it a consideration. But not anymore.

Well into the sixth year of Bhairavi's marriage, Kesari Devi's second daughter-in-law Goma was with child once again while Bhairavi was still childless. The stigma of a barren womb churned a storm that was gyrating inside her, tying her guts, nerves and emotions into knots. Though not a word of hers gave voice to this storm, every part else of hers did. She continued to remain fair of skin but it was no longer the fairness of the milk she milched but the fairness of a shroud upon a lifeless body. Her once full face had now shrivelled and her little, dew-drop eyes sunk into their sockets. They glistened no more. She no longer liked to adorn herself with rings on her earlobes and nose and strings of beads around her neck. Kuntal, however, heard every word of what these other parts of Bhairavi's had to tell. As Goma grew rounder with child, Bhairavi grew thinner with the absence of one. And the day Goma delivered her child, a dead one, Kesari Devi threw Bhairavi out of the house. She yelled, 'It is because of the shadow of infertility that has darkened the house that another womb has failed! Send the evil omen to her mother's, Kuntal, or wherever she wishes to go. For I shall not let her stay on here to eat up my descendents. Send her away! Before she preys on the next!'

Kuntal suddenly sprang up with a huff from where he was sitting and rushed past his brother to come and stand directly in front of Kesari Devi. His breath got faster and his eyes turned red with rage.

And the look in those eyes was not that of the indulgent youngest son facing his mother to plead for his wife.

'Really?' he charged instead, 'indeed! What then of all those lives that arrived like worms, year after year, for six long years since Bhairavi's shadow has darkened the house? If at all it has done so? What of them, really? They were not eaten up by Bhairavi's shadow, were they?'

Taken unawares, Kesari Devi took a step back. The domination and spite of all these years that were fuelling a rebellion in Kuntal had come to its peak.

'Who, anyway, wishes to stay here? Not I atleast!' And he stomped into the house and dragged Bhairavi out with him by her hand. Kesari Devi stood dumbstruck. This wasn't how she had expected events to turn. What she had expected was that Kuntal would beg and plead and seek mercy to let Bhairavi stay on and Kesari Devi had thought she would relent then, if only Kuntal brought home another wife to bear him a child. But far from pleading, Kuntal had that day snapped the umbilical cord. He was leaving. When he walked past his brothers and mother pulling Bhairavi after him, things suddenly started to sink into Kesari Devi. That Kuntal was leaving. What if her elder sons picked up the cue? It wasn't Kuntal whom she wished to leave. It was Bhairavi. And before situations fell apart, she gathered her composure and amended her ordain. 'Leave if you so wish, Kuntal,' she shouted after him, 'But remember, a mother cannot stop having concern for her children. Oh! I forget! But then how will you see through that, when you have none of your own to feel that concern? Leave if you have to, this ancestral roof, but I will yet allow you to raise your own separate shelter in the farthest corner of our field from here. Remain there and don't ever let that woman's infertile shadow be cast upon the fields and wombs of this home. Go leave if you still have to. But as long as that banshee is with you, don't expect any share of the harvest. Don't expect any support of any kind. From anyone here. Krishna! Kailash! You better understand that and make your wives understand as well! And so if you still want to leave, Kuntal, go! Leave!'

And Kuntal Newar left. He, taking Bhairavi with him and she, taking her goat Shamlee with her. And Kailash carried his stillborn child away, wrapped in an old saree, to bury it somewhere in the mountains. The herbs Goma had asked the hamlet's midwife to get for her to abort the foetus had done their work.

It was late afternoon when Kuntal and Bhairavi left Kesari Devi's home. He didn't know where he was walking to, but he kept on walking, holding Bhairavi's hand all along. None of them spoke a word. With Bhairavi's other hand, she walked her goat with a length of rope. Kuntal didn't notice Tara approaching them. She was returning home from the fields with her cow. Bhairavi saw her at a distance but couldn't find her voice to say anything to Kuntal. She had got so used to thinking many times over before uttering even a word that many a time, by the time she knew she would be allowed to speak, her wish to speak had died away. Her voice had learnt to withdraw into the silence of her hollow womb. So it was now. While she fought with her dilemma of whether she should ask Kuntal if he had seen Tara coming towards them, Tara was already standing right before them.

'Kuntal?' Tara asked, looking straight into his eyes, 'Is it what I understand?'

'Yes,' He replied.

Darkness was slowly descending and Tara saw that the children had nowhere to go. At a certain age as that of Tara's, after an entire lifetime's wisdom of raising children and then grandchildren, women get to know things without these being told to them. So it was with Tara now. She gently held her hand forward, took in it Kuntal's hand and led Kuntal, Bhairavi and Bhairavi's goat Shamlee to her hut. Little, flickering lamps started appearing here and there, high and low on the slopes of the hamlet of Tilibham. 'I cannot keep you for always, Kuntal,' Tara said after they had walked for a distance towards her hut, 'but I can keep you till you make some arrangement.'

Tara's sons helped Kuntal make those arrangements while her grandchildren doted on Shamlee. But Bhairavi continued to remain the lost, confused and subdued person that she was made to become over all these years at the home of Kesari Devi.

Kuntal, Bhairavi and Shamlee took refuge with Tara's family for two days and three nights. Early on the morning after the third night, Tara and her eldest son walked with Kuntal and Bhairavi to leave them at their new home.   It was a home where only Kuntal and Bhairavi would live, along with the goat she loved like her child. Even this child of hers was with child now. Shamlee was pregnant. They raised their home at the outer edge of Kesari Devi's field. It was a windowless square shed of about eight feet on all sides and a low cut-away on one side for a door, where even Kuntal had to bend to pass through. The mud floor and bamboo roof completed the shed. Years ago when Kesari Devi took a young Kuntal to the fields with her, it took about half of an hour for Kuntal's little feet to walk him home from there. Now there was a cluster of wild banana plants next to a cluster of tall sugarcanes at that place. Kuntal and Bhairavi raised their little hearth just beyond those clusters which stood as some kind of a fence between them and Kesari Devi's home. Here Bhairavi and Shamlee lay to sleep on opposite sides of the same unplastered bamboo wall at night. She, on a floral cotton bed-sheet spread out on a reed mat upon the mud floor inside the shed and Shamlee, on a clump of grass outside. When the crisp, chill winds stole into the shed through the long, narrow slits on the wall, Bhairavi curled up and turned towards Kuntal and snuggled into his chest for warmth. She dug her feet under his to keep them warm. And Kuntal gently drew her in. On nights that were too cold, Bhairavi brought Shamlee too into the shed with her and Kuntal. While the goat sat on the clump of grass and pressed its nose into its belly, Bhairavi pressed her nose and mouth into the warm flesh on Kuntal's bosom. And Kuntal put his arm around Bhairavi. But she could yet breath. A long felt suffocation had suddenly lifted from her and in the spacelessness of that small shed Bhairavi found her space. And her sleep. And while she slept, Kuntal stayed awake. Wondering how to feed and fend for the woman on his bosom, for the woman who had placed all her trust in him, had thrust her face into his chest and breathed out all her sufferings there and slipped away into blissful slumber. Kuntal lay awake, wishing he could find some land to till, wishing he had a bullock to pull his plough. Shamlee watched Kuntal through the darkness. Bhairavi's breath grew deep and long, of a sleep that came to her after years. At times, her breathing appeared like tiny grunts, muffled that her breath was. Kuntal gently lifted her head from his bosom and lay it on the bed-sheet on the mat. Then slowly, so not to disturb her, he pulled himself away from her and quietly went out of the shed. He didn't know how long he stood outside in the stillness of the night. A deep dark shade of navy blue brushed everything that lay all around him, as far as his eyes could see. Soft blotches of pale yellow moonlight fell on the mountain peaks like buttermilk dropped accidently upon them. A chill breeze floated in from the north and he braced himself. As if there was a purpose in it all. In his coming out of the shed and letting the sediments of a life left behind be lifted by that breeze and be blown away. He didn't remember when or from whom, but he had once long ago heard of a clearing somewhere by the ruins of princess Ambaa's palace. Maybe he could go see it, he thought, standing there in the stillness of the night. Maybe he could till it.

Kuntal stood there the rest of the night and watched the sky turn into a much thicker shade of navy blue than before and then slowly paling away to grow ashen, then blue and finally swathing everything with a tinge of orange. The night sky took Kuntal's mind and thoughts with it as it moved through changes that were deep, dark and ashen to finally arrive at a new dawn. The dollops of buttermilk on the mountain peaks too had turned orange. The wind was still crisp and clouds pregnant with rain still hovered but chirps of birds and voices of dawn had started echoing through the mountains. Kuntal stretched his arms above his head and clasping the fingers of one hand into the other, turned his palms heavenwards. He then slowly turned towards their shed, his and Bhairavi's shed, lowered his head and stepped inside through the opening they considered a door. Bhairavi was still sleeping. Kuntal came out again, picked the hoe from where it was standing just outside the wall and started walking towards the clearing by the ruins of princess Ambaa's palace.

All of a sudden, the anguish and resentment in Kuntal which the cool night breeze had helped ebb had soared again. 'Barren land, Kuntal, is of no-one's use. Remember that!'...

~

That night, after returning from the clearing by the ruins of princess Ambaa's palace, Kuntal lay down quietly with Bhairavi by his side and Shamlee lay down on her clump of grass. Kuntal's heart ached when he proposed to Bhairavi to buy a bullock to till the land by the ruins. His heart ached, because to buy the bullock they would have to sell Shamlee. The decision was hard but it had to be taken. And so it was.

But they would wait for some time. Till that time as would be needed for Shamlee to deliver her babies. So that she would fetch a higher price. And till such time, Kuntal walked up to the clearing by the ruins of princess Ambaa's palace every dawn to dig out whatever undergrowth he could with his hoe. Sometimes he used both hoe and khukri. Because he had to do it now when the earth was soft from soaking in the rain.

While in Kamakhya in the faraway Nilachal hills, the ambubasi fair was at the peak of its religious revelry.

END OF CHAPTER 3

CHAPTER 4

HOME

Maili, however, didn't stop taking out Kuntal and Bhairavi's share of rice from the big basket in the corner of the kitchen when she prepared to cook the family's meals. Only, she didn't cook their share with that of the rest. Instead, she set aside the two fistfuls of their share in a small cloth bag and tucked the bag away behind the low pile of firewood. Then every sixth or seventh day she would get one of the older children to smuggle out that rice to Mohini's house. Mohini's house was close by, just where the narrow path took a sharp bend down the slope. Mohini then took the rice over to Bhairavi. As she did so, Mohini sometimes added a couple of eggs from her hen coop or a few cobs of corn with the rice. Once she even took a few chickens and the mother hen and left them at Kuntal's yard.

'Feed them, Bhairavi, let them grow and breed,' she said while returning. Bhairavi smiled and nodded. She picked up a chick gently onto her palms. It looked like a ball of coloured cotton. And as she looked at it, it looked back at her and chirped. If it turned out to be a hen, it too would be expected to grow and lay eggs. What, Bhairavi wondered, if the chick too was infertile? There'd be one hen less to lay eggs. That would mean fewer eggs to sell or roost and thereby less earnings for them. Bhairavi gently put the chick down on the ground and it scurried away to the rest of the brood.

'It's okay, Chick-Chick,' Bhairavi said, 'I know you'll lay that egg if you're a girl,' and she smiled to herself, discovering an inexpressible joy in her freedom to say what she pleased, to whom she pleased, without having to think over and over again whether she should speak or not. Or whether she would be chastised for speaking. She continued, 'And even if you don't, it's just fine!'

Thus slowly, she began talking to the chickens and the goat, the plants and the birds. She realized she still had her voice and that she wished that voice to be heard. And when she stood by the fence and called out to Kuntal, she loved to hear how her voice rang through the fields, skies and mountains carrying his name with it. How she laughed when the echoing mountains called her back. She was seeing life anew in her new home. Her home. And not the home of Kesari Devi.

Bhairavi put out an old, tattered cotton scarf under a shrub in the yard for the mother hen and her brood to rest at night. The leafy branches of the bush hung low to almost touch the ground so when the fowls sat at the root of the bush, they were well protected. But Kuntal left a large wicker basket overturned on them, for fear of the mountain fox. Soon Chick-Chick indeed grew to be a hen, a beautiful one. There were also two roosters among her siblings. But because they started pecking and clawing at one another, Kuntal took away one to the market to sell. The lone rooster that stayed back now reigned over Chick Chick and all the other hens. It chased them all and mated with each, filling Bhairavi's yard with frequent and frantic crowing and clucking of the fowls. Even Shamlee was slowly getting heavier. Life was filling into her new home. Her home.

Bhairavi had so much to do each day from early morning to dusk that she could keep no track of time as it went on its own unhurried and unslowed pace. Kuntal erected a fence around their shed with a yard of a manageable size inside. He put up the fence with sticks and branches which he collected in the clearing by the palace ruins. The lower part of the fencing was more closely woven to keep the goat and fowls inside. Then while he went to prepare the clearing near the ruins of princess Ambaa's palace for cultivating, Bhairavi set about plastering the bamboo walls of her house with water and mud. Sometimes she brought in grass for Shamlee from the lower reaches of the slope where there was an abundance of juicy mountain grass. At other times she walked down to the mountain spring and fetched water. As she found herself talking more and more to Shamlee and the hens and playing about with them, she came to realize that she ceased to remain conscious all the while of her barrenness. When she served meals to Kuntal, he saw that her eyes were coming back to be the dew drops they once used to be and her cheeks were filling up too. She no more thought a million times before uttering a word, there was no one from whom she needed to restrain herself from being the way she was. Soon the hens started laying eggs. Kuntal and Bhairavi left some for the mother hen to sit on and roost and collected the rest to sell. They needed the money for salt, mustard oil, kerosene and soap while Maili continued to send rice and sometimes potatoes. The last time she sent rice, Maili and Goma's older children came by to leave it at Kuntal and Bhairavi's shed. When Bhairavi saw the three children coming, she ran towards them but suddenly halted at a short distance away. Seeing her stop, the children themselves moved closer to her, but no one spoke a word. The one who held the bag of rice walked to the door of the hut, left the bag there and came back to stand with the others, near Bhairavi. All four stood in silence, an awkward reticence crawling up to their midst. Some unseen, imperious force all of a sudden came to loom into the yard, questioning every thought, criticizing every move and crippling the heart's little liberties and joys. Bhairavi's hand instinctively reached for the soft round part of her belly. The consciousness that was leaving her had once again come to remind her of her barrenness. It felt as if the children from that home brought with them Kesari Devi's unseen presence into Bhairavi's yard. It was at that very moment that Kuntal emerged from inside the shed.

'Boy! O Boy! Look who's here!' he shouted with joy seeing his nephews and niece. That one carefree shout spread instantly like a happy song among the restrained group of family members standing, until now, like strangers. The children rushed forward to Kuntal, clung to him, each speaking above the other and no one hearing anything. They had so much to tell! 'What if your grandmother finds out that you came here?' Bhairavi asked after a while. 'She won't,' replied the youngest. The eldest added, 'But you know, uncle Kuntal, she saw aama handing the bag of rice to me the other day. She looked the other way but did hang around the yard pretending not to notice. She waited till I walked out. I could sense her eyes on me as I walked towards grandma Mohini's house. I guess she knows.' Bhairavi walked into the shed and quickly prepared a scramble of the only two eggs left at home and offered it to the children. How they relished it! She had a strong urge to ask the children to keep coming but instead found herself quietly seeing them off till the detachable part of the fence in the yard that served as a gate.

As the days went by, Kuntal's palms had grown blisters and his skin acquired a deep dark tan, yet his heart had grown a kind of bond with that virgin land he was hoeing, which gave him the blisters and the tan. He would raise corn and maize there. He would split bamboo lengthwise into halves and use them as channels to bring water from the brook by the palace to water the clearing. And then, if the water stayed, he would also consider growing rice. Then someday, maybe he would take in the harvest from his field and celebrate, maybe dance the jyapu again.

Little clumps of moist earth fell off the edges of his pyjamas which were still rolled up to his shins as he walked back home through the fields. The rains were good that year. Krishna and Kailash had already begun preparing their field. It was once his too, but no more. Kuntal wondered what they would grow. In rains like that year's, Kesari

Devi normally chose to grow rice. He continued to walk, a thousand thoughts racing through his mind, taking the speed away from his feet. The soles of his feet had cuts and bruises but Kuntal hadn't noticed them. What he instead noticed was that Bhairavi was content. And when he thought of her, his pace homewards quickened. When he reached home, he saw that Shamlee had delivered her babies. Two of them. They were both black, like their mother. Kuntal would now have to make a shed for Shamlee and her kids too. Because they would not be able to put all three goats inside the hut with them, nor would they be able to leave the newborn babies out. Because unprecedented monsoon rains kept lashing by. So he decided to put up a shed of thatch and mountain grass against the southern wall of their own makeshift shelter. Because the rain drenched winds spared that side of the shelter. However, for that night and the next, Shamlee and her kids stayed inside with Kuntal and Bhairavi, while he worked on the shed with split bamboo, grass and reed that he gathered on the way back from the clearing by the palace ruins. Towards late afternoon when he walked back home across the fields and mountain slopes from the clearing, he sometimes wondered why he was doing what he was, what and where it would all lead to, if at all anywhere. If all of it was even worth doing. Then while his thoughts still played in his mind, he would reach the merrily undisciplined fence that marked his yard with its tiny, one room hut. Bhairavi would most often be out there in the yard, either weeding or planting something, or talking to and feeding the chickens, or with one of Shamlee's babies in her arms. Sometimes Kuntal found her plastering the walls of their shelter with mud. She no longer remained scared all the while, of having unknowingly done something wrong. Kuntal realized that though he and Bhairavi remained just two, his household had expanded. With goats and chickens. For sometime now, two stray dogs had also started visiting and soon they started staying on at nights too. 'Pashupatinath has sent watch dogs for us,' Bhairavi would say in a light hearted banter and laugh unrepressed. And when she laughed thus, she did so without guilt and without fear of being chastised for showing the audacity to laugh despite not having borne a child.

'When was the last time that I heard her talk and laugh like that?' Kuntal would then wonder.

The next day after returning from his digging, Kuntal put in the finishing touches to the shed and stuck uneven but firm sticks into the ground to form an enclosure with the shed as its roof. Then he entwined grass to make a thick rope and used that length of rope to hold the door of the enclosure together. So on that third night, both Kuntal and Bhairavi moved Shamlee and her babies into their new shelter. Sensing Bhairavi's attachment to them, Kuntal gently slipped an arm around her waist and said, 'They anyway won't stay here for long, so this place will do just fine for now I guess.' 'I know,' she replied, 'but do you realize that when they leave we will need to put up a bigger shed? For aren't we supposed to bring in a bullock then? We've been saving for one, haven't we?' Kuntal drew her closer to him and held her there for long. She was growing, he thought, as a woman. Growing as someone capable of taking up the reigns of a household, her own household, because she was given the opportunity and space to grow. It was only now that she was starting to live her life with Kuntal. She now allowed Kuntal, even initiated, that little teasing and caressing before they buried themselves deep into each other, locked in love for the sake of love and not for the sake of bearing children.

In the mornings now Kuntal was no longer the first to wake up. Because now their yard came alive even before the morning sun brushed the mountain peaks with yellow butter. The hens and the rooster would all be pecking about while Shamlee and her babies would get restless, wanting their enclosure to be opened. It was these little noises of life, contentment and sometimes lovemaking of the fowls which woke Kuntal now-a-days. On some such mornings, he lingered on in bed upon the cotton bed cloth spread over the mat till Bhairavi too woke up but didn't yet open her eyes. Instead she shifted closer to him. During such mornings Kuntal and Bhairavi fell into tender, laid back and drowsy love-making listening to the fowls do the same outside in the yard. Their love making would then make them spark away from sleep a little at a time, then more rapidly until both panted into complete wakefulness. That particular morning was one such sluggish start to an equally sluggish day. Kuntal didn't feel like going to the clearing by the palace ruins but he had to. He had worked really hard to free that land from nettles and undergrowth and thereby make it ready for cultivation. It was the rainy season and he could not let the rains go waste. He could not afford to. Tara had spared some corn for Kuntal to sow. So he owed it to her too. He had to go. Though he didn't wish to. He reluctantly went but decided to return early. Despite the looming presence close by of a palace that lay in ruins, of a place from where some swore they heard the sound of anklet bells and tiny hammers on copper sheet float into the valley even now, despite the eeriness of it all, there was a certain quiet about that clearing by the palace ruins. A quiet that was almost comforting. It was the kind of tranquillity that was scary for the scared but serene for the unscared. Birds, crickets and little creatures of the mountainous wild arrived there to peck and sniff at the worms that got dug up for the first time ever by Kuntal's hoe. The birds chirped and made their own little noises which reassured Kuntal of life that was living at present, unlike the ruins which stood as a reminder of life that was living in the long gone past. These creatures gave Kuntal company. So despite the uncanny quietness of the place, Kuntal found solace there. Sometimes he walked Shamlee and her babies to that clearing with him to feed on the grass and help him weed the place. And at other times, the dogs lazily followed him to the clearing. They sniffed and pawed at everything that challenged their curiosity on the way and in the process, often went astray from the narrow foot track. But soon they sniffed back to reach Kuntal. Sometimes they waited there with him to follow him back home. But sometimes, one of them would wander away and reach home before Kuntal did, or after.

And now a small part of the land was all ready to be sown and all set to bear fruit. That land, Kuntal knew for sure, wasn't barren. It just didn't have the opportunity to bear. That day he planned to fence the area with whatever twigs and branches he could collect in and around. He took with him the little pouch of corn that Tara had sent. If he still had time after the fencing, he would scatter the corn and cover them with soil. Then maybe he would take a break. But for now, he had to go there despite the lethargy of the morning. So he picked the hoe and the sickle, tucked the pouch of corn into his waist band and left for the clearing by the ruins of what was once princess Ambaa's palace. Walking down the edge of Kesari Devi's field always filled him with renewed zeal to strive harder to make things work out, away from his mother's shadow. So maybe it was good, he thought, as he walked past her field, that he had to walk that way whenever he went to the clearing by the palace ruins. It kept his anger and the subsequent desire to make it on his own, ignited. People often asked him, 'Kuntal, they say souls yet to be liberated still hover around the ruins. They say, Brajbhushan's soul still works on his copper sheets and the *tonk-tok-tong* of his little tools beating on the copper sheets are still borne out of the ruins by the winds. True, is it? Have you ever heard them? Heard any sound else, for that matter?' Kuntal honestly had not heard anything that sounded like the beating of tiny hammers on sheets of copper. Or anklet bells or laughter of little girls. But yes, sometimes, though rarely, he did feel the unearthliness of the place crawling up from all sides towards him like a soft hum. During such times, he felt a breeze coming from the wrong direction. He felt eyes on him. He felt breath on his nape. But again, he thought these just might be because of all the stories he heard about the palace and about the long gone royals in that palace since the time he learned to listen and to remember. Nothing more than that. Or were they? He shuddered sometimes even when an ant crawled up his naked leg. But now his reasons for telling people that he did hear Brajbhushan on a number of occasions were entirely different. He didn't want others to come close to the clearing. He wanted even the stray goatherd to stay away. For he had to keep that unclaimed land to himself. To till it and make it bear fruit. So when people asked, he said, 'Yes, I hear Brajbhushan sometimes. That, and ankle bells too. There have been times when I sweated and hurried home.' And the word spread far into the valley and to villages higher on the mountains. Just as Kuntal desired. Not that he never felt a cold shudder and a sweat go down his back together but thoughts of

Kesari Devi's taunt had the power to wipe them both and keep him going.

After that day's fencing and sowing, he would have to take time out to take the goats down to the market to sell. He had to have a bullock. And a plough. Otherwise getting that whole place ready for sowing with only a hoe, a sickle and a khukri would be absolute madness. Moreover, he could not let the rains pass by.

And so he went that day to the clearing by the ruins, though he didn't wish to. He finished fencing a fourth of the area, scattered the corn and gently rubbed them into the soil. It was already late in the afternoon when all of that work was done. Though he had hoped to return home early that day, it took him longer than usual. His limbs were loosening with fatigue. But he was happy that the sowing was done. Even if just on a small portion of the land. It would be his own harvest. Even fertile land did not get ready to bear fruit when not given an opportunity and not gently and persistently worked upon. Anything sharp and hindering, be they nettles and weeds, killed the paddy even in good soil. Kuntal had toiled much to break the soil loose and prove its fertility. He once had a fleeting thought of how this land and Bhairavi were so alike. Craving for love and waiting to yield wholeheartedly.

As Kuntal walked back home, many a thought creased his brow. The goats alone would not fetch enough for a bullock. If they even somehow did, it would only be for an old, sickly one. They had saved up a meagre amount from selling eggs and firewood but it was just that. Meagre. If he even asked for a loan, he didn't know whom to ask from. And if he let too much time pass by in thinking of arranging for the money, the monsoon rains would quickly aid a regrowth of the weeds and nettles over which he sweated and grew blisters. He had to act fast. As he walked on, his hut slowly began to appear in the distance. Little stalks of corn and maize sprouted through the soil in the fields all around his fenced yard. The rains made the growth of wild banana and bamboo near his hut more luxuriant. Kuntal sometimes used those banana leaves as an umbrella. There was crispness in the mountain air, yet there was a certain rejoicing, of life and growth. For a passing moment Kuntal wondered, 'Was all this some kind of a harbinger? Ah! Illusion!' The closer he arrived home, the more expanded a view he got of his hut and its yard. He could see Bhairavi looking at the goats. When she heard his hands at the gate of the fence she turned and walked towards him. Then, as if reading his mind, she put a hand on his arm and asked, 'I was thinking, Kuntal, if we could borrow a bullock for a few days instead of borrowing money?' Because even Bhairavi had a fair idea of how much the goats would fetch and how much a bullock would cost. Kuntal remained quiet but thought over what she suggested. Yes, he thought, she was growing as a woman with a mind of her own. Because she was given the opportunity to. 'I suppose we can, yes, Bhairavi,' he replied after a moment's consideration. She let her hand fall from his arm and clasped his fingers. He tightened his own around hers and they walked towards the bucket of water behind Shamlee's enclosure. At this place Kuntal arranged for a short length of a halved tree trunk, with the flat side up and the rounded side pushed partly into the ground to keep it steady. This served as Bhairavi's wash area. Here she washed whatever utensils they had, their clothes and herself as well. Stepping up on that halved tree trunk, Kuntal released her hand to wash his hands and feet but Bhairavi remained standing beside him. 'Maybe we can ask Mohini mai? Or her sons?' She kept standing, looking at him, expecting an answer. But Kuntal remained quiet. He was thinking. 'Mmm, maybe we can, yes,' he replied, not very confidently though. Bhairavi moved towards the hut only after she got his answer. She smiled as she walked slowly past the goats' enclosure. 'If that works out,' she said looking indulgently at Shamlee and her babies, 'We can keep her. And her babies. We can sell some milk as well.' The fatigue that completely overtook Kuntal now was a sweet, deliciously pacifying kind, one that tired the muscles but eased the heart. There was still enough daylight outside for him to have walked up to Mohini's house to ask them about borrowing the bullock. But the soles of his feet were aching. He would instead just lie on his bed and go there the next day. 'Mohini mai should not mind,' Kuntal said, stretching out on the bed cloth over the mat, 'And yes, probably Shamlee will get to stay on with us.' 'With the babies,' Bhairavi added, her eyes glowing.

Harbinger? Kuntal wondered again.

END OF CHAPTER 4

CHAPTER 5

BIRTH

Mohini's land had already been tilled and sown. They would not require the bull now, not in a while. So it was arranged that Kuntal would come in the mornings, take the bull and also the plough, till the land by the palace clearing and when done for the day, would take the bull and plough back to her. Providence was strange. It provided when it wished to, took away when it so wished. But it nevertheless stood by. Watching. Sometimes giving, sometimes taking. That day it gave. The bull. Without any hindrance. Kuntal wanted to rest that day but when things were snugly falling into place and when a bullock had been bestowed upon him, he thought he ought to make the best of it. Or else Providence might just as well decide to take back what it had bestowed.

Kuntal felt an incredible force surge through him as he led the bull into the clearing by the ruins of princess Ambaa's palace. A force he never felt before. He was tilling on his own, though on land that he couldn't really claim to be his, with a bullock and a plough that were borrowed. Yet he was on his own. He hoped and prayed that there would be good yield. Everywhere.

The bull did not need much coaxing during that first day of tilling. But the plough did. Stubborn roots of aged shrubs, bramble and undergrowth which remained undisturbed under the soil for long now refused to dislodge. But since Kuntal did some weeding earlier, the roots eventually gave in, although reluctantly. 'Remember, kyeta,' Kesari Devi used to say when she taught him how to plough, 'the first tilling of a land always has to be forceful. Let the plough penetrate deep. Push hard. Then however virgin the soil, she will yield.' Kuntal pushed hard and let the plough penetrate deep. The rains had moistened the soil so the tilling did not require as much force as Kuntal anticipated. In places where there were no obstinate deep roots, there the plough glided in easily and the bull moved fast. On that first day of ploughing Kuntal ploughed a considerable portion of the land. And as the days came and went by, more and more land was tilled. However, there were times even in broad daylight when the breeze stopped blowing and the leaves on the big trees around became still. During such times, even his own shadow made him shudder as it lay crippled because of the uneven mounds of earth on which it prostrated. He would then stop on his tracks and listen. To hear if any sound came from the ruins of princess Ambaa's palace. There weren't any. And yet, he expected some sound to come by. Had he heard something, he would have felt more comfortable than not having heard anything at all but yet having to wait and listen as if something would emanate. And when no sound came, it only added to his nervousness during such afternoons. That afternoon was one of those times. So as soon as he was done for the day, he quickly went to leave the bull and the plough at Mohini's place and headed straight home.

That night there was a light drizzle. Bhairavi had started keeping the chickens inside Shamlee's enclosure. Now that Shamlee would stay on, Bhairavi christened her two babies too. She called them

Dairu and Kajlee. She hadn't named them earlier because she feared that the attachment and their subsequent going away would hurt. And she was not ready to bear anymore of being hurt. Not when she was trying to leave behind all the misery she was made to bear and was seeking out her life and laughter.

Early next morning Kuntal once again walked up to Mohini's place for the plough and the bull and led it to the clearing. As days passed, he started making little, random conversation with the bull as they walked to and from the land they were working on together. The bull sometimes nodded and sometimes shook his head and yet at other times snorted, making Kuntal laugh. A bond started to grow between the two, man and beast. Soon, Kuntal no longer had to lead the beast. It knew its way and so the two of them just walked side by side. At the clearing, Kuntal's tilling was progressing closer towards the edge of the land where the hillock with the palace ruins started to rise. Kuntal had by then grown accustomed to the stillness of the place. He had also grown accustomed to the occasional cacophony of the mountain birds, the way they all joined in together when one started to chirp. Some even mated while the cacophony was on. As Kuntal grew more and more familiar with every tree and rock around the slope of the hillock, he no longer feared his own crippled shadow and no longer shuddered in anticipation of voices from the ruins of princess Ambaa's palace. His plough buried its front into the soil and moved ahead effortlessly, turning up clods of fertile black soil as it moved. Then one morning, while still tilling, the plough suddenly stopped. Kuntal shoved it in with a big thrust but it didn't slide in. He gave another shove, a stronger one this time, yet the plough did not move. It struck something hard and wouldn't move ahead. Kuntal stopped the bull and pulled out the khukri from his waistband. He then dug into the soil at that place. What the plough had struck didn't seem like rock to him. He pushed the khukri deeper and finally dislodged from the earth and pulled out what seemed instead like a piece of metal. It was indeed metal. It was in the shape of a banyan leaf, a remarkably large one at that. Soiled and muddied, it was stained a queer brown. It seemed to have been originally flat but later beaten upon. Kuntal picked it up and turned it over and over in his palms. There was some kind of an etching on it but he couldn't make out what it was. Because the ridges in the etching were filled with mud which got deeply embedded and had become hard as stone. Kuntal had to jab really hard at all that mud to dislodge it. He slapped the sheet with one hand on to the other palm to shake off whatever loose earth stuck to it. Then he nonchalantly tucked it into his waistband to take it home. He could put the metal to use, he thought. Maybe make a ladle out of it, with a handle of finely scraped bamboo. Or maybe make a trowel for Bhairavi to dig and weed her little vegetable patch where she planted a little sapling of chilli, another of lemon, a few sprigs of the long, serrated coriander and some herbs. A little distance away, she had also planted a small kurvak plant. She knew it would take time for the plant to show up with the first red blooms but she was willing to wait. She watered and nurtured the plant with such love that Kuntal saw in her earnestness a fear, lest the plant turned infertile like her. As for the sheet of copper in his hands, he thought of a number of things, as he walked on, that would possibly be made out of it. After the day's ploughing was done, Kuntal left the bullock and the plough at Mohini's place on his way back and headed home with the piece of metal shoved into his waistband. Reaching home, as was a habit, he walked straight to the bucket of water by the halved tree trunk beside Shamlee's enclosure to wash the mud and filth off his limbs. He sat on the block of wood and taking out the banyan leaf shaped piece of metal from his waistband, started to scrub off the mud from it. But the stains on it were adamant. They seemed to have got lodged from years and years of remaining under the soil, undisturbed and unseen. Kuntal could not wash off the stains but he could make out for sure that there was some sort of engraving on it. He was definite of that now. Though he still could not make out what the engraving was. The sheet itself looked like it was copper. He would scrub it clean at leisure later, he thought. But as of now, he flung it on to the roof of their shelter. He would bring it down once he finished the ploughing and sowing, when the corn would grow on its own and would not require for him to be constantly at the field. It would be at such times that he would bring the piece of metal down from his roof, scrub it clean and make something out of it. So Kuntal tossed it and the piece of metal landed gently on the hut's grass roof.

Kuntal, though, would forget about that copper sheet, shaped like a banyan leaf with Dakshyayani's yoni engraved on it.

That evening Bhairavi scrambled an egg with chilli and onion for Kuntal. In it she added a few sprigs of the long, serrated coriander from her tiny vegetable patch. She also made a curry of tapioca to go with the steamed rice. 'Have our hens started laying again?' Kuntal asked, as he sat for supper. Bhairavi smiled and sat close to him. 'Not as yet,' she replied, 'but they should soon.' She wiped the mud floor in front of Kuntal with one hand and sat the plate of rice there with the other. 'The children had come,' she said, 'and Goma sent two eggs and a few pieces of tapioca with them.' Kuntal started eating in silence. Darkness was gathering outside. Inside, by the flicker of the feeble kerosene lamp, Bhairavi watched the play of light and shade on Kuntal's tanned face. He was handsome. She blushed. Even through the dimness of the light, Kuntal saw through the corner of his eyes how her cheeks slowly filled with colour. He took a morsel of rice and some scrambled egg in his hand and held it up to her. She brought her mouth forward towards his hand and took it in, holding up his hand with her own. Kuntal started giving her more. For those few moments, every ounce of misery had lifted from Bhairavi. There was a bullock and a plough to till the land without having to barter the goats. A part of the land had already been sown and there were babies in the house. What if those were just goats and fowls, but they were babies nevertheless. Maili and Goma's children too had come and enlivened the yard during the day. And now Kuntal was feeding her. Her little heart filled with an aching pleasure and bliss in it. It had been really long since she felt this way. She took in all that Kuntal was indulgently feeding her. She took in all of it.

She took in all of him.

Days and nights that were drenched in rain and warmed in sun came and went by, soaking Kuntal in sweat and toil. The bullock came and went each day. Soon the ploughing was complete and the sowing was done. So the bullock was no longer needed and once the need stopped, the bullock no longer kept coming. Kuntal seemed to miss him. Kajlee and Dairu too had grown. And from afar Bhairavi could no longer differentiate the chickens from their mother because they too were almost as round and fluffed up. Her vegetable patch expanded. Kuntal went to his corn field only for light work like some weeding and some mending in the fence where stray sticks fell off. Slowly, the rains ceased. Autumn was on its way. The mountain and its valleys were getting crisp. Kuntal wondered how they would fare during the chill winter months. Meanwhile, Bhairavi thought she lost track of time and must have somehow been mistaken when her monthly cycle of bleeding didn't yet occur. She thought it was well past a month and overdue but it just couldn't be. She thought she made some mistake in calculating her cycle. It just couldn't be that she missed her periods as a consequence of having had conceived. For she could never conceive. She was barren. But then she missed the next one too. This time too she brushed it aside. Only when she missed the third, when nausea and laziness gradually started to leave her weary in the mornings and when she started craving for spicy, tangy, chutney did she tell Kuntal. She probably was not barren after all. Not anymore. But she couldn't be sure. While the corn grew and rose in Kuntals's field by the ruins of princess Ambaa's palace, at home Bhairavi thought she felt her belly and bosom grow heavy. Bhairavi wondered if she could truly be with child, with Kesari Devi's grandchild from Kuntal.

Soon autumn arrived and in Tilibham, it was festival time. To observe and celebrate navaratri, the nine nights and ten days dedicated to Durga, the Goddess of fertility, of female power. As if to celebrate apparent life in Bhairavi's womb. In those nine nights and ten days, the Newars of Tilibham worshipped the ten different forms of the Mother Goddess Durga, one form for each day. However, every year on the eighth day of navaratri, which they called Ashutwami, the Newars of Tilibham worshipped a living goddess, a pre-pubescent female child. This custom was an ancient one in the village of Tilibham and the Newars there called it the Kumari Puja, the worship of the Kumari, the pre-pubescent girl child. Though it indeed was a custom that had prevailed since very ancient times in Tilibham, it however, was not one that went back in time past and beyond that of princess Ambaa's. Village elders never referred to the practice being prevalent before the times of princess Ambaa and her days in the palace near Tilibham. Aamas, who were the nuns of the Durga temple of Tilibham, too said that the worship of the living goddess in Tilibham began only to make true a prophesy that was foretold at princess Ambaa's palace.

....you are the force of Creation and yet, need to be sowed upon... you are the virgins that man will worship, my darlings, and they shall call it the Kumari Puja...

No Newar though knew how true it was, because no one from the times of that doomed clan lived to witness even the first ever Kumari Puja at Tilibham. But now it no longer mattered to people in and around that quaint little Himalayan hamlet as to when it began or how it began. All that mattered was that Kumari Puja and the autumnal navaratri were of great religious rejoicing among the Newars of Tilibham. Apart from the spiritual zeal of the occasion, there was also much spirited dancing of the jyapu. The Newars danced and prayed all of those nine nights and ten days, oblivious of the fact that far away at the Kamakhya temple in Assam's Kamarupa, fervent preparations were on for the same nine nights and ten days of worship and celebration in dedication to the same Mother Goddess. At Kamakhya too, a group of senior priests called the Bordeuris, performed the rituals at the sanctum sanctorum, at Dakshyayani's yoni, inside the temple's innermost chamber, the 'garbhagriha'. At Tilibham, aamas along with priests whom they called bubas performed the rituals leaving the temple doors open for devotees who flocked in from farther down the valley and from higher in the mountains to sit through the rituals and watch it being performed. They believed that even sitting and watching the navaratri rituals being performed brought fertility to the barren womb, groom to the marriageable girl, cure to the terminally ill and abundance to the poor. And because Bhairavi wished to go to the temple of the Mother

Goddess once during the navaratri celebrations, Kuntal decided to take her there on the eighth day of navaratri, on Ashutwami. And that was also the day of the Kumari Puja.

Tilibham's only Durga temple was freshly painted, its floors washed and its fence redone for the autumnal navaratri celebrations. A hundred and fifty ancient steps of cobblestone reached up to a high flat land where the temple was perched. A high mast was now erected at the centre of that yard and festoons of brightly coloured paper flowers were hung from that mast and looped to the posts of the fence around the temple. The fence too had shimmering paper garlands and streamers hung on it. New grass mats were brought in to be spread in the courtyard for devotees to sit through the navaratri rituals. The Newars believed that three drops of blood from Sati's body and a clump of her hair fell there when Shiva roamed the mountains in those parts in a fit of grief and wrath at the unnatural death of his beloved. The temple was built around a large female figure carved onto a megalith that stood ensconced into the mountain on one side of the flat land. The figure was nude and sat cross legged. Legends in Tilibham went that many years ago a woodcutter found a similar image of a nude female engraved on a small round piece of ancient red copper in a crag in that same megalith, entangled among what seemed to him like a clump of fossilised hair. He also noticed three strange dark marks around that clump. He had picked the piece of copper and taken it to an old hermitress who lived nearby with her disciple. 'The piece of copper would have rolled down the face of the rock and fallen to the ground,' the woodcutter told the hermitress, 'It would have then got buried, never to be found, had it not been for some thread like raised marks on the rock-face that held the piece of copper from rolling to the ground.' The hermitress listened well and asked, 'Were there also some deep, dark marks around that clump?' 'Yes there were,' the woodcutter replied, 'Three dark marks surrounding that clump. Yes!' The hermitress immediately knew that it was the clump of hair and the three drops of blood that fell from Dakshyayani's body. She knew it to be so because it kept appearing repeatedly in her dreams, as if insisting of her some divine wish to be fulfilled. And rightly assuming so, both the hermitresses and the wood-cutter then had the large replica of that nude image sculpted on the rock where that small piece of copper was found. As they sculpted, they took great care to leave the fossilised clump of hair and the blood stains untouched and just as they were discovered. Then when the carving was complete, the woodcutter began to leave wild flowers at the base of the sculpture and the hermitress began to light earthen lamps there, thus leading to the birth of a shrine. And the piece of copper began to be handed down from the hermitress to her successive disciples. As time went by, seasons and the elements roughened that naked, unsheltered deity on the face of the megalith. Woody roots of bushes crawled all over it and mountain birds made nests in the crags on the rock. For centuries the deity remained thus beaten by wind, snow and sun until the first thatch shelter was put up during the first navaratri observed in Tilibham. That too was hundreds of years ago. And the small round piece of ancient red copper, with the engraving of the nude female on it, came to rest on the heart of the aama who took upon her to selflessly look after every ritual and requirement of that Durga temple of Tilibham. The copper came to rest *above her heart, the core of her virtuous life*. Then on as the years went by, word about the mystique and miracles of the temple began to reach far and wide across the Himalayan mountains and the flow of devotees coming to visit it began to grow more and more with each passing navaratri. With that the temple too began to grow. Then after all these ages, by the navaratri of that year the temple came to have three major chambers apart from the sanctum sanctorum. The outer, large chamber was for devotees to gather during hymns and yajnas. The second chamber was for the aamas and bubas to sit during special prayers and the next one, which was comparatively smaller, was meant for some kind of preparation of the devotees before entering the main, innermost shrine which was the sanctum sanctorum and which housed the sculpted face of the ancient megalith. It was in that innermost chamber that the rock sculpture of the mother goddess Durga prevailed in all its rugged, nude and stone-grey glory, smeared with red vermillion. In that same yard, a little towards the temple's left, was another shrine built around a small cave. This shrine, though, was not ensconced into the side of the mountain. Instead, it was a long, rounded and brownish stone that emerged from the ground on the extreme edge of that flat high land and had a natural shelter of a living rock that jutted out from a fault in the mountain from below and which, through the ages, had arched in over the brownish stone, forming a cave-like structure over it. The Newars dedicated the shrine to Pashupati because they found embedded on that brownish stone, a small piece of red copper with strange, ancient engravings of a pair of serpents coiled around a shivling that looked uncannily like that same brownish stone in the cave. And just like Tilibham's Durga temple, this cave too attained a temple around it through the centuries. It had one big outer chamber, one smaller and circular middle chamber with no windows and finally, the innermost chamber comprising the cave with its shivling. However, the piece of red copper with the engraving of the serpants was reverently taken off from the face of the brownish stone and it stayed on with the priests who successively took care of the temple. The possession of the piece of copper was seen as a sign of immense spiritual mastery as well as responsibility bestowed by the divine. And thereby it was made to rest *upon the core of another human's life, upon the warmth of virtuous life-line,* from where it came to watch over the shrine and the hamlet as a guardian. Even since those early times, a pair of cobras black as the darkest hour of a moonless night had always waited upon this brownish stone that the Newars believed to be a shivling. As if representing the serpent couple engraved in the piece of copper. The female of these two had a bright yellow mark around her body, a little below the hood, like a garland of yellow marigolds that got embedded because she could never take it off. Maybe it was because of this garland-like mark that she came to be known as Gunnikaparini. The fairy's daughter with a garland. Her mate, Pangeshu, crawled out of the inner sanctum sanctorum only twice each year. And he took those two jaunts after the Garhalachmi Bulaunu rituals every year to go out in search of the next Mata Taleju incarnate. The Newars of Tilibham observed the Garhalachmi

Bulaunu rituals to call upon the goddess of hearth and home to enter and stay in their houses to bless, protect and provide. Many had seen Pangeshu and Gunnikaparini lying entwined by that stone inside the cave, many had even seen them slithering over one another in sensuous love making and many others had seen them just lying limp as in sleep. Never threatening. There were yet others who had climbed the hundred and fifty steep stone steps leading to the twin temples not to pay their obeisance but just to see the cobras there. Often enough, they got disappointed because they never saw any. What made the Newars of Tilibham believe that even the cobras were immortal and divine was that ever since Tilibham came to be, there have always been just the two reptiles. No one ever saw them either birthing or dying, nor in infancy or old-age. If such had even happened, it must have happened during those periods when no one saw them around the brown stone in the small cave. The Newars there also believed that Durga and Pashupati, wife and husband, should never be separated. Because together they created life and kept Tilibham alive. Separated, their despair would spell despair upon the whole of Tilibham. The Newars there of course didn't know that even far away in Assam's Kamarupa, Shiva had his own abode on the small hillock of Umananda, surrounded by waters of the Brahmaputra river, near his beloved Sati whose yoni lay in the nearby shrine of Kamakhya. Elsewhere too, shrines that came up from Sati's disintegrated parts had a shrine of Shiva close by, watching and loving his Sati every moment. The Newars of Tilibham were however, unaware of it all.

And so that day, the temple of Pashupati was also spruced up. The brass trident on top of the temple's dome was polished to a dazzle equal to that of the rising sun. Also spruced up and decorated was the quaint little cottage adjacent to the temple of Durga. This cottage was the abode of the goddess on earth, of the goddess incarnate, whom the Newars revered as the Kumari. The procession which brought the chosen Kumari to the temple's cottage from her home seven days before the beginning of navaratri was in itself a festival in Tilibham. Priests of the Pashupati temple, whom the Newars addressed as bubas, led the procession. And the bubas were led by the head priest, Hajoorbuba. Aamas, drummers and dancers, devotees and villagers, all joined in the procession that marked the commencement of the navaratri celebrations in that small hamlet. The Kumari would stay in a sanctified room of that cottage from that moment. There she would be groomed for a fortnight for the goddess to descend into her being on the eighth day of Ashutwami. And she would stay on in the cottage till all the rituals of the Kumari Puja were over and till her transition back to human from divine was complete. Leaves from the mango tree were tied into a string and hung over doors and windows of the Kumari's cottage. These were also entwined on the posts that supported the awning over the broad, mud floored veranda that went all around the cottage. For now, there was a bustle of activities around that little hut. Inside, aamas were hastening about in preparation of the Ashutwami rituals as well as in preparing the little girl for her transition into the divine from human. As the aamas hurried about in their yellow sarees worn with yellow full sleeved shirts and yellow headscarves, it seemed like streaks of sunrays brought themselves down on earth to the temple even in the hours after sundown to crisscross the entire yard in adornment for the Ashutwami celebration. And outside, there was an incessant flow of people, mostly women and children, waiting patiently with fruits and sweet meat to get a glimpse of the Kumari.

All of six years, cheerful and endearing, the chosen little girl was unscathed of body and strong of mind. All through navaratri, the Newars of Tilibham revered her as an incarnate of the Mother Goddess on earth but on the day of Ashutwami, she would be worshipped as the Goddess Herself. But till such time, she was faithfully looked after by the aamas who had devoted themselves to the worship of Goddess Durga and the care of her temple. During the Kumari's stay there, the aamas saw to all of her human needs too. They even carried her in their lap and sang lullabies and rubbed her back gently to put her to sleep. For the whole of that week she was fed rice cooked in milk and honey. She also got to eat the fruits she liked. And because she showed a fetish for sweetmeats, she was given those as well. But from the midnight of the seventh day of navaratri, she would go on a fast. The regimen of the past week made her capable of undergoing that fast along with a mild transition from little girl to a Goddess of infinite compassion and power. That transition would reach its climax on the dawn of Ashutwami, the eighth day of navaratri, when she would finally be made to sit on the seat of Goddess Durga.

From the midnight of the seventh day of navaratri, under the constant watch of the oldest and the chief nun Thuloaama, the aamas scurried in and out of the cottage and the temple of Goddess Durga, preparing the little Kumari to sit at the altar of the Goddess. Like every other aama, the old yet stunningly beautiful Thuloaama too wore the same yellow saree with the yellow full-sleeved shirt. But like the rest of the aamas, she did not wear a head scarf to cover the hair on her head. Because she had no hair. Not a single strand. Not just on her head but on her entire body. She had no eyebrows or eyelashes either. Even her fingers and toes were bare and without nails. Tilibham's old folks used to tell their grandchildren, 'Be guarded against anything living that has nails and hair. To the rest, be devoted with your life and soul.' So to her they were devoted like not even to themselves. And as if to make up for the absence of the yellow headscarf, she wore a necklace of brown translucent beads with a copper pendant hanging from it a little above her bosom, slightly moved to the left so that it rested upon where her heart was. And it was that same piece of copper with the strange and ancient engraving of the deity in her absolute nudity, sitting with her legs crossed over one another that formed the pendant that she now wore. It was the engraving that was Brajbhushan's first ever, etched out on a piece of left-over copper. It was also the same image that was sculpteded onto the face of the megalith that now formed part of the temple's innermost chamber. Meanwhile, inside her cottage the little girl sat on a low stool made of a seat of tiger-skin that sat on a grass frame supported by the legs of a tiger. She was being anointed with a fragrant paste of sandalwood, basil, turmeric and curd. All this while, two different sets of bubas and aamas concurrently started invocations and incantations at the two temples of Pashupati and Durga. They were pleading to the Mother

Goddess to descend into the Kumari. They were also pleading to Pashupati to convince and cajole his consort Durga to be benevolent and comply with their request. All the bath-paste from the Kumari was then slowly washed off first with milk that aamas poured on her head and let flow all down her unscarred, pre-pubescent, virgin body. Then they did the same with water which had been collected from melted snow fetched earlier during the year from the highest peak in Tilibham. All along, the drone of chants seeped through the walls of the Kumari's cottage and also floated all about the temple yard. Darkness still hovered outside, because daybreak was yet a while away. The little girl showed amazing calm through that entire ritual of the divine bath. Then on, her little body was gently wiped with a new red towel and moisturized with buttermilk which Thuloaama alone had to churn. This too was a custom at the Kumari Puja of Tilibham. From here on would begin the ritual of adorning the Kumari, the ritual of Sajaunu as the Newars there called it. The whole of the previous evening aamas got together and made garlands of small, yellow marigold, interspersed with tiny white blooms of the fragrant mountain jasmine. They put these garlands round the Kumari's head like a tiara, around her tiny, dainty wrists like bracelets, around her ankles and even around her soft upper arms like the armlets around the arms of a danseuse. They then draped her in a beautiful shimmering saree of red and gold and painted the edges of her tiny, fair feet in red. They also placed a brilliantly red, round dot at the centre of her forehead from where the hair was neatly pulled back and tied into a braid at the back of her head. The braid too had little flowers of jasmine stuck all along its length. Her bright eyes were made brighter by kohl drawn along the lash lines. By the time the incantations at the temples of Durga and Pashupati were over, the ritual of Sajaunu too was complete. This synchronization of timing, bubas said, was the most important part of the rituals. The Kumari's feet were not to touch the ground upon which mortals walked. Hence, aamas would then carry her from her room in the cottage to a little wooden palanquin and in it they took her to the two temples one after the other. The palanquin itself was all covered with soft yellow linen curtains and flowers. The Kumari was taken in it across the yard, first to the temple of Pashupati. There she was again carried down from the palanquin to the innermost chamber of the temple and made to sit on a low stool next to the brownish stone shivling. And because her feet were not to touch the ground, so even while she sat on the stool, her feet were made to rest on a fresh green banana leaf spread on the floor in front of her. They believed that only divine intervention and possession by the Goddess over the tender aged mortal could bring such calm and mystical poise upon a child who would otherwise be too restless and exhausted to sit through hours and hours of such rigorous and deep spiritual rituals oblivious to hunger, sleep or other physical needs. While dawn was yet to break into the valley and into the village of Tilibham, the Kumari, sitting beside Pashupati as his wife incarnate, was going through the final stage of her transition to the Goddess of fertility and female power on earth, to Mata Taleju. More chants followed. At times they felt like songs sung without too much of a rise and fall of tune but with great depth of voice. And at other times they felt like monologues which began in the head and rang out through the ears instead of ringing in through the ears and reaching the head. Whatever they felt like, they held the mind in a complete trance. Such was the power of the chants that now resonated through the entire Himalayas and the abode of Shiva. Back in the yard of the twin temples, the pace and passion of the chants were gaining rapid momentum. Soon, the fervour and ecstasy in them reached a climax to the accompaniment of the sound of gongs and cymbals, drums and conch. Outside, a rooster crowed somewhere in the valley, allowing the first rays of the Ashutwami sun to drift into Tilibham. Unprompted and unaided, the little girl slowly rose to her feet. She turned towards the shivling, bent very low in front of it and with her left hand, picked a pinch of vermillion from its base and smeared it on the parting of her hair. A part of the vermillion stained her forehead too. She then stood up and turned to face the bubas and aamas. All through, Gunnikaparini and Pangeshu lay calmly and together in a dark corner of the cave. The sunrays gradually got brighter outside. From the outermost chamber of the temple and from the yard, people watched mesmerized and curious as divinity and immortality entered the human and the mortal. The little girl continued to look like the little girl that she was and yet, mysteriously, she ceased to look like one too. She continued to remain in her three feet of height and had her dazzling six year old eyes. And yet, she looked captivatingly different, with a kind of unseen aura about her. In those six-year-old eyes, the look was that of a woman who was ageless. And in those three feet of childhood, the poise was that of a woman who was older than the beginning of time.

The Kumari's transition to Goddess was complete.

From this moment, the Newars of Tilibham would venerate her as Mata Taleju. For that was what the Newars of Tilibham called the Mother Goddess. The Goddess would own her for a day, the day of Ashutwami, till midnight. She would now once again be carried to the palanquin amidst hails of 'Jai Mata Taleju!' right across the yard to the temple of Durga. During this short ride from the temple of Pashupati to her own temple in the same yard, aamas, bubas, devotees and all present showered the palanquin and the Goddess in it with petals of flowers and rice. On reaching the steps of the Durga temple, the palanquin bearers gently lowered it and aamas once again carried the child Goddess out of the palanquin and to the altar inside. There she would reign till midnight. She was now Durga. She was the Goddess of Fertility. She could create and she could destroy. She could bless and she could curse. She saw the cosmos in its entirety from the beginning of time till infinity. But, only till midnight. Till then of course she was the Goddess. She was Mata Taleju. So on that day a little wooden chair with a broad, cushioned seat was placed beside the rock sculpture of the nude, stone Durga at the main altar. There were red bolsters on either side on the chair and a red cushion at the back. That was Mata Taleju's throne, till midnight. Sitting there, she would receive prayers and grant wishes, she would bless and touch to heal, she would receive offerings of buttermilk and fruits and give flowers in return. When there were children, some even older than her mortal age, she would hand them little round cookies made only of powdered sugar called batashas. She also doled out bananas and apples from what she received as offerings from other devotees. She would treat and talk to them with the age and manner of a woman old enough to be their mother. Because she, now till midnight, was immortal and ageless. She, during this while, had divine powers to see into the past and the future of those on whose heads she placed her left palm, still stained red with the vermillion from the base of the shivling in the cave. She saw through people's intentions. When she looked at them, they could not hide their most well guarded secrets from her. Many therefore feared to go and stand before Mata Taleju and many, for just the same reason, went and stood before her. To know what their subconscious was holding as a secret even from their own selves. Because the Newars of Tilibham believed that it was in reality the Mother Goddess who spoke through the little Kumari.

By dawn, back at the temple of Kamakhya in Assam's Kamarupa, morning rituals of the eighth day of navaratri were over and the temple was thrown open to devotees and pilgrims. And in Tilibham, the yard of the temples of Durga and Pashupati was swarming with people. Their bodies bathed, their hair oiled, each made the best effort to keep filth of body and mind back at home. They all carried offerings, each according to capacity, to place before Mata Taleju. Even if the Kumari's own human mother came to see her, she would be just another devotee in front of Mata Taleju. Upon entering the yard, they all gathered under the festoons, some sitting on the grass mats, some waiting for their turn to go inside to pay their obeisance to Mata Taleju. Yet others were coming out of the temple after having done so. While inside the temple, rituals continued. The crowd grew bigger as morning slipped into afternoon. Towards late afternoon, young and old would together dance the jyapu under the festoons, none matching steps with the other, yet all merged in oneness of joy in their faith in Mata Taleju. Waiting devotees who were unable to resist the foot-tapping jyapu joined in with merry spontaneity in an equal zeal.

Kuntal brought Bhairavi to the Ashutwami celebrations in the temple during the morning. While they were leaving home, the two stray dogs sauntered into their yard. One scratched vigorously behind an ear and dropped himself near their hut's door while the other sat at the gate of the goats' enclosure. Not really alert and watchful, but they looked like they would rise to the occasion if at all the occasion itself happened to come by. Kuntal noticed that Bhairavi wore her string of coloured beads for the first time after having come out of Kesari Devi's house. The beads now rested in ample space on a bosom that was growing and allowing the beads more room. She wore her nose ring and earrings too. She looked beautiful. Very beautiful. Her eyes lit up once again like drops of dew just as they used to earlier. Kuntal slipped his hand into hers and they started walking towards the temple. Slowly. Because they were in no hurry and also because Kuntal believed, not without some amount of surprise and impossibility, that Bhairavi was with child. People from other nearby villages too were flocking to the temple that day. The closer Kuntal and Bhairavi arrived at the temple, the more people they saw, some entering the temple while others were leaving, and some leaving to come back again later in the evening for the jyapu. Bhairavi climbed the steps one at a time, pausing often to get her breath. And all through that climb of the hundred and fifty steps, Kuntal never let go of her hand. The fragrance of flowers and incense greeted them as they approached the temple. There was also the smell of smoke, like that which emanated when raw cotton yarn was smeared with buttermilk and burnt in earthenware. Like in lamps. Bhairavi's heart started thumping. She couldn't understand if it was joy or apprehension. She had brought with her a packet of incense sticks and a few flowers to offer Mata Taleju.

Upon reaching the temple yard, Kuntal and Bhairavi sat down for a while in a corner of the grass mat before going in to see the little goddess. There were a lot of people whom Kuntal knew. Some he talked to, some he nodded and smiled at. Some came forward to talk to Bhairavi as well. She had almost forgotten what it felt like to meet and talk to people. She was being initiated into it all over again. Having had rested for a while after the long walk and the climb up the steps, they slowly got up to go inside the temple of Durga. To meet Mata Taleju. Bhairavi's heart started thumping again. What if the Mata placed her left palm on her head and said she was still without child? And that what she was going through was only an illusion? She clutched the offerings close to her womb with one hand and with the other, clasped Kuntal's wrist. Slowly the two stepped into the innermost chamber of the temple where Mata Taleju sat next to the stone carving of the nude Durga sitting cross-legged.

'Bhairavi!' called out Mata Taleju, a smile on her baby lips, 'Come, child, come in. Come closer!'

Bhairavi went weak in the knees and she wondered whether everyone present in the chamber heard her heart beating against her breasts from inside. Both Kuntal and Bhairavi knelt and sat on the floor in front of Mata Taleju.

'I have been anticipating you two,' Mata Taleju said, 'so, by what name will you call the child growing in your womb?'

Sensing that Bhairavi went into a state of absolute stupefaction on hearing that, Kuntal took it upon himself to reply to the goddess. Though he too was taken aback at the suddenness with which their doubt was laid to rest. He folded his arms and brought his palms together, bowed his head and said with all the courage and reverence he could muster through his confused emotions, 'Jai Mata Taleju! Mercy, Mata, but since we do not know whether we will have one at all, and even if we do, we do not know whether our child will be a boy or a girl, how may we to know by what name we shall call it?'

Mata Taleju chuckled like a six year old. 'Your child is already seeded. Call her by the name of Paarvati.'

'It'll be a girl?' Bhairavi was at last capable of coherent speech.

'It'll be a girl,' Mata Taleju repeated, 'beautiful, and no ordinary girl.' She then gestured Bhairavi to come forward. 'Bhairavi, won't you give what you brought for me?'

Only then did Bhairavi realize that in her anxiety she forgot to offer Mata Taleju the flowers and incense sticks she brought for her.

'Now go, light these incense yourself and stick them into that halved banana there in the corner. Go.' Bhairavi did as she was told.

Then when she knelt to place the flowers at her feet, Mata Taleju placed her left palm gently on Bhairavi's head.

'The one breathing in you and whom you shall call by the name of Paarvati is no mere human, Bhairavi. Listen well! Like you bow in reverence before me today, so shall others do before her. She shall take you beyond these mountains, to a lesser one, there towards the east,' and she pointed outside to her right with her right hand, keeping the other still resting on Bhairavi's head, 'because she shall sense a calling that shall traverse the worlds of god and man, into past, present and future. She shall follow that call.' Mata Taleju then paused and closed her eyes but her hand remained on Bhairavi's head. When she resumed, she continued to keep her eyes shut as if to look at the Universe in the days to come inside those closed eyes. 'Paarvati! She shall be strong of head and gentle of heart and take to the Goddess that which is rightfully hers but that which has not yet reached her. She is destined to threaten furore in the worlds of god and man. She is destined to cross over to another world. She shall, if the Goddess receives her offering. And if the Goddess does so, then a bloodstone there in the lesser mountains towards the east shall acquire human form...'

'Jai Mata Taleju! Will the Goddess receive her offering?' Bhairavi asked, quivering.

Mata Taleju suddenly opened her eyes and brought her hand down, 'If such is willed, then there shall come great unrest in the heavens, on earth and in hell as well. Disease and death shall ravage through mankind! Fires of hell shall blaze on earth! Oceans shall churn themselves once more into mighty tides to sweep across continents! Great hills shall come crumbling down and angry blisters on the face of the earth shall squirt out fire and ash! Blood...'

Nervous to the point of tears, Bhairavi blurted out, '....shall flow?'

'...shall stop flowing!' Mata Taleju said without pausing, but looking far away right through Bhairavi and Kuntal into such time and space where only she could enter. 'If such is willed and such comes to be, fertility rituals shall cease to be observed. Beliefs of the ancient past shall be thrown asunder. And when the cleansing is complete, a new order shall come to prevail in the Universe! If such is willed!' Kuntal suddenly became conscious of the outer chambers of the Goddess's shrine being thronged with people. Outside, daylight was getting brighter. And yet, there was silence. Inside as well as outside. But through the window he could see that people's lips were moving. They were talking, laughing and walking about. Noisy arrangements continued to be made for the evening's jyapu and dhimei. And yet, he heard nothing. Mata Taleju's was the only voice he heard and it was only that which rang through his ears and his heart right into his gut where it formed a hardness impossible to absorb.

But Mata Taleju went on. 'You shall only wait and allow for things to happen on their own. Things and events shall take their own turn when their rightful hour arrives. But till then, it shall remain dead as in stone yet bleeding as in life. Living dead. Bloodstone.

All of it shall begin upon that predestined hour when that one divine call comes through. And it shall be that fateful call which this child in you, whom you shall call Paarvati, shall seek to follow!'

'Mata Taleju, what are we supposed to do then?' Kuntal asked.

'Nothing,' she replied, smiling, 'nothing, just wait and let things come to be at their own pace. The Universe knows its time. It also knows when to make you do what you ought to do. Till then, Kuntal, do nothing. Just wait.' And Mata Taleju brought her glance back to earth, to that present moment, to look at Bhairavi and Kuntal. The look in her eyes was once again that of a six year old. Soft, mischievous and vulnerable, yet veiling a supremacy. Of omnipotence.

'The universe is greater than the individual,' she continued, 'let it decide for whom it may, be it for the divine or be it for you. Let it decide for what it may, be it for peace or be it for tumult. Do nothing, Kuntal, let the Universe decide. You have been a devout companion to Bhairavi, go prepare for the arrival of Paarvati in your lives,' and as she continued speaking the next words she touched the parting of her own hair with her left hand, collected a dusting of vermillion from there and smeared it horizontally right across Kuntal's forehead and said, 'Look! what I see here,' she said, 'I traced out for you to see as well. Your line of lifeblood. It is a long one. Paarvati shall yet bring you joy. Rise now! And go!'

The next night was the last night of the autumnal navaratri at Tilibham. Bubas and aamas had already initiated Mata Taleju's transition back into being human. It was a ritual as crucial and exhaustive as the transition from human to divine. Once the whole intricate ritual was complete and the transition was done, the little girl fell into deep slumber. She slept like a child. Of six years. Lying on her belly, her head resting sideways on one cheek and one hand pushed under her pillow. She was all human now and yet, in her sleep, she looked so angelic. Almost divine. Seven days and eight nights from the last night of that navaratri, on the day the Newars of Tilibham worship the goddess of hearth and home which they called the Garhalachmi Bulaunu Puja, the little girl would once again be put into the wooden palanquin and be taken home to live her life as a human, as before. All memory and trace of whatever elapsed on the day of Ashutwami would be erased from her being. She would remember nothing.

Then on, the aamas and bubas of Tilibham's Durga and Pashupati temples would be on the search for the next Kumari who would eventually transform into the next Mata Taleju, for the next Ashutwami during the navaratri celebrations. They would be on the lookout for such a virgin who ought not to have attained puberty as yet, born out of humble seed in a fresh, hitherto unused and unstained womb and born a female. The female ought to be neither a bastard nor born out of incest, nor conceived by divine, extraordinary or non-humanly simulated insemination. At the same time, she ought to be unscathed of skin and nail, undiseased of the mortal body, pure of soul, and black of hair and eyes. They would be on the lookout for such a pre-pubescent girl to take her into the Mother Goddess's cottage as the next Kumari. She would then be reigned in as the next goddess incarnate and the custom of the Kumari Puja, the worship of the Kumari, would go on. The search itself was one that called for immense penance and prayer on the parts of Thuloaama and Hajoorbuba and elaborate preparations on the part of all other aamas and bubas. Every step of the search was steeped in such mystique and marvel that it was impossible to realize where and when worldly rituals ended, and where and when divine intervention took over. So to find out such a pure and tender-aged female, an hour before midnight on the first Monday after one lunar month from the Garhalachmi Bulaunu ritual, bubas and aamas of both the temples gathered in the closed, circular, central chamber of the Pashupati temple. There they burned fresh green leaves of the stone-apple tree along with four pieces of raw, undried twigs of a hand-span's length each from that same tree in a round earthen bowl. 'This bowl,' Hajoorbuba told young bubas, 'represents the earth and its bowels, and the smoke that arises from therein represents the souls that are liberated and which go in search of the divine Mother Goddess. Just like in the Universe, both soul and smoke arise to seek the truth that would be spoken through the words of Mata Taleju. Watch and know, bubas, that it is only the raw, undried twigs that emit the kind of smoke which could rise from the earth to seek the divine. It is for this reason that we are to keep the leaves and the twigs raw and still alive with moisture.' The burning ritual was performed in the closed chamber so that no breeze could either influence or prompt the smoke from the fire as to which way to go. And so the smoke was left on its own, unhindered and unchaperoned, allowing it to find its own pace and direction. As for the four pieces of twigs, one each was burned to appease the gods Brahma, Vishnu, Pashupati and goddess Durga. The smoke found its own direction even inside the closed chamber and it would be in the direction that the smoke went, whether north, south, east or west, that the next goddess incarnate, the pre-pubescent virgin would be found. Hajoorbuba and Thuloaama would then cajole Pangeshu and Gunnikaparini to go out in the direction as determined by the stone-apple smoke, each on a different Monday and together only on the third monday, to crawl out of the temple in search of the goddess incarnate while they themselves followed Pangeshu and Gunnikaparini at a distance. And invariably, on all three occasions the reptiles arrived at the same door to mark out the next Kumari to be hailed in as Mata Taleju. It was thus the cobra couple that eventually led them to the next Kumari. The Newars of Tilibham believed that Shiva alone knew where to find his wife incarnate and so it was left to him to send his agents to look for the next Kumari.

Like the rest of the bubas, Hajoorbuba too was always seen in a long brown robe with the sleeves coming down to cover the longest finger on each hand. While at work, the bubas often rolled the sleeves up to a convenient reach along the arm but during rituals and ceremonies, the sleeves always kept the hands covered. Hajoorbuba too wore a necklace to make him stand out as the head priest. This necklace was a long one, longer than Thuloaama's. It had bright red beads with a similar copper pendant like hers hanging just above his naval. Only, the engraving on this pendant was not that of the nude deity but of a pair of cobras around a shivling in a cave. It was Brajbhushan's second engraving on the piece of the thrown away sheet of copper, the one that was found embedded on the brownish shivling.

And thus that year's Kumari was ushered back home, navaratri got over and so was Garhalachmi Bulaunu. Meanwhile, seasons changed in the mountains.

When Kuntal's corn was ready for harvest, Mohini's son helped him bring in the yield. Soon the snow started capping the mountain peaks and frosting the valley. Kuntal had to cover the goats' enclosure with thick jute sacks. The chickens too were put in there, upon a clump of dried grass. As the chill grew, so did Bhairavi's belly. During the coldest days and nights, Bhairavi stayed mostly inside their hut. And then slowly, the harshest part of winter too had passed by. The chill was starting to move away as gradually as it had moved in. The snow was now starting to melt and seeds that lay frozen but preserved on the ground beneath the snow were starting to burst forth and sprout into blades of new grass and blossoms of tiny wild flowers. Spring was round the corner. Just like the melting of the snow, one early afternoon Bhairavi's water-bag too broke. And the seed germinating in her womb sprouted, like a preserved seed within the frozen earth. Bhairavi's child was born. Like the arrival of spring into the lives of

Kuntal and Bhairavi. All of a sudden everything seemed so unreal, magical and joyful in Kuntal's life that he hadn't realized when he broke forth into an impromptu jyapu. For the first time after years. He hadn't realized that he danced for really long in happy abandon, drowned in ecstasy, relief and disbelief, drowning anguish, fear and stigma. It was the birth that belied barrenness.

Paarvati was born.

END OF CHAPTER 5

CHAPTER 6

DEFIANCE

The prophesies of Mata Taleju spread through the mountains and valleys even far beyond the little hamlet of Tilibham. People heard about it, discussed and gossiped about it sometimes in whispers behind closed doors and sometimes in noisy arguments at the market place, got curious about it and feared it and then with time, slowly forgot about it. Thus, whispering voices and wagging tongues carried the prophesy to Kesari Devi's ears too. But unlike all others, she alone kept thinking about what Mata Taleju had said of her grand-daughter from Kuntal.

'*.....So shall others bow to her....*'

'What strange powers will this girl have? Maybe others will bow before me as well?' she wondered, 'For haven't I borne the father of this child? She has my blood in her. Tilibham will know her first as Kesari Devi's grandchild and only then will know her as Kuntal

Newar's daughter. Doesn't her sole and entire identity lie with me? Even now as she lives, she does so on my mercy. On my land. As such, should not I too rightfully bask in the glory of that power? Maybe others shall bow before me as well?' Every time such thoughts crossed her mind, Kesari Devi didn't realize that she pensively stood up and ran a palm against the damp mud walls of her room, dampened by the cow's urine. 'Will such powers turn these mud walls into walls of brick and mortar?' she wondered. And even while her hand ran slowly along the wall, she looked up at the leaking, reeking thatch roof above her head and her gaze ran along it as her hand did along the wall. 'Will such power turn this moss laden thatch roof into one of tin sheet?' There were, however, other thoughts that eclipsed this possible turn of her destiny towards a house where she and the cow would no more share a damp, dung smeared wall between them. Thoughts, that she had thrown the woman who had mothered that child out of her house. What if those who bow to the child now make Kesari Devi too bow to her? Or harder still, to the child's mother? When such thoughts came, once again without her realizing it, her hand abruptly dropped from the wall and her gaze dropped from the roof. A sense of deep foreboding and fear of an uncertainty that was worse than her present situation made her fall on her haunches. And then resting her disturbed head into her palms and resting her elbows on her knees, she sat alone and in silence for long hours. That silence was a morbid one. Goma and Maili had never seen Kesari Devi feeling thus threatened and in fear of another from her own family. Between them, they even talked that Kesari Devi began keeping mostly to herself these days and didn't bellow around at the daughters-in-law as she used to. They of course didn't know that she remained thus by herself and in deep contemplation because Kesari Devi was trying to take a decision on the most crucial matter in her life so far. She was trying to decide whether to give in and ask Kuntal and his wife to return to her fold with their child, even if it was a female child, or whether to carry on indulging in her pride and power and let them be where they were. But time, while Kesari Devi took it to take her decision, would not stagnate. It passed by, adding months to Paarvati's age. Paarvati was growing. So was Bhairavi's homestead. Still standing within that same fenced yard the hut itself grew bigger in size with an added room while Paarvati started to turn on her belly. When a part of the early layers of thatch rotted and slid off with the rains and the snow, Kuntal added new thatch on the roof over the existing sparse layer. They no longer slept on a mat on the hard earthen floor because they now had a wooden bed, though of the most simple kind. It was actually just a few boards of cheap wood bought for a throw away sum and nailed together, then rested on four legs of thick, sturdy, mountain bamboo. Also, Goma and Maili's children started visiting more frequently. And each time they returned home after such visits, Kesari Devi would ask with disdain, 'Baah! So what's there to go see this girl every other day? Isn't she just like any other?' And one of the grand children would promptly reply, 'Her feet are soft like freshly churned butter and how she chuckles when she sees us!' Another would add, 'She has started recognizing us. Her eyes are black like the sky on a no-moon night and yet there is so much light there when she smiles at us. You know, her hair too is black like that same midnight sky.' 'Oh?' was all Kesari Devi said then with a scoff. But this was how she got to know what she so desperately but discreetly had been wanting to know. She would furtively throw questions to no one in particular only to incite the children to talk about the child and the place she stayed in. And also about, 'All the other people staying with that girl,' as she referred to Kuntal and Bhairavi.

Paarvati was slowly able to keep herself steady when propped on pillows. She would sit back comfortably and kick her legs in play. Once after Goma and Maili's children visited Paarvati, Goma heard Kesari Devi say in front of the children, 'Whoever that girl looks like, how should it matter to me?' and she waited with bated breath for a reply from her grand children. Goma kept herself out of Kesari Devi's sight but within her earshot. And because Kesari Devi said that it didn't matter to her anyway, none of the children bothered to tell the old woman whom Paarvati resembled. They didn't realize that she in fact waited restlessly to hear just that. A while later, when no one said anything, she said, 'O Pashupatinath! I only hope that girl doesn't look like me. Or...does she?' And the sigh that followed belied what she said. The youngest of the grandchildren in that house then popped in, 'She is very pretty, yes she sure is!' Kesari Devi clenched her teeth for she was still left dying to know whether Kuntal and Bhairavi's daughter bore any resemblance to her.

Soon Paarvati started to crawl. The weather was turning comfortably warm and Bhairavi sometimes let the baby loose in the yard while she kept a watch sitting near Shamlee. The chickens came tottering about Paarvati while she herself headed straight towards Shamlee's kids Dairu and Kajlee. As she watched all the movements and listened to all the happy cacophony of the babies of fowl, goat and human, a kind of absolute bliss filled Bhairavi's soul. And her hand instinctively started scratching Shamlee's neck gently, very lovingly. Like Shamlee, she too was a mother now. At the gate of her yard she saw the two mongrels, sitting and lazily but indulgently staring at all the random activity in the yard. A couple of days back, Goma had visited. That was her first visit to Bhairavi and Kuntal's house. She brought with her a small jar of honey for Paarvati. The moment Goma stepped into Bhairavi's homestead, she could feel the difference between this home and Kesari Devi's. It was only then did she realize how suffocating Kesari Devi's house was. The same mountain breeze blew through the two yards and the same Himalayan sun shone on them. But the breeze at Kesari Devi's seemed to wring the soul and the sunshine there seemed to singe the spirit. At Bhairavi's house, that same breeze seemed to soothe the wringed soul and balm the singed spirit. Bhairavi held her by the hand and led her inside, near the bed where the baby lay asleep. She offered Goma a wooden stool, a low one, to sit on. Goma pulled it close to the edge of the bed, sat on it and stared at the sleeping Paarvati. She sat there and waited till the child woke up on her own. When Paarvati slowly opened her eyes with some sleep still remaining in them, Goma raised herself from the stool just so much as to bring her own face close to that of Paarvati's. On seeing Goma, the baby kept looking dreamily at her for a while. Then she slowly raised her hand towards Goma's face and felt it with her soft, freshly-churned-butter-like palm and smiled. Goma's eyes filled with tears. As she continued to look into Paarvati's dark but bright eyes, she wondered, 'Did all that had happened, happen because of me? Had I not aborted that last foetus, would Bhairavi not been thrown out of the house? Had this child then grown amidst the love of uncles, aunts, brothers and sisters and....a grandmother?' Goma's heart weighed down with guilt and ache. She took Paarvati's tiny foot in her hand, as if seeking forgiveness for having deprived it of its rightful share of love and belonging, and took her own lips to it and planted a gentle kiss on the foot. The baby wriggled its toes. The kiss tickled Paarvati and she chuckled. That made Goma smile through her tears and as she looked at that angelic face again, she thought, 'Or, had Bhairavi stayed on at Kesari Devi's stifling house, had this child even been conceived at all? Would Bhairavi have come out of her barrenness? Had I not killed mine, would this beautiful little child been conceived and born?' Goma didn't realize that she was merely a medium that the Universe used to carve out its plans. For when the Universe decides to create its own chronicle, it uses other humans as tools in the process of creating that chronicle. This time round, the Universe used Goma as that tool. Had it not been Goma, it would have been someone or some situation else. But oblivious to the plans of the Universe, Goma now took her hand away from the baby's foot and placed it on its head, as if bestowing her blessings upon the child because a part of her believed that it was she who caused it to be born. Then she opened the jar of honey, lightly touched the surface of the translucent contents in it with a finger and whatever honey she picked up thus, she gently smeared onto the lips of the baby. She then watched as the baby sucked and licked on it, making her little pink tongue click and slurp within her toothless gums. How sweet that sound was to Goma's ears! Almost like the honey that she brought. As she watched, Goma's heart started filling in with a sense of having been forgiven, if ever she was responsible for getting Paarvati's mother thrown out of the house. At the same time her heart also filled in with a sense of having blessed Paarvati, if ever that ouster led to this miracle birth. There was now no more honey left on the lips but the child continued to lick in anticipation of more.

Back at home, Goma didn't really make an effort to keep her visit a secret from Kesari Devi. So soon after that visit, one day when both her sons and their wives were around, Kesari Devi said aloud, 'I only hope the grownups in this house don't make a beeline for that girl over there in the far, wretched corner of my field. Of my land.' She paused for a moment and then said, 'Oh well, even if they do, how should it matter to me? I am above petty things like these, they don't bother me an ounce.' She paused again, this time a while longer. Then said in words that were well rehearsed in her mind but made to appear like she didn't even care about what she was saying, 'Hmph, let them go if they so wish, let them. Silly stuff for silly people to do!' Krishna winked at Kailash. Kesari Devi then resumed with a wave of her hand, 'Go! Whoever wishes to go see whomever, go see! Go! But mind you, chores and errands here in this house should not fall behind because people are wasting time elsewhere!'

Soon Paarvati took her first faltering step. Both Kuntal and Bhairavi were there to see her take it. And for an extended family there was Shamlee, Kajlee, Dairu, the fowls and the two mongrels, filling in for aunts, uncles, cousins and a grandmother, to see her take her first steps. That one step led to two, then more and soon she started running about the yard. Then one day after she started running around, Maili came over to see her. Maili had used the silver from a bracelet she was wearing and which was a part of her wedding trousseau, to get a pair of beautiful little anklets made for Paarvati. She also had tiny tinkering bells attached to the anklets so that Bhairavi would be able to keep track of where the baby was. So when Maili came to see Paarvati, she brought these anklets as a gift for the little girl. In the yard when Maili bent to put the anklets around Paarvati's ankle, her hands touched Paarvati's feet. And the child balanced herself by resting her left palm on Maili's head. Maili felt a strange mix of a flow of forgiveness and blessing calm her head under that little soft palm while her own hands were at those little feet. As if seeking the child's blessings. And receiving them too.

'My little Paarvati, forgive me!' she said to herself, 'I should have raised my voice to stop your parents from being thrown out with nowhere to go. I should have. But I could not find my voice. It was stifled and lost. It had long since feared to rise above a whisper. And I feared for my own self rather than for Bhairavi. As the eldest daughter-in-law in that house I should have resisted and stood at the doorway keeping Bhairavi and Kuntal from crossing over. But I could not. For I dared not. Though I should have. I have sinned against you. And against Bhairavi. I cried and spent sleepless nights with guilt crawling all over me but even my sobs were stifled. I could cry only in the dark and in silence. For child, that house stifles all other voices except one. That one voice alone reigns there. And yet, child, this is no excuse. I have but wronged you. Forgive me, my little kanchi!' As these thoughts passed her guilt ridden conscience, tears welled up in Maili's eyes. Little waves of tremble flowed through her as she sobbed onto the child's bosom.

Maili brought forward Paarvati's other foot to put the anklet and Paarvati let her hand fall onto Maili's shoulder for support. When Maili was done putting both the anklets, the little girl began running about the yard, amazed and amused at the tinkering sound which followed her everywhere and which stopped when she did. That was also the last day that Maili brought Bhairavi and Kuntal's share of the uncooked rice that she always set aside. Because Kuntal and Bhairavi were no longer in need of that share of rice from Kesari Devi's hearth. Back at home that evening, Maili too made no effort to hide from Kesari Devi the fact that she had visited Kuntal and Bhairavi's place. She, like the rest of Kesari Devi's family, was slowly finding her voice. And through it, her existence.

It was no more a secret to Kesari Devi that her daughters-in-law, and she supposed her sons as well, had been visiting Kuntal and Bhairavi. In that, she sensed a crack in her dominion. She too despaired to go and see this girl who was said would come to great power. But she refrained, lest it became obvious that she had surrendered to that crack in her authority. Once again, without her realizing it, her hand reached out and ran along the damp walls of her hut. If going to see that girl stood these walls a chance of turning into walls of brick and mortar, then should she go? Never before did the thought of being given only a choice between her authority on one hand and changing the urine-dampened walls to brick and mortar ones on the other come upon her. But now that she was actually faced with one, it surprised her that despite the dent in her power and ego that it caused, she still preferred a change in the walls. And so this one question stabbed her ego again and again, 'Should she bring Kuntal, his wife and that girl she bore back to her fold?'

Paarvati, meanwhile, started speaking. Among her first words were '*Tamlee*', '*Dailoo*' and '*Kalli*'. Then she started asking questions. About many things, of which some Bhairavi and Kuntal answered, some they laughed at and yet others that made them remain silent till Paarvati grew older, so that they could answer her once she was old enough to understand the answers to those questions. There were yet other things she asked but things they wanted her to find out for herself. Soon the child turned one.

That evening when Kesari Devi sat for her supper along with her sons and the grandchildren while Maili and Goma served and waited upon them, the younger children merrily chattered away about how Paarvati ran after the chickens, how her anklet bells brought the mongrels sniffing to her feet and how that made the little girl laugh in glee. Kailash and Krishna sat and ate in silence while the flickering flame in the lone kerosene lamp shed only as much light as was needed for people to see what they wished to see in that little kitchen and conveniently threw enough darkness to hide what they didn't wish to. And so it was that the brothers didn't see the eagerness in Kesari Devi's eyes to know more about Paarvati, while the old woman saw the adoration in the children's eyes for that same banished child. None of the grown-ups made any effort to divert the children from talking about Paarvati. Even Kesari Devi heard them out but then she retorted, 'These days the house gets to hear nothing but gibberish about that girl. I know that even people other than the children from this house have started visiting there. Baah! Such wastage of time and energy. Going and coming all this distance every other day, leaving household chores undone. And if done at all, then messily and in a hurry to save time for that...that girl. Instead, someone go tell Kuntal to return here with that woman and that girl she bore. Tell them, I have asked them to come back here for the sole reason that people staying here don't waste their time on these visits. Yes, just for that. So that while I am eating my meal, I will not have to listen to what that girl laughs at or how she runs after useless chickens.' She paused and put a morsel into her mouth and chewed it slowly, as if ruminating well on her next words. 'Also, tell them that I have forgiven the years of barrenness and am ready to have them back in my refuge,' she added, 'Go tell them so. That will save time for chores in this house.' Thus having said all that was churning inside her giving her sleepless nights and fatigued days, Kesari Devi felt as if a long overdue, loathsome task was at last done with. That night she slept in peace. Outside her walls she heard the cow swishing her tail to chase away flies from her back. But that night, that swishing did not annoy her. She just slept.

It never occurred to Kesari Devi even in her most abominable nightmares that Kuntal might refuse to come back to her hearth. But he did. He had defied Kesari Devi's will. And that one defiance made her run her hand along the damp walls once more. Between dominion and walls of brick and mortar, maybe Kesari Devi after all had an option of neither.

END OF CHAPTER 6

CHAPTER 7

ASHUTWAMI

The harvest kept coming in from the clearing by the ruins of princess Ambaa's palace. Kuntal once more found himself breaking into an impromptu jyapu when he brought in the yield, whatever little it was. And to his sheer joy he saw that little Paarvati matched steps with her father and soon she too started dancing the jyapu in happy abandon, along with her mother, when the harvest came in. It brought to Kuntal's mind his own childhood, when he too learned the jyapu without being taught but by simply falling in step together first with his father and then with his brothers Krishna and Kailash. Even as he danced, he realized that the wheel of creation constantly moved, that the Universe never stopped in its cycle, whatever the loss or the triumph. The first red buds appeared that year on Bhairavi's kurvak plant. Year after year of ploughing rendered the soil in the clearing soft and loose so that Kuntal no longer had to work as hard with the lone bull as he had to in that first virgin year and until a couple of years thereafter. The stillness of that place in broad daylight and souls that probably loomed in the vicinity keeping watch over the fallen pillars and the empty niches of princess Ambaa's retreat chamber no longer made the hair on his body stand up while he worked alone in the clearing. On rare occasions he even found himself humming as he worked. There were no more blisters on the soles of his feet and on the palms of his hand.

The year Paarvati turned four she started going to school. To the same school that Kuntal, Krishna and Kailash had gone but never completed their studies. Now, however, Kuntal had high hopes that Paarvati would someday complete what he did not and then go on to study further. Of the three teachers who taught Kuntal, Parshuram Newar was the only one still left teaching the children. Tonkoprasad Rai had slipped into senile dementia some months after he returned from a pilgrimage to Kamakhya in Assam, though he still appeared at the school every now and then. His wife mentioned that he sometimes spoke in a delirium. And when he did so, he talked about an unfulfilled pledge of an offering he had made at the Kamakhya temple during his visit there. During those moments of hallucination he told his wife that he had to go there again because the devi was waiting for him. He was filled with guilt that was born out of his disloyalty, for not keeping his commitment. His conscience shamed him day and night for having betrayed the devi who placed her trust on him. It was this guilt and the emotional stress it caused that brought forth his slow drift into dementia, his wife thought. Tonkoprasad Rai's wife, poor thing, was therefore doing her best to keep him in whatever sanity she possibly could, till she managed to take him on another pilgrimage to see his devi at Kamakhya. Badrinath, the third teacher from the times Kuntal went to that same school and who was the most senior among the three, had passed away some years back. So the school of around thirty five children was now being managed single-handedly by Parshuram Newar.

And the year Paarvati turned five was the first year that she was taken to see the navaratri festival on the day of Ashutwami, the day when Tilibham celebrated the Kumari Puja at the Durga temple.

When Paarvati was younger, she did go to the navaratri fair in that same temple yard with her parents but never on Ashutwami. So that was her first year to be at the Kumari Puja. Brilliant sunrays of a late, autumn morning reflected upon the triangular pieces of glitter-paper that made up the festoons above her head. Each year there was newness in the fair for Paarvati, a kind of newness that had a loving familiarity about it. The same festoons yet swinging down lazily in a new pattern, the same jyapu, but danced by new people, the same flowers, the same fragrance of incense, the same new clothes and stalls all around, and yet they were fresh flowers garlanded in a new way, the stalls had new toys and sweetmeats and the faces around her were new. Even from a distance she would be thrilled at the sight of the festoons that covered the temple yard like a canopy spreading out from the high central pole. Kuntal used to carry her on his back and when the reflection of the sun's rays upon the festoons of glitter-paper caught her eye and made her wink, she shrieked with delight. She didn't know what navaratri was observed for nor did she know the significance of the eighth day of navaratri, of Ashutwami, in Tilibham. She just loved to see the stalls, the crowd, the festivity, and the pigeons that watched the merry hullabaloo from the dazzling domes of the Durga and Pashupati temples in the same large yard and the carefree dancing of jyapu by people of all gender, age and size. Each year she went into the altar of the Durga temple with her parents and while they knelt for long in the inner chamber before the nude rock sculpture of the Goddess as Thuloaama chanted blessings and gave them flowers to take back home, Paarvati raised herself after a quick bow, turned around and kept looking outside at the happy din created by emotions that were a blend of spirituality and gaiety. How Paarvati loved the small, flattened treats made entirely of powdered sugar, which the aamas put into her little palms. The aamas gave these treats to her parents too but to her they always gave two extra. One on each palm. Her parents touched their foreheads with the treat before eating it and Bhairavi taught Paarvati to do the same. But Paarvati could never resist the temptation of having a bite first. And while the sugar from that first bite melted into her mouth, she let the remaining bit touch her forehead. Paarvati was confused, because Kuntal called the treat batasha and Bhairavi called it prasad. But by the time she was out of the Durga temple and into the spirit of the fair in the yard, she forgot about her confusion over batasha and prasad, remembering only the lingering sweetness of pure sugar in her mouth. It vaguely reminded her of something divinely smooth and sweet she had tasted, like in a dream. Like having licked something similar around her lips. But she wasn't sure what or where that was, whether it was even real. For she was only an infant when Goma wiped her lips with honey. After taking her sugar treat from the Durga temple each year, she followed her parents into the Pashupati temple in the same yard and repeated what Bhairavi did. She knelt down, joined her palms and bowed till her forehead touched the ground in front of the brownish stone shivling. Pashupatinath. The Pashupati temple too was spruced up and freshly painted and decorated with garlands of marigold, but because navaratri celebrated the Mother Goddess, it was the Durga temple that was done up more elaborately than the Pashupati temple for those ten days. Those of course, were the years when Bhairavi and Kuntal took Paarvati to the navaratri festival on days other than Ashutwami.

That year however, it was on the eighth day of navaratri that Paarvati had gone to the Durga temple. The day of Ashutwami, the day of the Kumari Puja. When Paarvati arrived at the temple holding Bhairavi's hand and walking alongside Kuntal, the year's goddess incarnate was already seated at the altar on the little wooden chair with its red bolsters on both sides and one red cushion at the back, in the innermost chamber of the temple. An awe immediately filled Paarvati when she saw Mata Taleju. She released her clasp around Bhairavi's fingers, quickened her pace and walked ahead, making her way past people of whom she couldn't see higher than the waists. When she reached the altar and stood directly in front of the year's seven year old goddess incarnate, her initial intrigue slowly gave way to amusement. Paarvati smiled at her. Mata Taleju smiled back. 'Is it your wedding today?' Paarvati asked her. Because she remembered having gone to a wedding and having seen the bride dressed up and adorned like Mata Taleju was at that moment. Mata Taleju only grinned and offered her a batasha. Paarvati took it and stretched out her other hand for one more. And received it too. Bhairavi and Kuntal meanwhile reached the altar and knelt down in worship before the child goddess. As she knelt down, Bhairavi recollected the last time she bowed before Mata Taleju. The time Mata Taleju assured her of the birth of her child. She also recollected with a faltering of breath, what the Mata that year told about her yet unborn Paarvati...*She shall take you beyond these mountains, to a lesser one, there towards the east.... because she shall sense a call. A call that traverses the worlds of god and man, past and present. She shall follow that call.*

All these years since Paarvati's birth, a part of Bhairavi always desperately wanted to come to Mata Taleju and plead her to place her left hand on Paarvati's head, to see what her future held. She was anxious to know what Mata Taleju meant when she said, ...*She shall take you beyond these mountains, to a lesser one, there towards the east.... because she shall sense a call* ...Did she mean that Paarvati would leave home and go away? And that Bhairavi would follow, looking for her, towards the east beyond the mountains of Nepal? *A call that traverses the worlds of god and man, past and present. She shall follow that call.* Would Paarvati be drawn towards one of the many Buddhist monasteries scattered about from there eastwards, in the high mountains? And renounce all attachments of life to embrace nunhood? This was the only meaning that Bhairavi could think of Mata Taleju's words, of Paarvati traversing the worlds of God and man. But then, what might Mata Taleju mean when she had said, *She is destined to threaten furore in the worlds of god and man*? Would Paarvati commit any heinous sin against man or challenge god's words? What did Mata Taleju mean when she said, '....*she is destined to cross over to another world*? Would that mean the world of the dead? A totally perplexed Bhairavi's heart cried out and shrieked within the silence of her soul to find an answer to all these questions and prophesies, an answer she was also dreading and hesitant to know. So that day as she sat in front of Mata Taleju, Bhairavi raised her head from the ground, but kept it bent, unsure of whether she truly wanted

Mata Taleju to place her hand or not on Paarvati's head, unsure of whether she really wanted to know or not, what destiny had in store for Paarvati. Now that the moment had actually arrived when she could find out about Paarvati's destiny if she so wished to, and bound with Paarvati's destiny, those of her own and Kuntal's as well, she was painfully scared to see the truth in its face. She was torn between her desire to know what lay ahead and of her fear of knowing that which lay ahead. She wanted her only child, her Paarvati, to stay on with her, grow up with her and live with her like other little children did. As Bhairavi's thoughts rushed like a storm and created a turmoil inside her mind, her eyes fixed their gaze on the little Mata Taleju. The look in her eyes was, however, bare. Because it wasn't her eyes that made her see what she saw at that moment. It was instead her mind that made her see. And through it Bhairavi saw a bride in Mata Taleju, draped in a bright golden red saree and adorned with flowers of the auspicious colours of yellow, red and white, her eyes lined with kohl and her forehead smeared with vermillion from the feet of Pashupati. While all other devotees perceived Mata Taleju in that little pre-pubescent virgin female child, Bhairavi perceived in her a bride. A bride like whom she would dress her own Paarvati someday when Paarvati would get married. Bhairavi would herself look after all rituals of Paarvati's sajaunu on her wedding day. She would herself prepare the kohl out of the blackened soot from an earthen lamp lit only with home churned butter. She would braid Paarvati's hair and tuck small fragrant flowers all through its length. She would not let her child traverse the worlds of God and man. She would not let her cross over to another world, nor to create furore in the worlds of god and man. She would draw in such vibrant aura into her love for her child that it would hold and keep Paarvati in the world of mortal man, in her world. So lost was Bhairavi in her own thoughts that somewhere during her gaze, Mata Taleju's face dulled and faded away before her and in place of that face, she saw that of Paarvati's. Paarvati, whom she saw dressed as that bride sitting on the small wooden chair with red bolsters in front of her and not Mata Taleju. And lost in a trance, Bhairavi remained thus seated and staring till

Mata Taleju smiled and said, 'Rise, Bhairavi, don't you already know what there is ahead for your Paarvati?' Mata Taleju asked Bhairavi as if reading her thoughts, while she put a few white mountain jasmines into Bhairavi's outstretched hand. 'That which is destined to be will yet be. I have spoken and my words shall hold. But despair not!'

Only upon hearing Mata Taleju's words did Bhairavi come out of her reverie. She stood up abruptly, picked Paarvati onto her arms and beckoning Kuntal to follow her, hurried out of the shrine pushing through throngs of people walking in, so that she and her daughter may merge into the revelling crowd of the festivity and get away unseen. She heard her heart beating inside her above the happy din of dhimei and jyapu, above the laughter of little children, above the voice of young girls giggling at the attention of young boys and above the haggling of prices at the stalls. She thought each one of those in that crowd too heard her heart beat. She tightened her embrace around Paarvati and looked pleadingly at Kuntal. Kuntal wanted to take the child from her so that he could make Bhairavi sit and calm down but Bhairavi wouldn't let go off Paarvati. For an instant she didn't trust Kuntal either. For a traumatic while, she saw in them all elements that were lying in wait to take her Paarvati away from her. So Kuntal just managed to lead her to a quiet corner of the grass mat spread on the ground in the temple yard and gently made her sit down. All along, she desperately held on to Paarvati. Kuntal sat down beside them. The crowd was never stagnant. All kinds of people, old and young, sick, healthy, crippled and widowed, childless, poor, rich and even those who committed petty crimes but with intentions that they thought were noble, arrived at the Durga temple that day to seek Mata Taleju's favour. They pleaded her to tell them what their future had in store. But Mata Taleju did not put her hand on the head of whosoever begged her to do so. She used her own will and discretion. It took a while for Bhairavi to calm down and when she did, Kuntal slowly took her hand and said, 'Come then, shall we go and get Paarvati some peanuts before going home?' As they descended the hundred and fifty steps of ancient cobblestone, there were many who were still going up those steps to the temple. But

Bhairavi saw none. Paarvati held a small stick with a big blue balloon tied at the tip of the stick. She turned her neck as far back as she could to take in every glimpse of the fair and the glittering festoons as she saw them receding higher and higher away from her and into the autumnal sky of Ashutwami. On her way back home, Paarvati asked many questions. About the little bride and why there was only batasha and no wedding feast, about the bald Hajooraama who did not even have eyebrows and eyelashes and whose fingers and toes had no nails, about the pigeons and why they let their droppings dirty the dazzling domes. She asked them why Mata Taleju kept her hand for so long on the head of the blind girl, saying things that made the girl smile. But before she got to hear all the answers to all her questions, she let her little head slowly ease into the fold of her father's neck and fell asleep.

Bhairavi returned home with certainty in her mind of the fact that the other part of Mata Taleju's prophesy, all of the rest of it that came after the prophesy of Paarvati's birth, would come true just as did Paarvati's birth. This Ashutwami, Mata Taleju only said, '..... *Bhairavi, don't you already know what there is ahead for her*?' Even though Bhairavi could not decipher the deeper meaning of her earlier words, she could decipher the meaning of the words Mata Taleju spoke this time. It meant that her words spoken during that last Ashutwami held good and steadfast. While Paarvati slept on their way back home on her father's arms, Bhairavi would lose her sleep for many more days and nights to come. Her fears and trepidations, though she did not know how exactly they would manifest, had been confirmed.

Ashutwami would never be the same again!

END OF CHAPTER 7

CHAPTER 8

CHOSEN

An hour before midnight, on the first Monday after exactly one lunar month had elapsed from the observance of the Garhalachmi Bulaunu rituals that year, Hajoorbuba and Thuloaama sat with five other bubas forming a wide circle in the round, middle chamber of the Pashupati temple. They had concluded the Garhalachmi Bulaunu on the seventh day from the last day of navaratri, the day the Kumari was sent home with all honour and grace to live her life like she did before her divine experience. But now at the centre of that circle of priests and Thuloaama was the earthen bowl with the four pieces of raw stems and green leaves freshly plucked from the stone-apple tree which stood precariously by the edge of the flattened mountain beside the cave. Even as the weather turned frostier with each passing day and leaves from most trees in the mountains were turning brown and falling to the ground, the last few leaves of that stone apple tree bravely held on. Those few leaves were still green and fresh as if it was summer in that part of the mountains. They held on thus to serve their share of the purpose towards the search for the next Mata Taleju incarnate. So now as the priests and Thuloaama sat around the earthen bowl, the rest of the floor in the chamber was left wholly bare. The chamber was bereft of any other flower, ritualistic offerings and objects or anything except the earthen bowl, lest their vibrations disturbed the smoke that would soon rise from the fire in the earthen bowl. Hajoorbuba sat with his back to the inner shrine and Thuloaama sat directly opposite him, facing the shrine. He then started the incantations. As he chanted, a slow, strange stillness began to flood into the chamber. And when Hajoorbuba was done, he gestured Thuloaama to light the leaves and the twigs in the bowl. She moved towards the bowl and having lit the contents in the bowl, retraced her steps towards her place in the circle without turning her back to it. They all sat in a circle with the bowl at the centre so that even the air from their breath would not direct the smoke from the stone-apple fire in any one direction but kept it shepherded to the centre. By the time the fire started, all movements and speech were stopped. All sat in absolute silence, absolutely still, not to distract and offend the rising smoke which slowly started appearing in the bowl above the leaves and twigs. Soon it started to rise. It rose higher above their heads as a wide, spread out mass but soon narrowed and came together as it rose higher. Even as the bubas and Thuloaama watched, the trail of smoke slowly started deviating from a central rise. It turned. Each year it headed towards a different direction and that year it turned towards the south east. And continued moving in that direction. More smoke from the base of that trail in the earthen bowl flowed on upwards uninterrupted. When the smoke finally touched the south eastern part high up the wall of the chamber, it hung there for a while before gently sliding down the wall like rain on a window pane and disappeared before it touched the floor. The direction had been marked. They now knew towards which direction to let out Pangeshu. Yet, they waited for all the smoke to rise, turn in that same direction and slide down towards the floor along the wall. When the last of the smoke had risen and fallen, Hajoorbuba started his chant once more and by the time the chants ended, the fire in the bowl was out. He then rose and turned towards the inner shrine and walked in quietly into the cave. The cobra couple were lying in a corner, unperturbed by the smoke rituals.

In that eunuch hour when it was neither night nor day yet a part of each made its presence felt, when it was neither dark nor bright but a steely grey, Hajoorbuba gently enticed Pangeshu to crawl out of the inner sanctorum of the Pashupati temple. Pangeshu let his long slender body lazily caress over the lying Gunnikaparini before slithering out into the cold, steel grey hour. It was that moment which the Newars of Tilibham referred to as the purgatory of time, a moment that languished between yesterday and today. So once Pangeshu was out and reached the steps that led down into the sleeping hamlet of Tilibham, he waited and watched Hajoorbuba. Standing close, Hajoorbuba nodded at him, turned to face towards the south east and stood facing that way till Pangeshu too nodded and slid down the cobblestone steps towards that direction in search of the next Mata Taleju incarnate. Back inside the Pashupati temple, Gunnikaparini glided farther into the corner and coiled herself in. No one really knew for how many centuries that tradition had been practised in the search for the next Kumari, the next Mata Taleju incarnate. For even the oldest of the old in Tilibham remembered hearing about this ritual since they were little children. They remembered having heard with rapt interest tales about that same neither hour, the same Pangeshu, followed at a distance in absolute silence by the same Hajoorbuba, Thuloaama and five of Hajoorbuba's juniors, identifying but a different pre-pubescent virgin each year. Tilibham was a tiny hamlet so by daybreak Pangeshu would arrive at a threshold. Till then he glided away into fields and narrow foot tracks, sometimes vanishing from sight under rocks and tall mountain grass. Sometimes he raised his head and a part of his gleaming body below it and then widened his hood. Then he turned his head this way and that as if to look out for the house he needed to reach. During such moments, Hajoorbuba observed from behind tiny scales just below the hood rising to form the pattern of a three pronged 'Y', like a trident. The scales in the trident changed colour from black to a brilliant red like that of vermillion. While the scales were raised and red, they radiated a gentle glow that formed a halo over the raised hood. It stayed thus for just a while and then the scales fell flat again and the red in them dulled and darkened till it merged with the black of the rest of the serpent. The halo too then evaporated. And Pangeshu resumed his journey in search of the Kumari, as if the trident appeared as a mark only to let him know that he was on the right track. But there had also been times when Pangeshu raised his hood and the trident didn't appear. During such moments, he retraced his path and kept moving along the ground and raising the hood again and again till the trident appeared. There had also been moments when he slithered away with such haste that he looked like a dark streak of satanic lightning upon the face of the earth. However, at other times, he just paused, letting the whole of his serpentine length feel the cold ground under his scaled belly. Pangeshu was allowed every whim during that journey. For the slightest offence that he took made him turn back and head towards the temple, up the steps and to the cave. No force on heaven nor on earth could then make him go out again in search for the Kumari, till a year passed by. So those who followed him indulged him his time and whim. Here and there, Hajoorbuba's long brown robe got picked at the hem by thorny bushes and brambles but such petty obstacles were not to distract him. He couldn't afford that. He kept his eyes only on Pangeshu. One of the bubas would free the robe and the priests continued to follow Pangeshu at a distance. Not a word was spoken during that whole journey. Meanwhile, shades of darkness floated above them wrapping the whole night sky. Gradually it would grow paler and softer till it would begin to turn orange at the far eastern horizon. Dawn would soon break. But till then, it was still the dark before dawn.

Kuntal and Bhairavi slept peacefully through that entire play of colours in the sky as the night swum by, with Paarvati lying in her mother's bosom. Outside, Kajlee, Shamlee and Dairu huddled up with Kajlee's babies. The mountains were getting colder with each passing night. Which was why both Kuntal and Bhairavi stayed longer in bed in the mornings. That night towards dawn, however, the two mongrels outside were making weird noises that were a mix of deep, low growls which came forth impulsively out of astonishment. This was followed by whimpers that came out as apology for those impulsive growls. And finally, they let out light, short barks of recognition. Night birds suddenly flapped their wings as they jolted from their perch and mountain rodents squeaked. It felt like the winds were whistling. But there was no wind. This blend of eerie noise went on for a while through the cold dark wilderness, till it woke up Kuntal and Bhairavi. Alarmed, Kuntal took out his khukri from under the thin grass mattress on the bed and stealthily stepped out into the yard. There was only enough light in the yard to just about make out the silhouette of nearby objects. Beyond, everything was dark and opaque. The mongrels too appeared as mere dark shapes against the haphazard trellis of the twig fence. Kuntal slowly moved towards the dogs. Both were sniffing around the same place upon the ground. They no longer barked. But there was some movement near the part of the fence that had a section that could be opened like a gate. Kuntal went closer. The dogs stepped back as if to make way for him. Seeing them thus calmed, Kuntal gained confidence to move closer and strained his sight in the dark to see what the thing was on the ground that caused fear in the dogs. And then he saw it. It was a snake. A cobra. When the dogs saw Kuntal, one twitched its ears and the other gave a mild wag of the tail before returning their attention to the reptile. Kuntal stood still for a while, not knowing how to react. The cobra raised his hood as he looked towards the hut where little Paarvati lay in blissful slumber, snuggling into the folds of her mother's warm body. Outside, as Kuntal stood watching, he saw a soft red halo rising above the head of the serpent against the pale sky of a dawn yet to arrive. What he didn't see was the scales at the back of the hood rising to form the pattern of a trident that changed colour to a brilliant vermillion red. He saw only the halo radiating from that trident. The serpent nodded his hood a couple of times towards the hut where Paarvati lay asleep. Meanwhile the halo slowly blurred and merged with the dawn that was now languidly spreading. The serpent gently lowered his hood and slipped away into the fields. His task was done. Kuntal froze. Even in that infant daylight, he recognized the cobra. Pangeshu.

Kuntal waited for the serpent to disappear from sight before he turned around and sauntered towards the house. Bhairavi would still be in bed with Paarvati, he thought. She would ask him why the dogs were whimpering. What would he tell her? What should he? He would wait, he thought, for more signs. And just like he assumed, Bhairavi was still in bed with Paarvati but when she heard Kuntal walking in, she sat up on the bed, twisted her loose, long hair into a bun with a quick and deft movement of her hands and asked, 'What was it, Kuntal? Why were the dogs making such noise?' Kuntal hesitated with the reply. 'Some small wild creature I suppose,' he said after a pause, 'Maybe some snake...' Later in the day he suddenly asked Bhairavi, 'When was Garhalachmi Bulaunu Puja?'

'Why, last month. It's been long, Kuntal,' she replied. Kuntal fell silent. So it had been a month. Moreover, the night the serpent appeared was a Monday night, the first after a lunar month from the Garhalachmi Bulaunu ritual. What little doubt he had about the serpent being Pangeshu had been cleared.

The rest of the week passed by like any other for Bhairavi and Paarvati. And during this while, the little girl had also learnt to write her name. Paarvati Devi, she wrote. When her cousins came over from the other house, the house of Kesari Devi, they loved to see her hold the slender white piece of chalk between her little chubby fingers and trace out figures on her little black slate with its wooden border. When she wrote her name, she did it without once erasing even a small part because she made no mistake. Her cousins were in awe of her intelligence. They then taught her to make sketches of Shamlee, the chickens, the dogs and the mountains on the other side of the slate. Bhairavi smiled inwardly and her heart filled with joy on seeing her little girl's prowess. She would let her study as much as she wished for, maybe more than anyone else ever did in Tilibham. And whenever she sketched mountains, Paarvati always drew a temple there. Bhairavi assumed that it was the Durga temple atop the flat highland. And below the temple, as if under the ground beneath the temple, she sketched a 'V' and drew a line from the base of the 'V' upwards to the opening, as if dissecting the angle at the base of that 'V'. This is what she drew below the temple.....

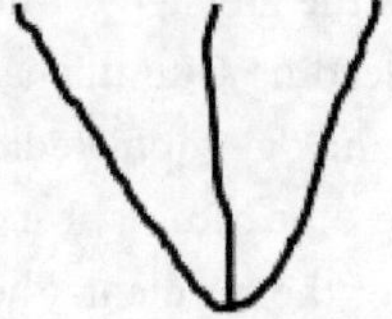

'Ah! That's a trident, a trishool. Isn't it Paarvati?' Kuntal would say looking at the drawing, 'Put it on top of the temple, not buried in the earth under the temple. Tridents don't stay buried in the earth, child, they stay atop domes and steeples.' Paarvati only smiled and left the 'V' where it was, the way it was.

As the week passed by, days and nights in the valleys of Tilibham turned colder. Sprinkles of the season's first snow started frosting the valleys. The next Monday, an hour before the night was at its deepest and darkest, and while Paarvati lay cosily snuggled inside a soft quilt, once again the stone-apple ritual began in the round, middle chamber of the Pashupati temple. The same number of raw stems from that same stone-apple tree and its leaves were being readied to be burned in that same round earthen bowl. Only this time, it was Thuloaama who sat with her back towards the inner shrine and Hajoorbuba sat directly opposite her. Also this time, it was Hajoorbuba who lit the fire in the bowl. Soon the smoke emerged and started to rise above their heads in the closed chamber and slowly turned towards the south east. Just like it did during the previous week's ritual to establish the direction in which to go out and look for the next Kumari. Thuloaama got up and gingerly walked towards the inner shrine of the temple, into the sanctum sanctorum. When Thuloaama put her feet on the ground her whole sole fell flat upon it. Because the small arch between the heel and the underside of the big toe was missing in her soles. The soft vibration of those flat feet that travelled in unseen, unheard little waves along the floor were so familiar to Gunnikaparini. How she loved the feel of those caressing waves upon her underbelly! Now as she recognized those waves caused by Thuloaama's footsteps, she needed no cajoling to come out. Unlike Pangeshu, she slithered out on her own from the inner sanctorum towards the footsteps. Thuloaama then walked out of the Pashupati temple leading Gunnikaparini into the yard in that neither hour when night and day copulated. It was pitch dark outside. Thuloaama shivered. She didn't know if it was because of the chill outside or the mystique of the moment. She walked across the yard and stood at the top of the hundred and fifty cobblestone steps. A cold breeze played at the hem of her yellow saree around her bare ankles. She was old, very old, but no one knew how old. And yet, beauty forgot to abandon her even though her youth did. Gunnikaparini's glistening body too swayed about at her feet like the hem of the saree, waiting for Thuloaama to tell her which way to go in search of the next Kumari. Thuloaama looked down at her, smiled and then turned towards the south-east. Gunnikaparini remained swaying for a moment longer. Then she nodded as if she understood and slowly lowered her head and slipped away down the steps. From there, the serpent would go down the steps on her own. From there, she would be the one to lead. Hajoorbuba and five other bubas stood in silence behind Thuloaama, waiting for Gunnikaparini to glide down away into the darkness. And when she did, they all followed her keeping their footsteps as light and noiseless as they could.

Gunnikaparini kept mostly to the narrow foot track among the bushes along the mountain slopes. She was more confident about which direction to move towards. Maybe she sensed the trail left behind by her mate and so knew whether she was on the right track or not. She also was more fearless of the dark, of the outside world and of her mission, than was Pangeshu. She rarely paused even in the thickets and thorny bushes. Of course, she did slow down sometimes but that was only to let those following her keep up pace. And she glided over the rugged lands of Tilibham towards the place where the next Mata Taleju incarnate was.

Kuntal lay restless and fidgeting in bed all of that while. He knew that if what he saw last Monday night was indeed Pangeshu then that night his mate would visit. Kuntal had not yet spoken about it to Bhairavi. But if that night Gunnikaparini too appeared then he would have to tell Bhairavi. He suddenly sat up in bed and looked at Paarvati. His little girl. 'Might it truly be thus that Pangeshu came to look for her? Might it be thus?' He wondered, fear slithering up his spine as would maybe Pangeshu. Every little sound from the darkness outside startled him. He strained his ears for sounds from the dogs. Any sound, the slightest sound. There was none, though. There was absolute silence except for a stray night bird and crickets. Darkness seemed to have swallowed all noise that night. And yet, Kuntal could no longer hold his suspense. He picked up his khukri and walked out of the hut, walking quietly towards the goats. One was nibbling at some grass and the rest lay huddled together. The fowls too were quiet. He then walked towards the gate. There was only one dog there and it was sleeping with its muzzle tucked under its bushy tail. Everything was peaceful. Winter had arrived at Tilibham and nights were getting longer. Far away in the horizon the peaks of the Himalayas pierced into the night sky with thick snow smothered on them. Kuntal usually loved to gaze at those mountain peaks at that time of the year. But that night even though he looked at them, he didn't really see them. Just then he heard a noise at the gate. His heart started to race. He turned and walked towards the noise. Slowly, quietly. But it only turned out to be the other dog returning from a nightly jaunt. Seeing him Kuntal's heart calmed down and he returned to the hut, relieved. It was only after Kuntal stepped inside the hut and closed the door that Gunnikaparini arrived at their gate. Her stealth and lightness were such that neither of the dogs heard her. She circled the entire yard once, along the outer periphery of the fence. It was only when she arrived again at the entrance of the yard after one complete round of the fence that one of the dogs let out a sharp, shocked bark. The other looked up at him and then let out a deep, low but long growl. Inside the hut, Kuntal was just dozing off when he heard the bark. He jumped out of bed and walked out. Bhairavi too woke up. 'What is it, Kuntal?' she asked sleepily. 'Nothing, just the dog,' he replied, 'I'll go see, you sleep.' But Bhairavi got out of bed and followed Kuntal out into the darkness. As Kuntal got closer to the gate, Bhairavi whispered from behind, 'That's a...a.. snake, Kuntal, a ... cobra!' Kuntal stopped in his tracks. He stretched a hand back towards Bhairavi. She took it and walked closer to him, so close that her breasts brushed against his back. She moved even closer till she pressed herself against him with her head held sideways so that she could see the front of the yard. Even in the faint light of the moon he could see clearly the yellow mark around the serpent's neck. 'Bhairavi,' he gasped, 'Gunnikaparini!' And he immediately felt her fingers tighten around his. Her other arm went round his waist and she brought her head away, shut her eyes and pressed a cheek against his back. 'Gunnikaparini?' she repeated, after she overcame the initial shock. The reptile lifted its head from the ground and spread out its hood wide. Then it nodded a couple of times towards the hut and kept swaying gently from side to side for a while. Bhairavi and Kuntal held fast to each other as they watched Gunnikaparini do her dance of identification. She saw Bhairavi and Kuntal but decided to ignore them. This time too, Thuloaama, Hajoorbuba and the five bubas stayed back in the dark, away from Kuntal and Bhairavi's sight. But they had almost found and located what they were looking for. It was only a matter of another Monday night now, the next Monday night. That night when the serpent couple of Gunnikaparini and Pangeshu would together arrive at that same threshold, Hajoorbuba and Thuloaama would wind up their search for the year's Kumari, the year's goddess incarnate. However, at Paarvati's threshold, it was only because of the dogs that the serpentine harbingers came to be seen. Had the dogs not been there, like in other households in other years, the chosen little girl's parents would have come to know of it only when a couple of bubas arrived at their door to make the announcement and to beg from them their daughter to let the goddess descend into her. The child and her parents were then ceremoniously taken to meet Thuloaama and Hajoorbuba at the middle chamber of the Durga temple where the priest and the nun elaborated and explained the rituals and conditions of the Kumari Puja to them. That was a moment of inconceivable honour and glory for the parents of the chosen little girl. The little girl herself, though, was of too tender an age to understand the excitement surrounding her. The parents rejoiced, for the world would come to bow to their child. She would reign over them all, she would be the goddess, she would be Mata Taleju incarnate. They rejoiced and wept for joy. And so it happened thus over the years, until that year.

That year, when on the next Monday at that same neither hour between night and day when Pangeshu and Gunnikaparini were together led out of the Pashupati temple, they slipped down the ancient stone steps, crawled over rocks and fields, grass and bare earth and sometimes even slithered over one another to arrive at Paarvati's threshold. And there they together did their dance of identification this time, raising their heads and spreading their hoods to nod first, then sway from side to side, all along looking towards the hut where Paarvati slept in total oblivion. Scales at the back of Pangeshu's hood rose in a trident and a halo hung there. This time the halo spilled over to float above Gunnikaparini's hood as well. The cobra couple had completed their mission for the year. They had chosen the year's Mata Taleju incarnate. They had chosen Bhairavi and Kuntal's daughter Paarvati.

That year because of the dogs, Bhairavi and Kuntal came to know about the divine choice even before the arrival of the bubas to make the sacred announcement that Paarvati had been chosen to be the Kumari, the goddess incarnate. Though Bhairavi and Kuntal did feel blessed and joyous, unseen corners of their hearts began to twinge. It was an ache born out of the fact that Mata Taleju's words, '*...Paarvati is no mere human, Bhairavi. Like you bow in reverence before me today, so shall others do before her....*' had come true. And because one half of the prophesy came true, it was now certain that the other half, '*....She shall take you beyond these mountains, to a lesser one, there towards the east, because she shall sense a call. A call that traverses the worlds of god and man, past and present. She shall follow that call....*' too would come true. And once again in Bhairavi's mind, the entire glory of her motherhood collapsed like a high mountain peak made but of dry sand. How could the same Mata Taleju, who had said that Bhairavi would beget a child to defy the barrenness of her womb, and indeed made her bear one, also speak in that same instance that her child thus born would go away from her just to follow a call? Leaving her to anguish over the barrenness at heart? How could she? What call could draw that child towards it with a force greater than that of her mother's love? Now that the truth of a part of that prophesy was ascertained, fear of the definite occurrence of the other part gnawed away at Bhairavi every moment since that hour when Pangeshu and Gunnikaparini together did their nodding ritual at Paarvati's threshold, the ritual they observed in confirming that they had identified the next Kumari. Mata Taleju's words, '..... *she is destined to threaten furore in the worlds of god and man...'* kept echoing in Bhairavi's mind. Soon after, bubas from the Pashupati temple arrived at their place to make the announcement. But in Bhairavi's mind, it was Mata Taleju's words that kept announcing the uncertainty of the days to come.

'*....living dead. Bloodstone...'*

'How could such contradictory concepts manifest?' Bhairavi wondered. But by then she knew that they would surely manifest because a part of the Mata's words had already manifested, in the birth of Paarvati. The second part of the words too was about to manifest, in that Paarvati had been chosen as the Kumari, just like Mata Taleju had said, '*....Like you bow in reverence before me today, so shall others do before her...'*

Soon Bhairavi, Kuntal and Paarvati would be accompanied from their home by bubas to the middle chamber of the Durga temple where they would be made to understand how they were to go about the sacred practices of the Kumari Puja and that their little daughter would be the Durga temple's goddess for those few days. Often the most painful part to be understood and accepted was that they would get to see their Paarvati just as any other devotee would and not as her parents. Paarvati would not consider them as such, not during those hours while the Goddess reigned in her.

It was late in the morning when Bhairavi, Kuntal and Paarvati arrived at the Durga temple, escorted by two bubas and two aamas. Even from below the steps they saw Hajoorbuba's brown robe. He was waiting for them at the top of the steps. From there, he graciously walked them into the Durga temple across the large yard holding Paarvati's little hand and leading her. Thuloaama was waiting for them in the middle chamber. She looked divine. Sitting down on a grass mat against a side wall, the morning light from the window above her head formed a soft glow around her hairless head. Some of that light filtered in and reflected on the translucent brown beads upon her bosom and upon the copper pendant above her heart. As she moved, the light in the beads flickered like lamps lit before a deity. She smiled and gestured them to sit in front of her. A young aama walked in and spread out another mat beside her for Hajoorbuba to sit on. The mild, soothing smell of sandalwood and jasmine wafted out from the innermost chamber. Pigeons and spotted doves hovered outside despite the chill in the air. Their blissful gurgling and cooing broke the monotony of the otherwise silent morning. 'Get our Kumari a few batashas, won't you?' Thuloaama smiled and requested the young aama. The aama nodded and walked into the inner shrine to the plate of offerings in front of the sculpture of the nude, squatting Durga to get the batashas. The morning prayers were over and the batashas were the offerings of that prayer. Paarvati followed the aama into the shrine.

'Pangeshu and Gunnikaparini had, on all three ritualistic Mondays, unfalteringly arrived at Paarvati's threshold, Kuntal,' Hajoorbuba spoke, 'and through them, Pashupatinath had chosen your virtuous little daughter. So it is her that we are to hail in as the goddess incarnate to worship on the eighth day of the coming navaratri, on the day of Ashutwami.' Hajoorbuba paused and looked at Thuloaama. 'Bhairavi,' she said, 'the daughter you bore shall be groomed, taught and made to understand the ways of this divine transition. She shall stay on with you like she has done till now and aamas shall visit her at home every three days to slowly get her accustomed to the practices, prayer rituals and chants of the transition. But know, Bhairavi and Kuntal, that seven days before the commencement of the next navaratri, Paarvati shall be brought away from you to stay here at the Mata's cottage with us. All her needs will be looked after with great love and reverence, Bhairavi, fear not. For she, to us, shall not just be another little girl. She shall live among us as our goddess.'

Bhairavi and Kuntal didn't speak a single word while the priest and the nun spoke. But once they had finished speaking what they had to, Bhairavi's eyes turned moist. She began to weep. She didn't know if she was weeping out of happiness for the divine honour bestowed upon her Paarvati, or for nervousness and grief. But tears nonetheless trickled down her cheeks and dripped down her chin onto her hands that rested on her lap. She couldn't believe that this was what Mata Taleju meant during that Ashutwami years back, at this same temple, when she said, '....*Like you bow in reverence before me today, so shall others do before her....*' And this Ashutwami, as prophesied that day, it would be Paarvati that others would bow in reverence to. Born out of Bhairavi's seemingly barren womb to Kuntal, Paarvati Devi had now been ceremoniously proclaimed as the chosen Kumari for the next navaratri.

END OF CHAPTER 8

CHAPTER 9

BHAIRAVI

Bhairavi looked down lovingly at the sleeping Paarvati. She no doubt felt blessed that her little girl had been chosen by Pashupati. It was a sign that she had given birth to a virtuous one, that she and Kuntal too had been righteous in their own way. She slowly pulled down the edge of the quilt which was touching the little girl's chin. She gently let it slide further down, very gently so as not to wake her up. Then Bhairavi gently lifted her frock and sweater and ran a hand softly on her chest and belly while her eyes followed her hand. There was indeed no mark, no spot and no scar of any kind upon her fair, soft skin. In Paarvati's short life of six years, Bhairavi gave her many a bath and many a massage with warm mustard oil. But never did she look out for marks and scars on her little body. Many a time she washed and oiled Paarvati's hair and yet, never noticed till that moment how deeply black her hair was. She wanted to see her eyes too but they were shut in sleep now. Bhairavi once again pulled down her frock and sweater and put the quilt back on her, upto the chin.

..........born out of humble seed in a fresh, hitherto unused and unstained womb and born a female..... neither a bastard nor born out of incest, nor conceived by divine, extraordinary or non-humanly simulated insemination...... unscathed of skin and nail, undiseased of the mortal body, pure of soul, and black of hair and eyes....

Aama Panchali and aama Ahalya soon started visiting Paarvati at her home. They both would probably be just a little older than Bhairavi but were far more aware of life's small and big courses and of life's spiritual meaning. After the initial shyness and inhibition disappeared, Paarvati began to enjoy their company. On their first visit she took them around their homestead, all across the backyard right up to where the goats' enclosure was, to show them where Shamlee and her family stayed at night.

'Kajlee and Dairu are her babies,' she introduced, pointing at Shamlee, 'and then Kajlee has her own babies too.'

Aama Panchali and aama Ahalya indulgently followed Paarvati around the yard. It was good, they thought, that the child was opening up on her own. On their successive visits, they all sat together and sometimes taught her beautiful hymns which she learnt really fast and was soon able to sing along flawlessly and with élan. They also taught her prayers and chants which she practised with them in their later visits and soon began to recite as effortlessly as she breathed. However, it wasn't always the nuns who taught. There were also times, light-hearted ones, when it was Paarvati who taught them. She taught them how to dance the jyapu. The more Paarvati grew fond of the aamas and their way of life, the more Bhairavi's heart sank. During one such visit, Bhairavi asked aama Panchali, 'Has it ever happened thus, aama, that a Kumari kept missing her home and her mother during all the days that she stayed at the Mata's cottage?'

Aama Panchali shook her head. 'Hm? No, not that I can remember. Not that we've heard of, Bhairavi, not that anyone ever has heard of. The Kumari is showered with so much love and her days are filled with so much to do that she is left with no occasion to miss home.'

Bhairavi sat quiet for a moment as she watched Paarvati. Then she asked abruptly, 'Has it ever happened that a Kumari expressed a desire to stay back at the temple even after her time there was over? Even after Garhalachmi Bulaunu? Has such ever happened, aama?' There was almost a kind of implore in her voice as she asked this, an implore to hear a no. 'No, Bhairavi, such too has never happened,' aama Panchali assured her, placing a hand on Bhairavi's arm, 'never,' she repeated, 'they all returned home just the way they left, with all traces of those moments of their brush with divinity wholly erased from their being.' Bhairavi calmed down, atleast for a while.

Sometimes when aama Panchali and aama Ahalya came, Paarvati brought out her slate and a piece of chalk and drew on it goats, chickens and dogs and showed her drawing skills to them. Sometimes she also drew a mountain upon her slate to show them. And when she did that, she drew a temple on that mountain and once again put the 'V' under the temple with the line in between the two arms of the 'V'.

Days and months slipped by and Paarvati started looking forward to the aamas' visits. Bhairavi wished she hadn't. For her own self Bhairavi wished she could hold on to time. Then one day she asked aama Ahalya, 'What if Mata Taleju placed her left palm on her own head? What then?'

'Nothing,' aama Ahalya replied, 'she need not even place her hand on her own head. She places that hand only on the heads of mortals. Humans. As for her hand on her own head, why Bhairavi, you forget that she is the goddess at that moment and not the little girl that you see her to be. What you see is just the little girl's mortal form that serves only as an abode which, for those few hours, has been taken over to be dwelt in by the goddess. You forget, Bhairavi, that within that form it isn't the little girl's soul with a mortal fate having a past and a future. It is, within that form, the goddess herself. And the goddess has no past, no future. She is infinite. She is time eternal and she herself creates the future. So even if she placed her left palm on her own head, what much would happen? What might she even need to know when she herself designs all that needs to happen?' aama Ahalya asked Bhairavi but not really expecting her to reply. Bhairavi, however, looked blankly into aama Ahalya's eyes and blurted absentmindedly, 'Nothing!'

Aama Ahalya nodded her head and said after Bhairavi, 'Yes, nothing!'

Bhairavi shook her head and whispered, 'Nothing. Nothing...'

That year when Kuntal brought in the harvest, autumn had arrived in the valley. It brought with it a nip in the morning air, a lazy afternoon sun and a breeze that tingled the bare skin into a light shiver. Evenings of course were cold. This was also the time when Tilibham readied itself for navaratri. The Durga and Pashupati temples were beginning to get spruced up, painted and decorated. With that, a trickle of visitors too began arriving at Kuntal and Bhairavi's yard. They were mostly from Tilibham but a few arrived from the adjacent villages in the valley as well. They were all there to see Paarvati. Aamas from the Durga temple now began coming more frequently, in greater numbers unlike just the two during the earlier days and they stayed on for longer periods as well. Soon, visitors got to meet Paarvati only in the presence of the aamas. Bhairavi's usually happy, content days of tottering about with unending yet fulfilling chores concerning every life in her homestead were suddenly thrown asunder. Often, she herself had to step aside to let the aamas be in Paarvati's privileged company. She missed her little girl despite being close to her, around her. She missed the tinkle of Paarvati's anklet bells following her all about the yard, incessantly talking to her, asking questions that were sometimes so childishly funny and sometimes so intelligently thought provoking even for an adult like Bhairavi. She tried to busy herself with things that were not really required to be done but those which she forced herself to do. She often found her hand feeling her body over her womb. It won't ever be called barren again. But she feared that a barrenness of a different kind seemed all set to wrap her heart and soul. She did feel a faint flush of joy and gratitude but that was only sometimes, only momentarily. What persisted all along was anguish over the unforeseen.

'But Bhairavi,' Kuntal tried to soothe her, 'Mata Taleju also told you not to despair, remember? During that Ashutwami before Paarvati was born? Hadn't she said, *Paarvti shall yet bring you joy*?' Kuntal tried to take Bhairavi's mind away from her anxiety that Paarvati would be gone forever when she would leave for the Mata's cottage a week before navaratri commenced. He talked to her of things they would do together once Paarvati returned home on Garhalachmi Bulaunu. 'Why yes! Hadn't you been telling me that the thatch needed to be replaced? You know Bhairavi, I've been thinking of bringing in grass from the far side of the mountain by the waterfall this time. The grass there is so much better. I can fetch and pile them up before the snow starts falling. And this time maybe we'll pull down every blade of old thatch and put up an entirely fresh new layer.' Bhairavi only listened quietly. Then after sometime she said, 'When you have partly seen the unforeseen, it is very hard not to be scared of that part of the unforeseen which you are yet to see, Kuntal, I am scared of that part. I am scared of the bloodstone. I am scared for I know not what Mata Taleju meant during that Ashutwami when she had said ..... *blood shall stop flowing*.' Kuntal came up to her and held her firmly in his arms. She rested her head on his chest as if from immense fatigue and then slowly said, 'It is only in the dead, Kuntal, that blood stops flowing!'

Bhairavi lay awake all of the night. In the silence through her sleeplessness she heard Paarvati's heavy breathing, one that comes from a deep, restful sleep. She had already been told that she would go to the Mata's cottage the next morning. It ached Bhairavi's heart to see that Paarvati yet slept so undisturbed and was looking forward to her stay at the cottage. In the morning the Kumari palanquin would arrive to take Paarvati there. When day at last broke after a night that seemed to have stretched to eternity, Bhairavi heard the sound of drums and conch blowing at a distance even before the palanquin came into sight. She heard hymns and the sound of merriment too. The sound grew clearer and louder as the small procession came closer. Like every other year, this year too there was great rejoicing because this procession marked the beginning of the navaratri festivities in Tilibham. The procession itself was a group of about two dozen men, women and children. And about half as many bubas and aamas. They were all led by Thuloaama to Bhairavi and Kuntal's yard. Four bubas bore on their shoulders the empty palanquin which was beautifully decorated with long strings of yellow marigold hanging from its newly painted sides and bright yellow linen curtains forming its side veils. Even as Bhairavi and Kuntal stood and watched, the yard filled up with people making it seem so small that there was hardly any space left for the dogs to move around easily. But they still moved around, brushing against people's legs and sniffing the shins of all the strangers in their adopted yard. Aama Panchali and aama Ahalya came with the procession to fetch their Kumari while Goma and Maili arrived for their Kumari Paarvati's send off. Thuloaama, aama Panchali and aama Ahalya led Paarvati to the short length of halved tree trunk behind the goats' enclosure, the spot that Bhairavi and Kuntal used for washing. There the aamas gave Paarvati a ritualistic bath with water they brought with them from the temple. They then put new clothes on her. From then on till the moment she returned home, Paarvati would be theirs. They and all other aamas would take care of her as Kuntal and Bhairavi did at home. Bhairavi only stood and watched. She would not be encouraged to go and meet her Paarvati at the Mata's cottage.

Someone from the procession came close to Bhairavi and bent to touch her feet. It stunned her and she instinctively stepped back, bending forward at the same instant to lift the woman bowing before her. When the woman stood up and Bhairavi came face to face with her, she saw that the woman was an aged one, much older than her. She joined her palms and bringing them to her forehead, said, 'You are indeed blessed, Bhairavi Devi, you are! This moment of glory! This moment of being chosen by Pashupatinath himself for the Mother Goddess to come and dwell in! Ah, this is not bestowed upon anyone and everyone, you do realize that, don't you?' Bhairavi didn't, till that moment. The woman continued, 'you must be a very spiritual and devout woman to have borne a child of such untarnished virtue! You yourself are no less virtuous!' And having said that, she again bent to touch Bhairavi's feet, making Bhairavi once again step back and merely look on. The dogs were as confused and lost as she was. They forgot to even bark at all the strangers engaged in strange activities in their familiar yard. Someone else came up to her and asked with great excitement, 'Aren't you happy, Bhairavi? All parents of the Kumaris are, especially the mothers. They get beside themselves with joy.' Bhairavi smiled. She didn't know if she was happy. Even if she was, she didn't realize it. She just stood still and stunned, staring on at all the preparations for the send-off. Not knowing what to give Paarvati to take with her so that she may remember home, Bhairavi hurried indoors and brought out her little slate and three pieces of chalk and put them into Paarvati's hands. The little girl eagerly took them and held them close to her. When it was time for her to go, Thuloaama gestured Kuntal to come and be by Bhairavi. Because in all her lifetime of being an aama, this was the first time that she saw the mother of a kumari thus lost and despaired at a time when she ought to have been euphoric about being the one who gave birth to the goddess incarnate and as such, claiming an equal reverence as the kumari herself. Even the slightest feeling of glory eluded Bhairavi. Thuloaama however knew the reason behind Bhairavi's sinking heart. And that was why she asked Kuntal to be by her when she came forward to take Paarvati by her hand and lead her to the palanquin. The rest of the bubas and aamas showered Paarvati with grains of washed but dry, uncooked rice and flower petals. Aama Ahalya went and stood near the palanquin with the same round earthen bowl where the stone-apple leaves and twigs were burnt on the nights before each of the cobras came out on their divine mission. That day too there was light smoke rising from it but the smoke was of sandal wood and small, sundried cubes of pine latex. Eaglewood essence was sprinkled on those cubes for their sublime fragrance to blend into the smoke and waft far, far away into the valleys and mountains, carried by the wind. That day the smoke was let to rise free and far to usher the kumari into the Mata's cottage. Aama Panchali and Thuloaama then gently put the child into the palanquin and the bubas lifted it from the ground onto their shoulders. Once again, sounds of the gong, conch and drums rolled through the morning mist and the beautifully decorated palanquin left Bhairavi and Kuntal's homestead with their little Paarvati sitting inside it, clutching her little black slate and the three pieces of white chalk. These would be the only things that would bind her with home, Bhairavi and Kuntal for the next twenty four days and nights. She waved at her parents as the palanquin moved away from them, rocking gently in rhythm with the bubas' steps. The dogs too joined the procession. Maili and Goma waited for the last of the procession to leave the yard and go some distance before they too left. Kuntal held Bhairavi very close, very lovingly, while she looked on till the palanquin disappeared from sight up the steep curve round the cliff. The hymns and the sound of drums and gongs too gradually receded into the distant mountains till even their echo could no more be heard. All of a sudden Bhairavi's yard felt very quiet and forlorn, very bare. Only she and Kuntal were left behind with the goats and the fowls. But then it had always been like this before Paarvati was born. It was then just them. And yet those days the yard seemed full and alive even with just them. That day however, with those same goats and fowls and some more, the yard still felt so achingly deserted. Especially after the morning's rush of people and activities. Bhairavi remained standing just where she was in her yard, clinging on to Kuntal. She stood numb and lost, tearless yet joyless, stifled with gloom over what would come in the days thereafter. For Paarvati, her daughter, born out of humble seed in a fresh, hitherto unused and unstained womb, born a female and yet to attain puberty, was gone for the goddess to descend into her. And she would be hailed as Mata Taleju. *Others would bow before her....*

Shamlee bleated and Bhairavi turned to look towards her. Shamlee had Dairu and Kajlee by her and Kajlee's kids were pushing at her udders standing under her belly. Only then did Bhairavi come back to her own self and the truth that her child Paarvati was gone, sink into her. The thought stabbed into her heart and slashed all the way down into her womb. She shivered. Because more of Mata Taleju's prophesy had come true. She always knew it would, yet a part of her refused to believe that it would indeed come to be. But that morning it just did. And while Shamlee and Kajlee had their babies with them, Bhairavi's was gone. It was that sudden and painful realization which made her turn her head and burying it in Kuntal's bosom, she broke down and began to cry like a child. Her cries seeped into Kuntal's heart and tore it into pieces. Grief over loss shook her whole body as Kuntal tried to bring in as much of her as he could into his embrace. 'Bring her back, Kuntal, bring my Paarvati back!' She sobbed into his bosom. But Kuntal didn't understand what she spoke. The words were muffled. Even if he did, he wouldn't be able to do anything but only listen helplessly. The chickens came out and pecked at the grains of rice on the ground that were showered on Paarvati. They ignored the flower petals that remained strewn about among the rice. A faint trace of sandalwood, pine-latex and eaglewood lingered in the air. But Bhairavi was oblivious to it all.

Her Paarvati was gone so that others may bow before her.

Mata Taleju's words once again held true.

END OF CHAPTER 9

CHAPTER 10

PAARVATI

At the yards of the Durga temple in Tilibham, every aama in her resplendent yellow saree was waiting to receive Paarvati, the new kumari, outside the Mata's cottage. A few bubas were waiting at the bottom of the cobblestone steps that led to the temple. From there, a different set of bubas would bear the kumari's palanquin up the steps to relieve the others who bore it uptil there. The moment the palanquin reached the highest of the steps, the sound of the drums got louder, their beat rolled faster and more ecstatically. Still clutching her slate and the pieces of chalk, Paarvati looked out of the palanquin and saw the Mata's cottage. It had been cleaned and done up with great care to receive the new kumari. The thatch on the roof was new, crisp and golden brown. It smelt of sun-dried grass. Little saplings of banana each having two wide, long leaves and one tender leaf still rolled up like a newspaper at the centre were erected on either side of the main door of the cottage and also at the four corners of the verandah. The ends of a string, from which hung mango leaves, were attached to the banana saplings at the doorway in such a way that whoever passed through that door would do so by bowing under that string of mango leaves. Floral patterns drawn with powdered rice ran along the entire outer edge of the floor of the verandah. Little earthen lamps dotted this pattern at equal distances, all set to be lit at dusk during the hour of prayer. From her palanquin Paarvati found the cottage very endearing and welcoming. It looked like the play house that Kuntal had made for her once next to Shamlee's enclosure. Only, the cottage was bigger and more elaborately decorated. This cottage would be her home for the next twenty four days.

The moment the bubas bearing the palanquin put it down near the cottage's verandah, Thuloaama blew the conch thrice, each time blowing into it long and steady and finishing up with a spurt of short but forceful exhaling. From that moment Paarvati would be addressed as Kumari. Aama Panchali carried Paarvati out of the palanquin and into the cottage and showed her around, just the way Paarvati showed them around when they first went to meet her at her home. As they came to the backyard, Paarvati saw the black goats there and she instinctively looked back and said in glee, 'Mai look! Shamlee and Kajlee are here too!' But there was no Mai and those were not Shamlee and Kajlee. And suddenly it dawned on her that she was not at home with her Mai. Yet, unlike on other such moments, she didn't break into tears and didn't wish to go back home to Mai. This was that exact moment which elicited in Paarvati the gradual but steady process of transition from human to divine. She remained stoic through that moment of seeking to be with her mother and wishing for the comfort of being near Shamlee and Kajlee, her playmates since she could remember. It was precisely this hold over her emotions and weaknesses that she was being prepared for by all the hymns, prayers and meditations that she was playfully taught by aama Panchali and aama Ahalya in the course of their visits to her home during the months after she was chosen. And in the next few days she would be groomed to have a greater control over her emotional needs and desires along with her physical ones. That day after sundown but before darkness set in, Thuloaama led Paarvati to the Durga temple for the evening prayers. This was the beginning of a routine that would continue till the evening before Ashutwami. As she was walked across the yard she saw that preparations for the navaratri festivities had already begun. Bubas sat in the yard stringing the festoons which would go up to form the canopy from the high pole at the centre. 'Kumari, you remember the devi here last Ashutwami?' Thuloaama asked her as they reached the innermost chamber of the Durga temple, 'Small and pretty like you?' Paarvati thought for a moment and looked around, trying to bring to memory what seemed like a dream that was receding into the depth of heavy slumber while her physical self moved towards conscious wakefulness. She felt like she had seen that chamber before but couldn't remember when. Or if she even saw that place at all. But she was almost sure that it wasn't the first time that she was walking through it at that moment. Only, whether that first time was in a dream or in reality that she wasn't sure of. Then she saw the little wooden chair with its fresh coat of red paint brushed over thickened, previous layers that took away the smoothness from the surface and instead gave it the feel and look of peeling skin over a healing blister. Suddenly it all came back to her mind. Though she still wasn't sure whether that vision appeared to her in a dream or it really was, she now could recollect details in the vision. The red saree, the vermillion, the batasha, everything.

'The bride! Yes!' she suddenly exclaimed.

'Yes, you do? So you will be that bride in a few days Kumari, with the red saree and the vermillion, doling out batashas,' Thuloaama said. Paarvati's days thenceforth ended with the setting sun but began even before it rose. In between ritualistic baths and chanting of hymns, the words of which she now pronounced and understood as clearly as she pronounced and understood the words mai, baba and Shamlee, Paarvati happily played around with the aamas in the yards of the Mata's cottage as they went about their chores of milking the goats, churning butter for the lamps and the thousand other odd tasks that came up during the preparation of navaratri and the kumari puja on Ashutwami. But there was no tinkering of anklet bells when she ran because her anklets were left behind at home with Bhairavi. She was also gradually beginning to realize the control she was gaining over her own physical and emotional existence. Through all of it, Paarvati still found time to draw on her slate. She drew the chickens back at home and she drew mai and baba. She also drew Shamlee and showed the drawings to the aamas. How they adored those drawings!

'Mai says Shamlee had been with her since before I came to mai,' she told the aamas one day. Then she paused, looked up and asked, 'Where has Thuloaama's Shamlee come from?' For Paarvati, every goat was Shamlee. Thus, Thuloaama's Shamlee too was a black one. All the Shamlees there were black. 'Thuloaama's Shamlee came with a devotee, kumari,' the aama explained, 'as an offering to Durga, to Mata Taleju during navaratri.'

'Like flowers, incense sticks and fruits?' she asked.

'Yes, like flowers, incense sticks and fruits.'

The winter sun put little rounds of a healthy, happy and deep pink on the little girl's fair cheeks. The tip of her nose always remained very cold but that never made it sneeze or run. Her dark eyes sometimes squinted against the strong mountain sun but she yet preferred the outdoors.

'But why Shamlee?' she asked again, 'Then do devotees bring chickens and dogs too?'

The aama laughed and hugged her. 'No dear,' she replied, 'they don't. You see those pigeons and doves there?' she said, pointing at the gleaming dome of the Durga temple. 'They bring those and Shamlees.'

'Aama Ahalya said that somewhere, in another Durga temple atop another mountain in a faraway land called Kamarupa, Shamlees are sacrificed on the day of Ashutwami. You don't here?'

'No, we don't here. Here Thuloaama puts vermillion and grains of rice on them and after saying her prayers, she offers Shamlee or the birds to Mata Taleju. Mata accepts the offering by touching them and then Thuloaama sets the birds free and keeps the Shamlees for milk.'

'And for Shamlees that don't give milk?'

'Shamlees that don't give milk are sold, so that rice, grams and fruits for the aamas and bubas, wicks for the earthen lamps and sugar for the batashas can be bought.'

Paarvati listened well. Then she went in and brought out her slate and with neat, deft strokes of the chalk held between her baby fingers, drew mountains with a temple on top and below the temple, as if underground, she drew the same 'V' with the straight line dissecting the angle at the base. The figure that Kuntal said was a trident and asked her to place on top of the dome and not keep buried under the temple. This was what she once again drew under the temple....

'See this temple, aama?' Paarvati asked, and looked intently at her own drawing. Then she looked up at the aama and said, 'Here, maybe, Shamlees are sacrificed?' Though she asked, she did not really expect an answer. Because Paarvati knew only three temples, the first two being the Durga and the Pashupati temples at Tilibham and the third, the temple on her slate. The first two temples, at Tilibham, had names. And they also had real, visual images to which she could connect those names. But the temple on her slate only had a visual image without any name and the temple that aama Ahalya mentioned had only a name, Kamakhya, but no visual image bound to it, not yet. So the little girl, in her little mind, gave the name of Kamakhya to the visual image of the temple on her slate. So she now knew of three temples with names that created visual images too of those respective temples in her mind.

'Maybe,' the aama responded after a while, 'maybe.'

'Maybe,' Paarvati repeated after her, looking down at her Kamakhya temple on the slate.

The seven days before navaratri seemed to go by very quickly for Paarvati. And they seemed to go by equally slowly for Bhairavi back at home.

That year, the night before Ashutwami, it was Paarvati's Sajaunu that began in the Mata's cottage. Just the way Bhairavi yearned to adorn her daughter on her wedding day. Prayers for the transition began at both the Durga and the Pashupati temples at that exact moment when Paarvati's divine bath began at the cottage. It was this bath that marked the beginning of her Sajaunu. Little by little, inch by inch, her whole virgin pre-pubescent little body was anointed with a soft, smooth paste of sandal, basil and turmeric. A faint hum of the chants from the temples drifted to her. The Newars of Tilibham believed that the white of sandal signified the purity of the kumari's body and mind, the green of basil signified her power to nurture and ability to grow, and the yellow of turmeric implied the light she radiated into the universe. Since midnight she had been on a fast. But there was no trace of hunger, fatigue or sleep in her. Instead, her dark eyes shone brighter and a calm started to descend upon her while another lifted from Bhairavi. She tossed and turned in bed wishing for the night to pass away at the blink of an eye but even that one blink evaded her. She imagined Paarvati's Sajaunu. The golden red saree, the flowers on her hair, the fragrant garlands around her dainty wrists and neck and that bright red dot on her forehead. And then her heart screamed through the chill silence of the navaratri darkness to reach out to Paarvati, to hold her close and shake her till the whole of the prophesy fell out of her little being. But that scream remained within her. It only echoed through a womb made barren twice over. People had come to her and said, 'Ah, the kumari's mother! You too are blessed, Bhairavi, you must be beaming with honour and joy!' But Bhairavi didn't hear any of it. She only heard the words of the prophesy ringing again and again in her ears and each time they did, the surety of its full occurrence only became more and more apparent.

It was still dark in the valley when a beautifully adorned Paarvati, looking like a child bride, was carried from the Mata's cottage to the Pashupati temple in the equally beautifully decorated wooden palanquin across the festooned courtyard. She was calm. The phase of the divine transition had already begun. A quick flash of her mai passed through her mind but then it came and passed by just as did flashes of all those people who thronged to see her during the past few hours at the Mata's cottage. The gentle swaying of the palanquin made her remember the swing her baba made for her once long back. Once again, a dream-like vision came over her wherein she saw that at the temple on her slate, the one she began associating with the name of Kamakhya, black cattle were gathered to be sacrificed. A few looked like Shamlee. Shamlee! And Kajlee and Dairu. And Shamlee's kids. All black! But once again, the vision just flashed by without any special emotion. It didn't torment her, it didn't pleasure her. Because she had now transcended all feelings of torment and pleasure. Once inside the Pashupati temple and after the rituals there were almost completed amidst the chant of prayers and the sound of gongs and conch, a rooster crowed far away in the valley heralding Ashutwami. At that precise moment, as did all kumaris there since the first ever kumari puja at Tilibham, Paarvati too rose and walked up to the base of the shivling, picked a pinch of vermillion with her left hand and smeared it on the parting of her hair. And with that came the final transition. Drums, gongs and cymbals were let to roar and clang to a high, orgasmic pitch before they slowly fell and stopped. Then standing there in the caved in rock, the innermost shrine of the Pashupati temple, Paarvati saw the rooster that crowed miles away outside, far below those hundred and fifty steps of cobblestone, spreading its wings and elongating its neck for another call. Though the rest of the people in the temple only heard it crow. The mother goddess had descended into her. She now ceased to be Paarvati and rose instead as Mata Taleju and would remain so till midnight. While she awoke into her new incarnate, back at home her mother Bhairavi gave in to ache, angst and apprehension. And just before the rooster crowed, unable to bear any of it any longer, she slipped away into slumber. It was a slumber brought upon by heaviness of heart and exhaustion of mind. She slept through that whole noon of Ashutwami while Kuntal waited by her side, moving out only to feed the chickens and the goats. And the mongrels slouched by the gate. That was a sparse and quiet yard that day while the temple yard atop the high flat land swarmed with people. Rising from that yard, hails of Mata Taleju and sounds of dhimei rang out into every direction of the Himalayas and farther.

Paarvati was then carried out of the Pashupati temple and into the Durga temple where she took her seat on the little red wooden chair by the side of the nude rock sculpture of Durga. Her tiny feet were made to rest on a broad banana leaf. Paarvati, the year's Mata Taleju, had ascended her throne.

Mata Taleju once again reigned, this once through little Paarvati.

'....... *Like you bow in reverence before me today, so shall others do before her...'*

So that day they would bow before Paarvati, and make more of the prophesy come true.

A soft tinge of sunlight melted into the valley outside swathing every nook and corner in Tilibham, homestead and field, the living and the inanimate, and crevice and cliff. Many more roosters and even more birds broke the silence of the mountains, ushering in Ashutwami. And the first devotees to walk in to see Mata Taleju with bowed heads and folded hands were an old couple. The woman's back was stooping with age and her brows wrinkled with worry, her limbs unstable. Her husband was older than her but was erect of posture and steady of limb. He led her gently to Mata Taleju. Despite her unstable limbs and infirm grip, the old lady clutched a pair of black pigeons in her hands. The birds had their feet tied with lengths of thickly entwined grass. The couple approached Mata Taleju with the kind of nervousness that came out of indebtedness and reverence.

'Aha!' Mata Taleju said when they reached her altar, 'I can see that your great grand daughter had spoken at last, Janaki, she shall now speak coherently till her breath lasts. And that shall be till she too sees her great grand children.'

'Jai Mata Taleju!' the old woman said, almost in tears out of gratitude. Her husband helped her sit down on the floor in front of Mata Taleju. 'Here, Mata,' she said with her head bowed and her shaking hands stretched as far as she could towards Mata Taleju, with the birds in them. 'As you sought last Ashutwami, I bring you your black pigeons. That the child had spoken her first word at the age of eight is only because of your mercy on her and us, Mata!' Having said that, the woman delicately set the birds down at Mata Taleju's feet. They wobbled as their tied feet touched the ground. Thuloaama smeared a little vermillion on the head of each bird, silently chanted a prayer and forwarded the birds to Mata Taleju. Mata Taleju picked a yellow marigold from the plate beside her and plucked out its petals. These she then sprinkled on the pigeons. At that moment, the pigeons attempted to hop and move and the strings that tied their feet gave way. The birds got free. Mata Taleju smiled with all the glee of a six year old. The birds hopped around for a while before taking a low flight out of the temple. They would join the hundreds that cooed and gurgled on the domes of the Durga and Pashupati temples. Mata Taleju's glance followed the black pigeons as they flew out of the temple and when her gaze went out of the temple yard and beyond, she perceived the two black oxen sacrificed at her altar at Kamakhya atop the Nilachal hills at that exact moment when the grass-strings around the black pigeons fell off. As if it was the grass entwining that had held the breaths and bodies of the oxen together till then.

More people walked in and prostrated before Paarvati even before the previous ones walked out. Thuloaama and aama Panchali were always near her. They kept filling the plates with batasha, flowers and fruits for her to dole out. After a while, a voice rose above the din to reach the inner chamber.

'Please! Make way!'

People turned around to see what it was as they moved to give way. Mata Taleju smiled. It was Tonkoprasad Rai at the doorway. His wife and son had brought him to receive Mata Taleju's touch with hopes of reviving his memory. When they arrived near her they helped him sit on the floor in front of Mata Taleju and then themselves too knelt down.

'Jai Mata Taleju!' the wife said with her head bowed, her palms joined, 'Have mercy, Mata, I beg you to place your hand on my unfortunate man's head. I beg you to please heal him.' Tonkoprasad Rai stared listlessly at the little goddess and uttered two incoherent words. 'Devi,' he said. Then after a long pause, said, 'Kamakhya.' Mata Taleju had not yet placed her left palm on his head but she kept looking into his eyes. His wife took it upon herself to speak for her husband. 'Mata, he probably wishes to say that he had gone on a pilgrimage to Devi Kamakhya's temple. He had pledged a black goat....' Mata Taleju turned her eyes from Tonkoprasad Rai to his wife and raising a finger to her own lips, gestured the wife to remain silent. Because Mata Taleju saw in his eyes what the wife did not. She saw the saadhvi in those eyes whom Tonkoprasad Rai thought of when he said, 'Devi'. She understood and smiled before raising her left hand and placing it on his head. She then closed her eyes to see his past and also his future.

A few years back when Tonkoprasad Rai went to the ambubasi fair at the Kamakhya temple in Assam's Kamarupa, he fell in love with a saadhvi there. The two were married by a priest at the temple on the day the temple doors were thrown open to devotees after having remained closed for three days when the stone organ of the goddess inside was bleeding. But even as the goddess bled and people in Kamarupa abstained from ploughing lest the penetration hurt what they believed also to be the bleeding earth, Tonkoprasad Rai had penetrated deep and often into the saadhvi. Mata Taleju saw that their wedding had comprised a mere exchange of garlands of red hibiscus and the applying of red vermillion on the parting of the saadhvi's hair by Tonkoprasad Rai. And then they were led thrice around the temple, jostling and stepping through humans, goats and monkeys and ducking from doves and pigeons. There were no marriage vows taken, no friends and family standing by. The entire wedding had taken less than half an hour. And cost Tonkoprasad Rai a thousand rupees. Thus impoverished by a full thousand and the added expense of buying the saadhvi a new saree and some fake silver jewellery from the stalls that lined the steps to the temple, to symbolically bring her out of her life of an ascetic, Tonkoprasad Rai was left with no more resources to buy train tickets for the two of them back to Nepal and Tilibham. Nor did he know anyone in faraway Kamarupa from whom he could borrow money. The saadhvi did know a whole lot of other saadhvis, yogis and ascetics but they were just that, saadhvis, yogis and ascetics with no money on them, not to even think of a thousand rupees. Mata Taleju saw through her closed eyes that as an immediate recourse all those years back, Tonkoprasad Rai found the situation convenient. For he wasn't really prepared to take a bride, married on an impulse, to his grown-up children and wife back at home. So he felt relieved when his new bride offered to stay back at the temple till he returned from home with money enough to buy tickets to take her with him. Still keeping her eyes closed and her hand on his head, Mata Taleju smiled. For she saw what Tonkoprasad Rai himself had not seen, that the saadhvi and the priest who got them married split the thousand rupees between them after Tonkoprasad Rai left. He also didn't know that the saadhvi sold the fake jewellery and the saree at a little more than half their price and kept that part of the loot all to herself without letting the priest know about it. When Tonkoprasad Rai got back home to his wife and children in Tilibham, he felt that the gods had sided with him because the saadhvi had offered to stay back and wait. He almost pitied her innocence. He didn't know that she had, in all that while, married and earned money and pity from many more susceptible pilgrims like him and left them free to return home without her. Outside Mata Taleju's altar, in the middle chamber of the Durga temple, people waited patiently for their turn to come. But Mata Taleju was not yet done with Tonkoprasad Rai. She saw the remorse, the guilt and the pressure caused thereby in him. It was these that slowly released the senile dementia in him. With time, Tonkoprasad Rai began to hate himself not only because he had made love to a saadhvi using the facade of a marriage but also because he thought she was still waiting for him. That he had betrayed her trust in him gnawed at his soul. Gradually, he also started loathing himself for giving in to his desires right there in the temple yard, while the goddess's stone organ bled inside. Hate for his own self filled him to such an extent that even during the chill Himalayan winters of Tilibham, Tonkoprasad Rai often woke up in the middle of the night with a cold sweat. And to atone for his sins, which he could own up to no one, he promised to the goddess at Kamakhya that he would go back to her with an offering of a black goat to sacrifice at her altar, to seek her forgiveness. Mata Taleju opened her eyes and brought her hand down. Tonkoprasad Rai didn't make it to Kamakhya, not within that promised year, not until that moment. And by then, the wretched pressure that was rising within him began to come out in the form of dementia.

'He mentioned the pledge to you?' Mata Taleju asked Tonkprasad Rai's wife, though she already knew the answer. 'He did. He did, Mata,' she replied, 'and his health and mind were falling apart all because of this unfulfilled pledge. It is your wrath on him because of his failure to stand by what he committed, isn't it Mata Taleju? Isn't it this that has made a mockery out of a learned school teacher? Pardon me for having the audacity to ask, Mata Taleju, but isn't it so?' and the woman broke down. Her husband looked at her and looked back at Mata Taleju with eyes that were hazy and recognized nothing and no one. 'Devi waits at the Kamakhya,' he said after a while. Hearing this, his wife broke out into loud wails, moved by her husband's sincerity to his pledge to the goddess and despising herself for her own inability to save enough money for yet another pilgrimage to the temple of Kamakhya and for the black goat. Mata Taleju picked a pinch of vermillion from the plate beside her and simply sprinkled it all over Tonkoprasad Rai. She once again placed her left hand on his head and said, 'His sickness remains for a purpose, that purpose being to erase all memories of his devi and the moments he spent with her. But till such time, his mind shall continue to dwindle and fall. There! I can see that he shall once again visit the grounds of the Kamakhya temple on the Nilachal hills to offer his black goat...' Thuloaama and aama Ahalya exchanged glances because the little goddess had said goat instead of Shamlee, her usual name for a goat. The goddess continued, '....to devi Kamakhya. And thenceforth, Devi Kamakhya shall be the only devi to rule his head and heart. His mind then on shall cease to fall apart but shall neither go back to the learned and sharp mind that it once was. Now rise and go!' Mata Taleju said looking at Tonkoprasad Rai's wife, 'You shall, in due time, come to have resources enough to take him to Kamarupa and Kamakhya.

When you do so, use that resource and take him there. His guilt shall abandon him and his heart shall return to you.' The woman's wails softened to sobs as she and her son helped Tonkoprasad Rai on his feet and together they walked out of the inner shrine. Mata Taleju watched till they stepped out of the temple. She could see his black goat being sacrificed, four winters from then. She could also see her own shrine at Kamakhya, the navaratri festivities going on in those distant grounds, the people thronging there and the severed heads of black oxen and goats which had been sacrificed as offering to her. She also saw Bhairavi and Kuntals's courtyard, Shamlee indulgently watching Kajlee, Dairu and Kajlee's kids while Bhairavi slept inside the hut. And when she saw the hut where Bhairavi slept, she also saw a piece of copper in the shape of a large banyan leaf tucked away among the damp, fungus ridden thatch on the hut's roof. She saw the yoni engraved on that sheet of copper, the yoni that made Kamakhya the shrine that it was. She saw what was to come from it all. She saw it all happening.

Meanwhile, more and more people arrived to see Mata Taleju. Some arrived to pay their gratitude for favours already received, some came to seek favours then and there, and yet some came just to pay their obeisance and keep the blessings aside to use in seeking favours later. This was what that made up the past, the present and the future of humans, Mata Taleju thought. For her though, all time, past, present and future, was one span of timelessness. Outside, people rejoiced in the Ashutwami fair. Children bothered their parents to buy them roasted peanuts and little round balls of sweetened tamarind till they gave in. Young and old danced the jyapu under the cheerfully festooned canopy and some just sat and watched. Towards evening, lesser people lined up to meet Mata Taleju but more gathered to partake of the festivities outside. The hundred and fifty stone steps had little earthen lamps placed on their edges. Lamps were also placed all along the fence that ran along the entire periphery of the high, flat land of the temples and also on the verandah of the Mata's cottage. The temples of course had many more lamps, some larger than those in the yard and the steps. When darkness set in and all the lamps were lit, the combined glow from their otherwise tiny flickers lend a bright orange haze that rose high into the night sky from the high flat land of the temple grounds.

When Bhairavi woke up late in the evening, Kuntal brought her out into their courtyard and the two stood there for long and watched that bright orange haze rising from where there little Paarvati was. The dogs sauntered close and settled near their feet. Descending darkness was never so haunting for Bhairavi and Kuntal. Back at the temple, rituals for Mata Taleju to leave her abode in Paarvati's mortal body had already begun, for soon it would be midnight.

Paarvati would then be carefully and lovingly brought back in the palanquin to the Mata's cottage where she would fall into deep slumber after all the rituals of her transition back into human would come to an end. And when she woke up from that sleep, every memory of those hours of being goddess would lift from her and dissolve into that one span of timelessness just like the haze that rose from the grounds of the highland and evaporated into the darkness of the night sky. And then seven days and eight nights from the last night of navaratri, on the day of the Garhalachmi Bulaunu, she would be taken back home to Bhairavi and Kuntal. She would no more remain Mata Taleju, no more remain kumari. She would just be her mai and baba's Paarvati like she had been before her brush with divinity.

But as of now, Bhairavi and Kuntal just stood and watched that orange haze. Each daybreak from then on for the next seven days, Bhairavi stepped out into her yard despite the chill morning breeze to watch yet another orange haze, that of dawn, which rose over the mountains and over the highland. It was her way of counting the number of days that remained for Paarvati to arrive back home. And on the eighth day at dawn, long after the orange haze of daybreak turned into a radiant morning warming everything under the sky, Bhairavi remained waiting in her yard till her Paarvati arrived. She let her eyes search as far up the cliff as was visible from her yard to catch the earliest glimpse of a palanquin.

And before the sun rose any higher, clutching her slate and two new pieces of white chalk, Paarvati was at last home! For a brief moment, Bhairavi forgot all about a certain prophesy that had been gnawing at her. For during that one brief moment all that she was aware of was that she was holding her little Paarvati in her bosom once again. No, she thought, she was not barren after all. She had her Paarvati.

Paarvati was home.

END OF CHAPTER 10

CHAPTER 11

YONI

On the first dawn back at home Paarvati rose with the sun. Thin beams of pale daylight seeped in through the slits along the reed and bamboo walls of the hut, weaving a pattern of alternate streaks of light and shade upon the face of her mother sleeping beside her. As if reflecting the alternate streaks of joy and foreboding that her heart bore. Even in her sleep Bhairavi held Paarvati close to her all through the night, in fear of losing her again. And now as the little girl woke up she lightly traced with her tiny, soft finger, a band of light across her mother's face. The sensation made Bhairavi open her eyes. Paarvati smiled at those eyes and her mother drew her close to her bosom. Both lay cuddled that way till the light outside grew brighter and they heard the fowls clucking outside in the yard.

'Shall we go and wake Shamlee?' Bhairavi asked Paarvati. The little girl immediately sat up on bed. 'Yes, let's go!' she said enthusiastically, 'and Dairu and Kajlee too. And Kajlee's babies.' Paarvati got off the bed, took Bhairavi's hand and led her outside. The morning was cold. Drops of frost still hung onto the leaves on the shrubs. In a few days these leaves will have a light film of snow sitting on them but that day it was only frost. And yet, Bhairavi felt the chill groping through her clothes to reach her skin. Paarvati, however, seemed to remain oblivious to the cold. The joy she radiated when she saw the goats once again stirred life around that little hut that remained dreary all the while that she was gone. 'Shamlee!' she shouted in glee. Shamlee instantly flicked an ear, stood up and walked closer to the gate of the enclosure. Hearing her voice, the mongrels too started thumping their tails but only one uncurled himself, stood and stretched himself before lazily walking up to Paarvati. The other dog was too sluggish to move his whole self away from where he was so he kept thumping just his tail instead and followed Paarvati around with his eyes. The moment Bhairavi unfastened the gate of the goats' enclosure Shamlee walked straight up to Paarvati and started rubbing her head ever so gently against the little girl's legs. She giggled and scratched the goat behind her ear. The fowls too moved closer, fearless around those familiar feet. 'Dairu! Kajlee! Here, here!' Paarvati called out as she walked towards the younger goats. Unable to resist the happy reunion, even the sluggish mongrel dragged himself to be a part of that moment. The sun shone brighter now and Bhairavi wondered if it was the morning sun or if it was having Paarvati back home that made the whole yard come alive with a lingering kind of warmth, the kind only a bright winter sun and a content heart can bestow. For a moment, it seemed to Bhairavi that nothing had changed. Paarvati indeed had to go from her but now that she returned just the way she left, nothing had changed. And life in Kuntal's home and hearth were bouncing back to the way it was before Paarvati was taken away to the Mata's cottage. Nothing had changed.

Now that Bhairavi busied herself with Paarvati, Kuntal no longer had to be by her side all the while to comfort her and take her thoughts away from Mata Taleju's prophesy. So he now had time to replace the thatch on the roof of his hut, which he had been thinking of doing for quite some time. He thought of asking his friend Dayal and his brother Dinesh to help him with the task and he thought of doing it soon enough, within one of those days before the snow came in. It had already started snowing higher up the mountains and the snow was coming down fast to land in the valleys below. So Kuntal wanted to get this long overdue task done before that. He had already dried the grass and piled them up next to the goats' shed.

The days slipped by and Paarvati settled into the loving comfort of her life as before with her mai, baba and the motley members of her foster family, the fowls, goats and the two dogs. Like before, she continued to take out her slate and draw on it.

'You know, mai,' she would say when Bhairavi went about her chores and Paarvati followed her all around, filling the yard once again with the tinker of her anklet bells, 'You know, mai, Thuloaama's cottage has so many Shamlees,' and she spread her arms as wide and far from her body as she could and said, 'these many Shamlees!' And she would draw as many goats as would fit on her slate and show them to Bhairavi, who in turn expressed great delight and wonder at the large number of goats. Then Paarvati sat down for a while to draw the temple she used to draw earlier with the divided 'V' below it. When she finished drawing she looked at it for a while as if to see that nothing was left undone and then once again ran after Bhairavi. 'Mai! Now look at this,' she said. 'More Shamlees?' Bhairavi asked without looking at the drawing on the slate

'No, no, not Shamlee, mai, look. This is….,' she took a moment to recollect the name that she started associating with the temple she always drew, 'Kamakhya! Yes, this is Kamakhya!' she said in one go when she remembered the name and with great enthusiasm thrust the slate closer to Bhairavi's eyes.

'Is it?' Bhairavi asked, 'but how did you know?'

'I know because aama Ahalya said that Shamlees were sacrificed at the temple of Kamakhya in faraway Kamarupa. This is that Kamakhya, mai, look.'

'But did aama Ahalya also say that this,' Bhairavi pointed at the temple on the slate and asked, 'is that same Kamakhya?'

'No she didn't, but I know it is.'

'Oh! How so?'

'Why! There's no other temple for that extra name to be put to, mai, and this temple here,' she tapped on the drawing upon the slate and said, 'has no name. So I brought together the temple without a name and the name without a temple, and there you are! We have the Kamakhya temple here!' She uttered the last words with immense glee. Her eyes shone as if triumphing over a deep mystery, as if solving a good part of a puzzle and being able to chart out a path to follow to complete the rest of the puzzle. Her mai smiled and sighed. Inwardly, it greatly disturbed Bhairavi to see that Paarvati continued to chant the hymns which had become a ritual for her during her stay at the Mata's cottage. Even though only playfully, she chanted the hymns while she hop-scotched on squares marked out on the ground or looked up at eagles in the sky above just as other children her age might have sung folk songs and nursery rhymes. This slowly started unsettling Bhairavi. Once again her mind began to move away from the comfort in the fact that Paarvati was home. For deep within her she was always aware that a part of the prophesy, the most agonizing part, was yet to come by. When she mentioned Paarvati's chants to Kuntal he merely brushed it aside.

'Now that's the last thing that should bother you, Bhairavi,' he told her, 'she had been chanting those hymns for more than a month now, they have become a habit with her. Just as over time they became a part of her little being, so also over time they'll depart from her being. Give her that time, Bhairavi, they'll come out of her. Just give her some time.'

Bhairavi listened in silence, feeling all the while in her guts this other sense called the sixth. The intuition. She had a bizarre feeling that the tryst with divinity had not completely lifted from Paarvati, that a faint trace of it got left behind in her subconscious. Bhairavi had no logical reason to believe in the truth of this feeling and yet, she wholly believed in her intuition. Her intuition was reason enough. At the same time she comforted herself by saying that after all it was just that, an intuition. Because never till now in the fate and history of Tilibham's Kumari Puja did it so happen that a kumari returned home with fragments of memories of her divine experience as Mata Taleju still lodged in her. Never. And yet, everything that happened for the first time had, till that first time, remained as having never happened. So it was exactly this that unsettled Bhairavi. 'Could Paarvati's be that first partially lifted divinity from a kumari that had never happened till then?' Bhairavi wondered, as angst pierced through every inch of her flesh.

Just then Paarvati came to her with her slate and showed her the temple on it once again but this time she was pointing at what Kuntal had always thought to be a trident buried underground, under the temple.

'Mai,' Paarvati said pointing at that bifurcated 'V' in the hills below the temple on her slate, 'this...' she paused and then said, 'is here.'

'What is where?' Bhairavi asked.

'This,' said the little girl, 'this,' and she tapped at the dissected 'V' with her chalk and said, 'is here.' Then lifting her gaze from the slate and letting it go in search of something all about that little fenced yard, around the hut and on the thatch on it while still tapping at the 'V' with her chalk, she said solemnly, 'It's here!'

By the next week Kuntal had arranged for Dinesh and Dayal to come and help him pull down the old, damp and moss ridden thatch from the roof of his hut and put up the new sun-dried and crisp ones in its place. There was no money involved in this assistance, only the day's meal. Ofcourse in return Kuntal would help them chop and pile up a few logs of wood before the harshest of the snow and winter arrived at Tilibham.   They would have to start work very early and finish it all before darkness set in.

On the agreed day Dinesh and Dayal arrived early at Kuntal's place. Bhairavi offered them steaming, salted black tea to energize them before they started work. Kuntal had already made a ladder out of bamboo and kept lengths of rope, wire and a khukri handy. The goats were left in their shed that day but the dogs found all the activity so intriguing that they came forward to sniff everything when

Dayal, who had already climbed up onto the thatch, started tearing clumps of the damp grass and throwing them onto the ground below. A very nauseating soggy smell, that of fungus, bird poop and dust all rolled into one, rose from that damp grass and filled the yard. The dogs started sneezing and retreated to the farthest corner of the yard but continued to keep a watch over all the activities. The roof wasn't really a big one because the hut which it sheltered itself wasn't a big one. Moreover, it was just a single sloped roof and not one with a raised centre with the sides sloping outward. So it didn't take Dayal too long to take down the grass. Most of it had turned black and sodden and was rotting. Bhairavi had piled all her utensils in one corner inside the hut and spread a saree over them to cover them from falling bits of rotting thatch. She had also rolled up whatever clothes there was in the house into one big bundle on the bed and spread another saree over it. She let Paarvati be outside in the yard near the washing place with the halved log, far from where the thatch fell. So the little girl busied herself with Kajlee's kids. Soon after, one brave fowl came to the falling thatch. Then two more cautiously stepped close and started pecking at the very tiny worms and maggots that fell with the inner-most putrid layers of thatch. This encouraged the other chickens too and soon all of them were scampering by the thatch which Dayal kept detaching and dropping from the top. All this while Kuntal and Dinesh wove the new crisp grass along split lengths of bamboo that made up the entire frame of the roof. When all the decayed and fungus laden thatch would be pulled down, they would prop up that entire frame of thatch at one go. So while Kuntal and Dinesh wove layers of new thatch on the ground, Dayal continued to drop the old from above. Everytime a clump of thatch fell, the fowls jerked and scampered away clucking noisily, only to return immediately. Paarvati intently watched all of the excitement from where she sat near the goat shed.

Just then something other than thatch fell from the roof along with a clump of rotten grass, something noticeably heavier and noisier than thatch. Because it was heavier, it reached the ground among the fowls before the disintegrating clump of thatch did. It fell with a conspicuous *thonk*. The fowls, which were now getting more and more fearless of the grass falling on them from above, were taken off guard and they created an abrupt ruckus, clucking loud as they fled helter skelter all around the yard. This alerted the mongrels and they too let out loud, instinctive barks as they came running to see what caused the *thonk*. The goats flicked their ears and Paarvati too came running to see what fell on the ground from the rotting thatch. It was a copper sheet. Stained black and brown, in the shape of a large banyan leaf, its surface uneven.

Paarvati picked it up and turned it over and over in her little hands. Still carrying it, she walked slowly and thoughtfully towards the washing place. There she gently placed the copper sheet on the flat, upturned side of the halved tree trunk and picking a mug of water from the tin bucket next to it, slowly started pouring water on it. As she did so, she stood up and raised the hand with the mug above her head and poured the water just as the aamas poured on her the day they gave her the ritualistic cleansing bath in that exact place before taking her to the palanquin to proceed to the Mata's cottage. No one saw her pouring water thus on the copper sheet. Nor did anyone hear her chanting the hymn of the ritualistic bath of the divine as she was cleansing that banyan-leaf shaped copper sheet, as if giving it its purification bath. When she was done pouring that mugful of water, she did the same with two more mugs. The mud, grime and stain that Kuntal failed to scrape off even with all his might using knives and pebbles more than five years ago before he flung it onto the roof, had all come off that day with just the pouring of water on them. Just three full mugs. The water fell on the copper sheet from a good height because she poured it from a level higher than her head. As such, the water touched the sheet and splashed back, sprinkles of which touched Paarvati after they touched the copper sheet. As if the same water that cleansed the copper also cleansed Paarvati. She then once again picked the sheet and walked into the yard. The copper sheet and Paarvati were destined to have a bond. Of whatever kind, but a bond nevertheless. By now Bhairavi was looking for Paarvati and was asking the men what made the animals raise such a hue and cry. But even before the men themselves found out what the furore among the animals was all about, they saw Paarvati coming towards them from the washing place. She was partly drenched. Little trickles of water ran down the loose strands of her dark hair.

'Look at you!' Bhairavi said, surprised to see her soaked, 'what were you doing there? Come let me change you into dry clothes. And what's that in your hands?' Without saying a word Paarvati raised the copper sheet in her hands to show it to her mai. Bhairavi gasped. 'Why!' she exclaimed, 'It's that piece of copper! Remember Kuntal?'

Kuntal remembered. He did. It was the copper sheet in the shape of a large banyan leaf, the one with an engraving on it, of the image of the yoni of Dakshyayani. The one he found in the clearing by the ruins of princess Ambaa's palace. By then the roof had been completed and Dinesh and Dayal were gone. Inside the hut Bhairavi was putting the clothes and utensils back in order. Sitting alone outside, Kuntal stretched out his tired limbs, looking back on those times when the copper sheet arrived at their home as an insignificant piece of metal. He didn't know then, nor did he know now, that it was the last engraving with Dakshyayani's yoni on it. Paarvati had found what she came to know was lying somewhere in and around her yard, around their house. She had found that which would draw her to her calling.

END OF CHAPTER 11

CHAPTER 12

MATA TALEJU

As the snow fell that year, it pressed down on the new thatch which till now lay sundried and fluffed upon the roof of Bhairavi, Kuntal and Paarvati's home. The snow allowed the thatch to settle and rest. In Bhairavi's heart on the other hand, something else pressed down that did not at all allow her to settle and rest. The piece of copper. Paarvati could not be convinced to part with it. When she wasn't carrying it in her hands, she put it away in some place that neither Bhairavi nor Kuntal found out. Now that there was no work in the fields and the cold kept them mostly in the house, Kuntal often asked Paarvati for the sheet of copper so that he could carve some tool or utensil out of it, so that a good piece of metal did not go to waste. Or maybe, he thought, he could just beat down the engravings and edges on it to make it smooth and round, to be used as a plate.

'We can make that into a plate for you, Paarvati, and it'll stand out charmingly from the rest of the plates in the house. See, isn't that red? Wouldn't you like a red plate?'

'This cannot become a plate, baba,' she said, with pain in her eyes at the thought of the image being beaten, 'don't beat on the engravings. It will hurt.'

'Hurt?' Kuntal asked, surprised, 'hurt where?'

'Hurt here,' she said, pointing at the image on the engraving.

Kuntal laughed. 'My little angel,' he said, 'how much compassion do you hold in that little heart of yours! But what is this thing, Paarvati? That it would hurt if I beat on it to flatten it?'

Paarvati laughed as well and said, 'Wait, baba, I'll show you something. Don't go away, stay here, okay? I'll be back in a moment.' And she ran into the hut and came out as quickly, bringing with her the black slate and a piece of white chalk while still holding on to the red piece of copper. Then she sat down next to Kuntal and using his knees as a table, put her slate on them and started drawing her temple. The one she often drew atop mountains with the divided 'V' below it. Kuntal noticed that her fingers were steadier now and the strokes of her chalk upon the slate were much freer and more fluid, the kind that came from repeatedly and passionately drawing the same thing for years. The kind that came from drawing not only with the fingers but with the heart and the soul. Even the form of the temple was more pronounced now. The dome, the different chambers within the temple, all of it. Then when she was done, she traced out the 'V' once again with the chalk and as she did so, she said, 'Look, baba, look at this,' and showed the 'V' to Kuntal. Then she placed the banyan leaf shaped copper sheet beside it and pointing at the engraving on it, said, 'Now look at this image, baba.' Kuntal looked. Stunned and speechless, he kept staring for a while at both the images, the one on the slate and the one on the copper sheet. Because they were the same. It hadn't yet dawned on him that Paarvati had been drawing that image below the temple which she began referring to as Kamakhya, long before she even saw the large, banyan leaf shaped copper sheet or the image engraved on it.

'They are the same, baba, don't beat it,' she said pointing at the image on the copper sheet. 'Baba, if you beat the image on the copper, it hurts the image on the slate.'

'But there is no life in either of the images, Paarvati, that they should hurt,' Kuntal tried to reason.

'Baba, some things hurt even with them having no life. Some things even bleed with them having no life,' she explained. She seemed old and mature enough to understand the laws that governed the Universe, both through the animate and the inanimate. And through the divine as well. Kuntal felt his limbs going numb. She continued, 'The shivling at the Pashupati temple on the high flat land up there hears prayers and answers them without having a life of its own. You believe that, don't you, baba? Though it is only stone. Lifeless, like you say of other stones that lay unworshipped. And you know baba, when you reach out with your soul to those with no life you begin to see life in them as well. So it is with the worshipped stone that lives even with no life, that can hear and respond, bleed and bless. Because you have reached out to that stone with your soul. Just so it is with this copper. Can't you feel the life here?' she asked Kuntal as she ran her finger slowly over the image on the copper sheet, 'it too can feel the hurt, baba, it will hurt.' And she walked in taking her slate, the chalk and the sheet of copper with her. Kuntal found no word and reason, either to respond or to argue. His mind froze for a moment while his pulse raced like it was beating for many lives all at once. Questions that never occurred to him earlier, did at that moment. Could that really be the Kamakhya temple of Kamarupa that Paarvati drew? Was there, after all, some truth in Bhairavi's fears upon seeing Paarvati still go about the chants of the kumari? And most desperately, was the final part of the prophesy going to come true? Even if it did, how might it be in any way related to a stray piece of copper found while ploughing in the wilderness? Kuntal slowly got up and walked into the hut. Paarvati's slate lay on the bed with the temple still on it, unerased. He looked at it closely and for long. His gaze ran intently over every part of the sketch of the temple. He was so engrossed that he didn't notice Bhairavi coming and standing behind him and looking at the same drawing over his shoulders.

'Kuntal?' she called.

He turned around, startled. Then he returned his gaze to rest upon the sketch on the slate and slowly, somewhat hesitantly and with reticence, lightly touched with his index finger that image which he all along thought to be a trident. And he asked Bhairavi, 'What does the Kamakhya of Kamarupa have deep within it?' He knew what the Kamakhya of Kamarupa had in its deepest part, deep within the innermost, cave like chamber. In the garbha griha. And yet, the mystifying turn of events that drew his most loved Paarvati into them suddenly made him doubt even that which he always knew, with conviction, to be the truth. He began to question what he believed in.

'What is there?' he repeated.

'Dakshyayani's yoni,' Bhairavi replied calmly. Inner turmoil always made her appear amazingly calm outside.

'This, then,' Kuntal said pointing at the dissected 'V' under the temple, 'is not a trident?'

'It isn't a trident.'

'Then what is it, Bhairavi?'

'If, like Paarvati says, it is the Kamakhya of Kamarupa, then this is the image of the yoni.'

Kuntal looked up from the image to look into Bhairavi's eyes.

'Dakshyayani's yoni,' she answered to Kuntal's silent, unspoken question. Not that he didn't know.

'And this,' Bhairavi said circling the air just above the drawing of the temple on the slate with her finger, 'is that Kamakhya.' She paused and asked, 'but how may this be related to the engraving on the copper sheet?' Bhairavi, however, did not expect an answer to this from Kuntal. Because she knew that even Kuntal probably had the same question rummaging through his uneasy mind. Just then Paarvati walked up to them and in her hands she had the banyan-leaf shaped copper sheet. Mustering all the courage she had at that moment to veil her anxiety, Bhairavi forced a smile on her face and cheer in her tone as she asked Paarvati, 'Oh! You're still carrying that red plate about with you? So then what do you intend to do with it?' The little girl didn't say anything in reply to that. Instead she climbed up on the bed, made herself comfortable and pulled the slate towards her so that the temple now faced her upright. Then very gently, she placed the copper sheet directly on the dissected 'V' she drew under the sketch of the temple she called the Kamakhya. 'There!' she exclaimed, 'look! This is where it should be, this is where I need to lay it. Mai, see, this is what I am to do.' And she keenly inspected her alignment of the copper sheet on the slate.

As the cold got harsher, Paarvati was made to stay indoors most of the day. Of course, she loved the mountain sun of the winters, the way it warmed her face while the chill breeze brushed past her ears and cooled them. She sat outside in the sun-swathed yard sometimes with Shamlee and the other goats and sometimes the mongrels came and slumped themselves at her feet. Sometimes she ate an orange while she sat there. And when she did that, she fed the peel to the goats as she herself leisurely sucked at the segments of the orange. She would then point at the snow laden mountains faraway, showing them to the dogs and telling them, 'See those mountains there? Maybe Kamakhya is somewhere up there. Aama Ahalya said it was on some other hill in some faraway land. So maybe there.' The dog let out a long, low noise that sounded like something between a whimper and a gentle roar. 'Yes, boy, that's why I like telling you all the things that I need to. You listen well and reply,' she said, patting his broad head and scratching him under the chin. Then bringing her mouth close to his ear, whispered into it, 'Shamlee is not a good listener,' and she giggled, covering her mouth with a palm. When Bhairavi walked past and heard those last words, her disturbed heart found some solace in the fact that the child was talking to her pets and not chanting hymns. But this solace was not to remain for long. To Bhairavi's dismay, Paarvati resumed chanting the hymns.

As the days and months passed and the snow started to melt while new shoots of tiny grass started to sprout upon the earth, the intervals between Paarvati's chants narrowed. She continued to sketch the temple on her slate and gradually, the details in that sketch increased. Soon the summers came and filled the mountain slopes with tiny but brightly coloured wild flowers. Red and yellow lantana and purple goatweed bloomed in abundance along the outer side of the fence of their yard. Paarvati often plucked these dainty little flowers while still standing inside the fence, thrusting her tiny hand through the fence. She then spread these flowers out on the temple upon her slate as if offering them at the temple's altar. Bhairavi's kurvak too was in full bloom that year. Everything else in Tilibham went on the way they always did. Even the white, fleecy sheep which looked like blobs of cloud among the grass on the mountain slopes continued to graze lazily in the valleys. But in Kuntal and Bhairavi's house things were no more the way they used to be. Paarvati kept the copper sheet with herself, nobody knew where. Bhairavi tried looking for it among her few toys when she was asleep or under the bedclothes when she was outside. Sometimes they saw the copper sheet in her hands and sometimes, on certain calculated days as Bhairavi realized later, she saw Paarvati pouring water on it by the washing place, holding the mug of water high above her head. Soon the summers too passed by and the nip in the air that arrived with autumn came to settle in the valleys of Tilibham. More stars started to blink in the night sky of that tiny Himalayan hamlet, some very far away from Paarvati and some not so far, for they seemed bigger and brighter than the others. Autumn also ushered in navaratri. And Ashutwami.

That year when Kuntal, Bhairavi and Paarvati went to the navaratri fair on the day of Ashutwami, Paarvati walked all the way from home and even climbed up the hundred and fifty steps of cobblestone by herself. Yet she showed no trace of fatigue. She had grown taller too since her last visit there. This year also, like the earlier years, she found something new in the same familiar festoons that hung over the temple yard, newness in the same stalls that vended toys and peanuts and there was an overall newness in the same lively, bustling ambience that she was so familiar with and yet, that evoked her curiosity each year. And when she saw the eager faces of the aamas coming out to greet her, familiarity rushed back to her mind. It carried fondness and a sense of belonging with it. When she looked up, bright rays of the sun touched a glittering piece of festoon and bounced away, throwing the light into her eyes. Instant joy surged through her but this once, she didn't squeal out of delight like she used to earlier. There was something new in the same old Paarvati, just like there was something new in the same navaratri fair at the temple grounds. She saw people with black pigeons and black goats flocking to meet Mata Taleju. Bhairavi brought a few blooms of red kurvak from the shrub in her yard, incense sticks and some butter milk she churned herself from Kajlee's milk to offer Mata Taleju. This time when Paarvati saw the Durga temple and entered its three chambers successively, there was not an inkling of doubt in her of whether she had, on an earlier occasion, seen that shrine in her dreams or in reality. Because this time she knew that she had been there and spent cherished moments within those temple grounds. She recollected with amazing clarity and certainty each of the shrine's nooks, corners, walls and windows. Yet, when she saw the year's seven year old Mata Taleju sitting resplendent in her shimmering attire of red and gold, adorned with fresh flowers like a child bride with the bright red vermillion on the parting of her hair and the red dot at the centre of her forehead, an uncanny sensation of chill trickled down her back causing her small body to go into a shudder. With that one shudder a speck of confusion got stirred in her senses once again, a speck of that same dream-like state arose in her once more, the one that she felt when she arrived at that same shrine as a kumari with Thuloaama. This time, however, the feeling was not for the shrine itself but for Mata Taleju. 'Was I on that chair like her?' Paarvati wondered. A hazy, faraway vision kept appearing and fading repeatedly in her mind, a vision where she saw herself as Mata Taleju during some past Ashutwami. She could even feel the drape of the saree around her body, flowers on her skin and a banana leaf at the soles of her feet. She felt as if she knew how it was like to have her left palm touch the heads of those who bowed before Mata Taleju. Unknowingly, the fingers of her right hand slowly ran over her left palm, trying to feel that skin as if that would confirm or at least in some way let her know whether that feeling occured in reality or in a dream. Meanwhile, a motley flow of devotees, young, old and infants in the arms of grown-ups, all walked past her. Somewhere deep inside her, she heard a cockerel crow. She instinctively turned around to look for one but there was none. And yet she saw the silhouette of a cockerel with its elongated neck. The vision was very hazy and it soon began to melt away from the edges like smoke before it vanished completely into distant memory. Paarvati hadn't realized that they were standing in front of Mata Taleju till she heard her name being called.

'Come, Paarvati, come,' Mata Taleju said, 'I know you love batashas!' she smiled as she said so, picking up quite a few from the plate next to her and stretching her arm towards Paarvati to give her the batashas. It was only then that all trace of those hazy visions were gone and Paarvati's mind became as clear as it was when she left home. With that, her heart too filled once more with unrestrained joy and excitement on seeing aama Ahalya and Thuloaama beside Mata Taleju. As Paarvati knelt down and put her hands forward to receive the batashas, Mata Taleju put her other hand below Paarvati's, to support them from falling down from the weight of the calling they were about to receive. Mata Taleju thus clasped Paarvati's hands for a moment with the batashas in them and leaned forward. Then very softly, almost in a whisper, she spoke into her ear, 'I never wholly departed from this abode, Paarvati, never wholly departed from you!' as she said so the Mata released her hand for a moment to let it reach up to Paarvati's head and let it run down gently from there along her side, 'nor would I ever wholly dwell in it again. But I shall hold this abode to my will. I shall hold you to my will, Paarvati, because there is a purpose to it all. Now that the image of Dakshyayani's yoni upon the banyan-shaped copper sheet has come to be with you, the Universe shall guide you to do that with it which it had been waiting centuries for. And thereby it shall lead you to your calling. You shall follow that call.' Mata Taleju then sat straight once more but remained holding Paarvati's hands in her own. She looked deep into Paarvati's eyes, reaching into her soul through them, telling her through those eyes what to do with the engraving of the yoni and where to let it rest. Paarvati too kept staring at Mata Taleju, allowing her eyes to be looked into, to be read and to be told. After a while Mata Taleju lifted her other hand and placed it above Paarvati's. The batashas were starting to get sticky between the palms while the middle chamber of the Durga temple was starting to get crowded. 'The bloodstone awaits!' said Mata Taleju, still looking into Paarvati's soul through her eyes before releasing her hands. Paarvati blinked as she brought her hands down and only when she looked at them did she remember the batashas. Bhairavi didn't hear what passed between Mata Taleju and Paarvati. No one did. But while others didn't wish to know what passed between them, Bhairavi did. She desperately did. And the despair manifested as creases upon her face and racing beats in her heart.

'Why, Bhairavi, you have once again forgotten to give what you brought for me!' Mata Taleju said cheerfully, 'come, bring them here. The smell of that buttermilk you have churned,' and she drew in a deep breath, 'ah! how divine it is!' she said. Those words of Mata Taleju's seemed to smoothen out the creases of anxiety upon Bhairavi's face, though not all of it, and the corners of her mouth stretched to form a weak smile. Somebody's pigeons were gurgling in the middle chamber. Outside in the temple yard, the navaratri fair was at its peak. Strains of dhimei rose above the happy din of the buyer and the vendor, of pilgrim and tourist, the devout and the grateful, energetic little children and fatigued old people. The hundred and fifty cobblestone steps never got a moment free from footfall. The mountain breeze brushed past the hanging festoons, causing a light but incessant ruffling and swishing noise as if the festoons sighed with a desire for some more caress of the flirting breeze. When Bhairavi had put her offerings, Mata Taleju gestured her forward and looking at her, said, 'The temple on Paarvati's slate, yes, that is my abode. She has unknowingly begun to call it the Kamakhya, but it indeed is that. It is the Kamakhya, Bhairavi, atop the Nilachal hills in Kamarupa. You notice the hills she draws on the slate on which the temple stands, don't you? Yes, they are the Nilachal hills.' Then Mata Taleju looked at Kuntal and said, 'Kuntal, that which you thought to be a trident below the temple isn't a trident. No. But now of course you know what it is. It is but only a symbol of that which lies elsewhere, turned into stone, yet bleeding. You also know where it lies. High on the hills, yet deep below the earth. To that shrine of the bleeding stone you shall take Paarvati, Kuntal, for she happens to be the chosen pre-pubescent virgin to carry that last of the engravings carved by the doomed princess Ambaa, to that shrine atop the Nilachal hills.

Paarvati shall carry that last engraving to where it belongs.'

The creases on Bhairavi's face reappeared with greater depth as she spoke, 'Jai Mata Taleju! Mercy, Mata, but what is the last engraving that you speak about?'

'Why,' Mata Taleju replied, 'It is that banyan leaf, but of copper, that destiny put away carefully on your roof, cushioned upon the thatch, and which all along stayed close to Paarvati to protect and keep a watch over her from above. It was only for this copper leaf above where you slept that the child came to be born.'

'Jai Mata Taleju, but why need the last engraving be taken to the Kamakhya?' Bhairavi asked again.

In response, Mata Taleju closed her eyes and said as if she was repeating someone else's words.

'Some faraway time, on a faraway land,
Unseen from where we now stand
Her yoni etched upon this sheet of copper
Shall Dakshyayani's shame surely cover....'

Mata Taleju then paused, opened her eyes and said, 'Because, Bhairavi, word once given long centuries ago is to be kept. Dakshyayani's shame lies in the Kamakhya temple and the image of her yoni, of that shame, etched upon that sheet of copper which Paarvati holds, is to be taken to the Kamakhya so that it may cover Dakshyayani's shame. That's why!'

Bhairavi froze. Her hands stiffened in a clasp. Agony birthed in her womb and circling round her navel, surged up to pierce her heart over and over. The pain was so intense that she felt as if the sickle with which she cut grass for Shamlee and the other goats swung inside her chest and beat against her back. She wailed her lungs out, or so she thought. Instead, all she did was sit in absolute silence, still like a rock. That unforeseen part of the prophesy, the one she had always dreaded to face, was unfolding.

As Kuntal helped her on her feet and they rose to leave, Mata Taleju gave each of them a batasha. Paarvati took hers in her right hand and held the other up for one more on that palm. Mata Taleju smiled and placed two more on it. Bhairavi and Kuntal touched their foreheads with the batasha before eating it and that day, lost in her own fears and trepidation, Bhairavi forgot to remind Paarvati to do so as well. And unable to resist the batasha, the little girl took a bite from it and while the sugar melted to let the sweetness spill in her mouth, she touched her forehead with the remaining bit in her hand. As they walked away from the altar, she turned back once to look at Thuloaama and aama Ahalya, to wave at them. As she did so, once more in the hazy chambers of her memory, like in a distant, fading dream, she saw herself sitting on the red chair in place of Mata Taleju. She could almost feel the softness of that red cushion she was sitting on and the feel of the uneven, overlapping red paint upon the arms of that chair. She was being held on either hand by her parents and led away from the innermost chamber of the Durga temple through the thronging devotees but all the while, she walked turning her head back, straining to look at the red chair and Mata Taleju, till people and their legs let her see the red chair no more.

Once again that day, Bhairavi came out of the Durga temple completely engrossed in her own anxiety and oblivious to the merriment of the navaratri festivities out in the temple yard. Sunrays played upon the festoons of glittering paper to send hundreds of tiny flashes of brilliant light every now and then as the festoons swayed in the breeze. Paarvati looked up. The festoons never failed to delight her. A blinding flash caught her eye and she blinked. She didn't squeal though, but the flash darted through her little mind and sparked in it the inevitable questions....*Had I too sat there on that red chair*

someday, in some past Ashutwami? Was I too someday Mata Taleju?
....doubts, thus, got sown in her little being.

Unlike other times, that day as Kuntal, Bhairavi and Paarvati left the temple yard, all three climbed down the steps of cobblestone in absolute silence, each trying to work out the doubts, fears and apprehensions gnawing into their own hearts. Paarvati climbed down the steps herself and as Kuntal watched her take the steps, he wondered if he did right by bringing home the banyan leaf shaped copper sheet with the image of the yoni on it, the last engraving as Mata Taleju had said. Now however, it could no more be undone. Or could it?

A week later, Kuntal stole out into the twilight hour before dawn and rapidly walked towards the clearing by the palace ruins, taking with him his hoe and the banyan-leaf shaped copper sheet that he coaxed out of Paarvati the previous night. Sleepy that the child was, she couldn't really fathom what was being coaxed out of her. And so she had given in. Bhairavi and Kuntal had since the last visit to the Durga temple, been trying to get the copper sheet out of her. And once he got it, Kuntal had hurried to where he found that copper sheet by the ruins of princess Ambaa's palace, buried it back into the grounds there and returned home even before Paarvati woke up. But by the time she did, the copper sheet with the engraving of Dakshayayani's yoni was back at home lying in their yard next to Paarvati. For the mongrels had followed Kuntal, dug out the copper sheet and brought it back home to their Paarvati.

'*She shall take you beyond these mountains,*' Mata Taleju had said of Paarvati even before she came to be, '*to a lesser one, there towards the east, because she shall sense a call.... She shall follow that call.... and if the Goddess receives her offering, then a bloodstone there in the lesser mountains towards the east shall acquire human form.... If such is willed and such comes to be, fertility rituals shall cease to be observed. Beliefs of the ancient past shall be thrown asunder...*' so prophesied Mata Taleju.

And now, all of it was coming to be, with Paarvati at the centre of the ensuing storm that swore to ravage heaven and earth alike.

For thus prophesied Mata Taleju.

END OF CHAPTER 12

CHAPTER 13

THULOAAMA

The wait, and the apprehension it caused, were at last over. The final words of Mata Taleju had, after all, come to prevail. With that, all fear over what the future held and all uncertainty over the prophesy's final words ever coming to pass by too had lifted from Bhairavi. What made Bhairavi panic all these past years was the wait that her worst fears would come true. It was a wait that had till then haunted her night and day. It was a wait that she often wished would end. It was a wait that made her stop living her life. So when that which she was fearfully anticipating had finally happened putting an end to her wait, the haunt and the panic that were caused by the wait too had ended. Instead, in that space within her there came to settle a resigned and aching kind of calm, one that made her surrender to the prophesy.

All of ten years now but taller and healthier for her years, Paarvati continued to walk down with other little children to the primary school in the valley below. And yet, Bhairavi noticed that her daughter was more matured than the rest of the girls her age, both in body and in mind. She continued to look for ladybirds among the wild rhododendrons and at the mountain peaks for snow, which her mai used to say was buttermilk that fell from the cups of the gods from heaven. Back at home, she continued to look forward to Shamlee's company and to that of the mongrels as well. But to them all and to her parents, she began talking more about the temple on her slate.

'Mai,' she asked Bhairavi one day, as she watched Bhairavi hang out the clothes she had just washed, 'Have you ever seen the Kamakhya temple?' Bhairavi thought a while before replying. 'Of course I have!'

'You did? When, mai?'

'I did, Paarvati, during all those times when you showed it to me on your slate.'

The little girl giggled. 'No, no! not the one on the slate. The one out there,' she said, pointing towards the distant, azure sky towards the east, 'the one on the Nilachal hills in Kamarupa.'

'No child, I have never seen it. Never been there.'

'Baba has?' she asked again.

'I'm not sure, but most likely, he hasn't either.'

Paarvati remained silent for a while and continued to stare in that same direction as if searching for the temple somewhere on the mountains in the east.

'But why do you ask, Paarvati?' Bhairavi asked.

'I ask, for I have to go there, mai, I see myself going there.'

Bhairavi had not expected Mata Taleju's words to unfold thus. They seemed to be coming true sooner than she had expected them to.

'And who or what compels you to go there?' Bhairavi asked.

'No one, mai, nor anything. But then there is no compulsion greater than when you owe yourself and your existence to someone or something,' Paarvati tried to explain Bhairavi, 'And I owe myself and my existence to that same Kamakhya, the one atop the Nilachal hills in Kamarupa.'

'You don't owe your existence to anyone, dear, you don't. You don't!' Bhairavi's panic was emerging.

Paarvati replied calmly, 'I do, mai, I exist because of that shrine.' She paused as if to recollect something and then spoke again, 'don't you remember Mata Taleju saying during Ashutwami that it was because of the copper banyan leaf that I came to be? And that I exist? Mai, the banyan leaf brought me upon the earth and protected me just so I may deliver it to where it belongs. It belongs to the altar at the Kamakhya. The one on the Nilachal hills. Take me there, mai. I need to go there. I need to take the last engraving there.' The girl was amazingly calm all through, while Bhairavi was almost in tears. Certain words of Mata Taleju during a certain Ashutwami before the birth of Paarvati rang in her ears once more, like they did so often of late.

.....She shall take you beyond these mountains, to a lesser one, there towards the east....... because she shall sense a call....

'Why don't you understand Paarvati, my child, Kamarupa is very far from here, far beyond our means to go and return home without losing our minds. Why, don't you see how master Tonkoprasad Rai returned from there?'

Paarvati did not feel the need to reply to that. Instead she said, 'Take me to Thuloaama, mai, she wishes to see me.'

As the months slipped by, a change, first subtle then significant, came over Paarvati. She began spending less and less time with her pets and more time with her slate and the sheet of copper with the engraving on it. Instead of the red and yellow lantana flowers and the soft, velvety purple goat-weed blooms, she now took to picking the scarlet buds and flowers of the kurvak. These flowers she then gently placed on the shrine she drew upon her slate. Adorning that image of the temple, sketching out details on it and comparing the image engraved on the copper sheet to the one she drew underneath the temple on her slate became her favourite pastime. Gradually, Paarvati began to perform all those rituals upon the bifurcated 'V' which were otherwise performed upon the images in the shrines where organs from Dakshyayani's lifeless body fell. In her mind, Paarvati had already begun the journey towards her calling.

'Mai, come let's go and see Thuloaama today,' Paarvati said early one morning.

'But I need to plaster the hut's walls today, Paarvati,' Bhairavi told her. The next time when Paarvati wished to go to see Thuloaama, Bhairavi said that she was not well enough to enter the precincts of the sacred yard of the temple. Another day when Paarvati asked to go see Thuloaama, Bhairavi had said, 'I would have, but the goats have eaten up the last of the grass and I need to go get some today. You don't want Shamlee and her children to stay hungry, do you Paarvati?' Paarvati remained silent. Earlier that day she had seen her baba off till the gate as he went out with the sack in which he brought grass for the goats from the mountain slopes further down. She also saw the sickle tucked into the belt around his waist. But Paarvati had by now seen through her mother's fears for not going to see Thuloaama. So that day she replied, 'Oh well then, I can walk up to the temple myself, mai, I know the way.' And Bhairavi knew she could no longer put off the visit.

As they walked down the narrow mountain path, Bhairavi asked her daughter, 'Now that we have come, Paarvati, won't you tell me what you wish to ask Thuloaama?'

'Nothing,' Paarvati replied, adjusting her slate under her arm. She carried a piece of chalk as well, to write on the slate. Then after walking some more distance, she said, 'It is Thuloaama who wishes to tell me...'

Bhairavi interrupted, 'Tell you what?'

'I don't know, mai, but in my dreams, Mata Taleju often shows me a piece of metal, round like a coin, red and engraved upon, just like the one shaped like a banyan-leaf and which fell from our thatch. Only, the one in my dreams is smaller. And in my dreams, Mata Taleju says that the round piece of metal rests, *upon the core of another human's life, upon the lifeline of a pious soul.* It waits, she tells me, to guide me to take the engraving that I have with me. The one that fell from the thatch, remember? Yes that. She asks me to take it to where it belongs.' Paarvati stepped aside to pick a cluster of dainty blue grass flowers that leaned towards the narrow foot track. Then she resumed, 'Just that, in my dreams, I seem to know even without Mata Taleju saying so, that the engraving on that other piece of metal is not just one organ but a whole woman and she sits with her legs crossed over one another. And that piece of metal is always surrounded by pale lights of the heavens, but in the colours of the earth. Then when I wake up, mai, I'm sure of only what Mata Taleju tells me and of nothing other than that. I'm not sure of that which I seemed to just know in my dreams, of that part which Mata Taleju doesn't mention. I'm not sure of that once I wake up.' She bent to look at the flowers in her hands.

'So how may Thuloaama help here?' Bhairavi asked as she too looked down at the flowers.

'I don't know but in my dreams, I get this feeling that Thuloaama wishes to tell me something.' She paused and then suddenly exclaimed as if something just dawned upon her, 'Mai! Maybe she knows about that other piece of red round metal!'

'Maybe,' Bhairavi replied calmly.

Bhairavi and Paarvati never saw the temple grounds as quiet as they did that day, without any of the jubilance, crowd and excitement that navaratri brought upon the temple grounds. That day the temple's dome seemed to reach higher into the heavens because there were no festoons to obstruct Paarvati's gaze. She never felt this serene standing in the middle of the yard of the twin temples. The only sound that floated in were the cooing of the pigeons around the temple and the infrequent, faint bleating of a goat from somewhere around the mata's cottage. A warm sun spilled down the domes and over the sleeping yard. Thuloaama was waiting for them at the entrance of the Durga temple. When she saw Paarvati and her mother arrive at the top of the steps, she sent for Hajoorbuba. Paarvati felt an ineffable lightness and joy in her little heart upon revisiting those grounds. Cherished memories brought a smile upon her face. When she saw Thuloaama, she ran across the yard into the open arms of the old priestess. Thuloaama hugged the child very close to her, long and lovingly, and let the child be there as long as she wished to. Then when the child stepped out of her embrace a button from her sweater got stuck into the necklace of brown beads on Thuloaama's bosom. When Paarvati looked down at her chest to free the button, her eyes fell on the pendant that hung from those brown beads. It was the same pendant that she had been seeing for years but only that day did she notice it. Even after freeing her button she continued to stare at it and just when she reached out with her hand to touch it, Thuloaama stood up and proceeded to enter the temple. Paarvati and Bhairavi followed her in as she walked into the middle chamber. Hajoorbuba had also arrived by then and he too entered the temple with them. Inside the temple, as they sat down, Paarvati's eyes remained fixed on the pendant upon Thuloaama's bosom. She noticed that the image in it was nude and a female and that it sat cross-legged. And when the bright rays of the sun fell on the translucent brown beads and made them appear to glow from inside, it immediately dawned on Paarvati that these were the *pale lights of the heavens, but in the colours of the earth*. Like the ones that were shown to her in her dreams.

'The pendant!' she exclaimed, though softly, 'it is that other piece of red metal, the one Mata Taleju spoke to me about in my dreams! And it appears exactly like I seemed to know in my dreams even without Mata Taleju telling me so. Yes, mai, yes! I'm sure now, mai, I am! I am! It is indeed that same piece of metal!'

'It is,' Thuloaama replied, 'and it rests here upon the core of my life,' she added, placing her right hand lightly over her heart, 'waiting for this moment.' Paarvati remembered the words, *upon the core of another human's life, upon the lifeline of a pious soul*. It was now clear to her that Thuloaama was that pious soul.

The early afternoon sun noiselessly flooded in through the row of windows, making brighter the brown translucent beads that held Thuloaama's pendant. They were sitting on small square rugs placed on equally small square reed mats. Thuloaama made Paarvati sit close to her, facing her. Then patting the child on the head, she asked, 'So it is your piece of copper that brings you here, doesn't it?'

Paarvati nodded.

'And what does the image on your piece of copper look like? You have seen the image on mine, now tell me about the one on yours.'

'You haven't seen it, Thuloaama?' Paarvati asked in return.

'You haven't shown it to me yet,' the priestess replied calmly.

'Oh! I thought you had. But nevermind, let me draw it for you to see what it looks like.' And she picked up her slate and began to draw the bifurcated 'V' that she always drew whenever she sketched out the temple she now called Kamakhya. Thuloaama looked intensely at what the child drew. Then she took the slate from her hand and placing it gently on the ground beside her, brought the child's left hand towards herself and placed it upon the pendant on her heart.

'Close your eyes, Paarvati,' Thuloaama said, 'look for what you saw in your dreams and listen for what you heard.'

The girl closed her eyes and Thuloaama remained holding her little hand over the pendant. The pale lights around her pendant first dimmed and then lit up with blinding radiance. Somewhere in the valley below, a cockerel crowed. But only Paarvati heard it. Then she slowly fell into a trance and still sitting, she saw Mata Taleju inside her closed eyes. 'In the first ambubasi that comes from now you shall be at my shrine atop the Nilachal hills, Paarvati,' Mata Taleju was telling her, 'and you shall take with you that banyan leaf shaped copper, that last remaining engraving, which I have placed in your hands. Take it deep into the bowels of the shrine. There, underneath the layers of red garment and flowers, you shall see my nudity. Cover that nudity, Paarvati, cover my yoni with your piece of the red copper.' Mata Taleju paused.

'And then?' Paarvati asked aloud but her eyes were still shut. Thuloaama and the rest heard her say that.

'And then,' Mata Taleju continued to reply to Paarvati, 'The drops of blood left over from a menstruation that would just get over shall stain the underside of that copper sheet. Gradually, these drops will dry out clinging on to the copper shield and shall become what a placenta is to the mortal's womb. They shall then together begin to feed lifeblood into that yet unseen but divine fetus that shall over time emerge as the new form of the goddess to be worshipped at the Kamakhya. Only,' Mata Taleju continued to speak to Paarvati in her trance, 'unlike in the mortal, this once the placenta and the fetus shall remain apart, unbound by an umbilical cord. Because when it comes to death and birth, the divine does not go by the laws of the mortal. Just as the yoni bleeds by the year's monsoons and not by the lunar-month's cycle.' Thuloaama's hand remained holding Paarvati's over her pendant. Every now and then, she patted this hand with the other, as if conveying some kind of assurance. Paarvati, though, didn't know of it. She only heard Mata Taleju's words still speaking to her. 'Thereafter,' she heard the Mata's voice say, 'you shall experience bliss like never before as you renounce your earthly body at the Saubhagyakund...'

'Saubhagyakund?' Paarvati asked in slurred speech, almost like talking in her sleep. This time too the rest heard her.

'Saubhagyakund, yes,' Mata Taleju went on, 'it is that body of water that lies next to the shrine, where gods had long, long ago frolicked and bathed. It is the pond of good fortune, Paarvati, it is the Saubhagyakund at the shakti peeth and you shall desire to give up your earthly form to the shrine, remaining under the waters of that pond. Because it was one renunciation that caused Dakshyayani's death and eventually for the yoni to fall at the Nilachal hills to give rise to the Kamakhya shrine, hence, it has to be another renunciation which will liberate the stone yoni from whatever agony that still remains in it and makes it bleed. Fire had destroyed, earth had sheltered, metal shall rejuvenate, water shall make to reborn and wind shall carry the news through the three worlds of heaven, earth and hell. The shrine that is but a yoni till now shall, only after receiving your form in the waters of that pond, come to have a whole bodied female deity which shall receive its divine lifeblood from specks of dried blood adhering onto the copper sheet you place on the yoni. But mind you, that shall be, if it is to be, only a hundred and two years from the moment of the renouncement in the Saubhagyakund. Though the yoni shall still remain the way it is now for a hundred and two years from that renouncement, it shall but gradually cease to bleed. With it shall cease the shame that Dakshyayani's yoni at that shrine endured till now because there was nothing to cover it from the gaze of the mortal as also from heat and cold. And *blood shall stop flowing*. Also back inside the temple, in the hundred and two years from that moment of receiving the shield, the stone yoni shall open up only enough to let rise from deeper underneath, a female form carved out of the elements of the earth. It shall appear in that same position in which you remain while you renounce yourself in the Saubhagyakund.' The vision faded for a while but reappeared soon and began speaking once more to Paarvati in her trance. 'And then once the deity has fully risen from the womb of the earth, the yoni shall narrow down.' Bhairavi and the rest sitting there saw Paarvati's body tremble for a brief moment. At that very moment Bhairavi saw that the image of the serpents which were engraved on the copper pendant that Hajoorbuba was wearing had stirred, though ever so mildly. But they definitely did stir. And in Paarvati's trance, Mata Taleju spoke on, 'Paarvati, remember, Dakshyayani's yoni shall cease to bleed and shall cease to feel any humiliation whatsoever only when a pre-pubescent virgin covers her nudity with the copper you have. Also, only if a virgin who has not yet attained puberty and who renounces herself at that water-body shall she be able to give her form to the shakti peeth at Kamakhya. Remember, this is what will come to be!'

Having said what it had to, the image of Mata Taleju in Paarvati's trance was beginning to fade away, growing smaller and hazier as it faded. 'The calling then, asks of two tasks?' Paarvati asked. This last question, however, she did not say aloud for she had gone too deep into her trance to even form coherent and perceptible words.

But before the Mata's image blurred away completely, she gave Paarvati the answer to her last question. 'You have understood well, Paarvati,' she replied, 'When the copper sheet will have covered the yoni, the yoni shall cease to bleed but only after a hundred and two years from that moment. That, though, shall be only one part of the calling. The first part. The other part shall comprise the renouncement of the pre-pubescent virgin in the Saubhagyakund.

And that renouncement shall lead to the rise of the female human form in its entirety, in the elements of the earth. But as I said, that too shall be only after a hundred and two years from the moment of the renouncement. However, only time will tell, Paarvati, as to what shall happen. Only time will tell!' Mata Taleju smiled, for she knew and saw more than what she told. 'Now rise and be in peace!'

Paarvati opened her eyes slowly and when Thuloaama lifted her own hand to release Paarvati's from the pendant, there was a drop of fresh blood on the nude image on the pendant, between the legs, in the yoni. Bhairavi shivered and quickly lifted Paarvati onto her lap. Still in shock, Bhairavi asked Thuloaama, 'What may this mean, Thuloaama?' 'Oozing from where it does, it means the blood of womanhood, fertility and creation, that which causes the observance of ambubasi in faraway Kamakhya. It foretells Paarvati's pilgrimage to that shrine when the Goddess there bleeds, during the forthcoming ambubasi.' Paarvati then looked down at her palm and raised it for her mother to see. Bhairavi looked at it and gasped, 'Thuloaama! Look!' she exclaimed.

Stains of blood from the pendant's nude image had come off on Paarvati's palm too.

'And what might this imply, Thuloaama?' Bhairavi asked, restlessness clearly visible in her now.

'I fail to understand. She has not yet attained puberty, has she, Bhairavi?' Thuloaama asked.

'No, Thuloaama, not as yet,' Bhairavi replied.

'So why might this fluid stain the pre-pubescent girl?' Thuloaama wondered aloud.

Paarvati once again looked down at her palm. It was the left palm, the one she had placed on many a head that bowed before her during the hours that she sat as Mata Taleju incarnate. 'Only time will tell as to what shall happen,' she said, as if Mata Taleju visited that abode from which, like she had said earlier, she... 'never wholly departed,' and like she had also said, '...nor would I ever wholly dwell in it again. But I shall hold this abode to my will...!' And so at that moment only for a brief while she once more came to dwell in that abode just to speak out her answer to that question through Paarvati.

Back at the ruins of princess Ambaa's palace, at that very moment when the image of the serpents on Hajoorbuba's copper pendant stirred, a butterfly rose from the earth where Brajbhushan was cremated. It then soared away into the afternoon sky like a soul liberated, for Brajbhushan's earliest engravings had served their purpose of letting princess Ambaa's tale be told, heard and spoken of outside the valley of Tilibham. Because princess Ambaa's tale would, with the copper sheet on which she engraved Dakshyayani's yoni, reach the Kamakhya temple amidst a multitude of people from all over during the ambubasi fair. And every person in that multitude would come to hear of the engraved copper sheet and of the princess who carved it. They would come to know of princess Ambaa's tale and would come to speak to others of her doomed existence. And thus the tale would spread far and wide, because of a prayer once said long centuries ago by someone upon his deathbed.

......O Universe.......And if you make these come to rest upon the core of another human's life, upon the lifeline of a pious soul to keep these alive, then Ambaa's existence too shall relive, shall come to be spoken of, heard of and shall come to be known of! Do so then what pleases you, O Universe, I offer these back to you...!

So at that moment the butterfly soared away like a soul liberated while everything else around the ancient palace ruins continued to remain tranquil as ever. Since then villagers no longer heard the tapping sound of little brass hammers on copper sheets that they used to hear till that time, even centuries after Brajbhushan had passed away. But no more since that butterfly soared away. For a soul had been liberated.

Some days later at home, Paarvati came close to her mother and to Bhairavi's dismay, said gently, 'Mai, I don't belong here.'

A stunned Bhairavi replied, 'Then where do you belong, if not here with your mai and baba?'

'At the shrine in Kamakhya. It beckons, mai, my piece of copper is sought there, I am sought there. I need to shield with my sheet of copper the organ that rests in the deep, dark core of that shrine. I also need to make it whole from part, and which mankind shall then perceive as the human form. You know mai, it is always so much easier to believe in and put your trust into something or someone you can relate to, whose form you can imagine and understand. Just so, it is so much easier to believe in and trust a whole human form, one that you can relate to and understand and can visualize, instead of just one organ and that too, one that many shy away from. I need to make that part into whole, mai, I need to become one with the....' Bhairavi could no longer keep her calm and she stopped Paarvati half way. 'Become one with what Paarvati? With what!' she asked desperately, almost screaming in her distress, 'The stone? The bloodstone?'

'I need to become one with the goddess there, with the bloodstone. Yes,' she replied with amazing stoic. That calm in her was unnerving. It devasted Bhairavi. It tore her into pieces and singed those pieces with unbearable dread like maybe Dakshyayani was once upon a time.

'But you cannot, Paarvati,' Bhairavi said holding the little girl by her shoulders and shaking her, 'no you cannot! Because the bloodstone is divine and you are not. You are human. The goddess is immortal and you are not. You are mortal, Paarvati, only the divine and the immortal can become one with the divine and the immortal. You are neither, Paarvati, realize that. And as long as you are a human and a mortal, you can never become one with the divine and the immortal!' Bhairavi was in tears now, 'Please child, you belong here. With mai and baba. With humans and mortals.' She was turning hysterical as she pointed towards the goats and then towards the mongrels and said, 'Look! Look at Shamlee, Kajlee and Dairu! Look at Kajlee's babies. There, look at the dogs. They're all mortals and so happy by just belonging here!' Her words were getting incoherent and rapid. Distressed and frenzied, she began running from one end of the yard to the other, showing Paarvati the content birds and dogs there. Her hair came loose from the bun and her saree fell off her shoulder, dragging after her along the ground. At times she choked and stammered in her panic. She once more ran up to her daughter and pulling her towards herself, cried, 'You too belong here, Paarvati, how on earth can you merge with a bleeding stone?' At last she let her hands drop from Paarvati and herself dropped upon the ground in the yard, with her head in her hands. Her sobbing shook her entire being. It shook her world. Soon her sobs grew into wails.

Paarvati sat down next to her mother and gently laid her head on Bhairavi's arm, still as calm as ever. 'And when I become one with the formless goddess there, mai,' she went on regardless, 'my form shall remain no more my own. It shall then become that of the goddess.' Like it once did during an Ashutwami when Paarvati was worshipped as Mata Taleju.

'And how do you know that it shall be so?' Bhairavi asked through her wailing.

'I know,' Paarvati replied, 'from the nude deity who sits on Thuloaama's bosom amidst the divine lights of heaven and yet is one with the colours of the earth, with its mortals. I know from that deity when Thuloaama held my hand over the image of that deity. Thus, don't you see mai that in the beads on Thuloaama's bosom, the mortal merges with the divine? The colours of earth merge with the lights of heaven? So I know from that deity that I can merge with the bleeding stone.'

'Even so, your becoming one with the bloodstone won't in any way change the occurrence of the seasons and that of the rituals,' Bhairavi argued, 'So why change that which has remained thus in balance and in peace with Creation? Why disrupt that which lies in harmony with the laws of both the divine and the mortal thus for hundreds and hundreds of years?' Bhairavi tried to dissuade Paarvati from thoughts of surrendering her life and soul at the shrine of Kamakhya. At the same time, even through her emotional trauma, it bewildered Bhairavi to think how such profound reasoning and thoughts could prevail in such a small child as Paarvati. What Bhairavi didn't realize was that these itself were signs that her child had already embarked on her calling. Over the days, she continued to cajole and talk Paarvati out of her calling. Kesari Devi's words rang in her ears, 'But what will she know how it feels to be a mother!'

True, she hadn't known what it felt to be a mother when those words were spitted at her with scorn. But now she knew. What it felt to be a mother. The longing ache for Paarvati would start in her womb and rise to her breasts. She would do all that she could do dissuade Paarvati. And to dissuade the Mother Goddess too. Because Kesari Devi awoke the mother in her. She shall plead, beg and prostrate before the Mother Goddess, Bhairavi decided. She shall confront and claim her motherhood back. And if, she thought, the Mother Goddess would still not comply, then Bhairavi would destroy herself together with Paarvati at the shrine of the Goddess. She would let all of the coming eternity question the Goddess, for she being the mother of all creation had yet failed to defend the motherhood of a woman whose long barren womb the goddess had filled herself. So Bhairavi persisted in her efforts to dissuade Paarvati. 'Let that which lies in peace remain so,' she told her, 'Nothing shall change by your answering the call that beckons you. Nothing shall change, my child, nothing!' And having said thus, her hand unconsciously reached for the soft swell of her belly. If Paarvati surrendered herself, the only thing that would change was that having proved her barrenness untrue, Bhairavi would go back to being childless once again.

'Everything shall change, mai, everything that governs the laws of both the divine and the mortal shall change. It is but only a rule of Creation that every few centuries an adversity of immense proportion occurs to wreck the heavens and the earth, leaving them both bruised and battered, only to rebuild themselves and be reborn in a different manner. It is thus only in keeping with that rule, mai, it is thus keeping in tandem with that balance that this change shall come to be. That's all. So everything shall change,' the girl went on to explain, 'everything shall change when my form shall become that of the goddess, she shall begin to be worshipped in her entirety and not just in one organ as she is now being done. Also, the yoni there shall cease to bleed and hence, fertility rituals shall be observed no more. The ambubasi shall cease to be celebrated, because blood shall stop flowing. With no fertility rituals, a furore shall lash through all life and creation. Now isn't that one thing just about everything, mai? So if that one thing changes and stops, when blood shall stop flowing, wouldn't everything change? It will, mai, everything shall change!'

'*...blood shall stop flowing...*'

The words echoed through Bhairavi's disoriented mind. She had heard those words before. Mata Taleju had told her of the time when blood shall stop flowing. Yes, she did.

'So I ought to give myself at the shrine of the bloodstone,' Paarvati continued, 'I feel so much at peace when I think of the time I'll be done with that, mai, I feel so joyfully calm from within that there is a sense of exultation in that calm!'

'But why, Paarvati, why do you have to do this?'

Paarvati listened to her mother's question and answered, very slowly, 'To ease the pain of the yoni, mai, and to shield it from shame. And I have to do it exactly then, when the organ is just over with bleeding. So that stains of the blood may collect on the copper to give rise to a new form. So that the copper shield may become, mai, what the placenta is to the child-bearing woman. So that it may bring lifeblood into the divine fetus which over time shall rise as the new form of the goddess in the shrine of Kamakhya.' Bhairavi shuddered. It shocked her to hear the little girl speak with such ease and conviction about the way life began and grew in the womb of a woman. She could not imagine that her little Paarvati knew all of it and could speak thus. But Paarvati spoke on, 'And that form will be my form. It shall be the form of a female human. That's why I have to do this.'

How much ever she hated to believe all that Paarvati had said, Bhairavi was forced into accepting the fact that some greater powers had intervened to put such knowledge into her daughter's little being. For how else would the tender aged Paarvati, yet to attain puberty and still a virgin, who hadn't seen another woman with child and who herself was raised without siblings and neighbours, among a hoard of fowls, goats and dogs, come to know of such intricacies of the womb? How would she otherwise know of how life began in the womb and what fed that newly conceived life? How would she? Bhairavi had now resignedly accepted, more out of compulsion than out of understanding, the fact that a greater power was indeed taking Paarvati towards what she referred to as her calling. 'But why you, child, why only you! Why not someone else, some other Kumari from a past navaratri!' Bhairavi was beginning to get agitated once more, 'If the goddess truly sees everything and feels every pain in every faithful,' she said, distress spilling from each word, 'can't she then feel my pain and see that I shall become childless once more if that which she prophesizes should come true?'

Paarvati rose to her feet and embraced her mother who was still sitting on the ground. 'I have been chosen for this call, mai, that's why,' she said, holding her mother's tearful face lovingly in her bosom.

'You'll be able to part from your mai and baba?' Bhairavi asked, her words muffled because her mouth still remained pressed to Paarvati, 'and from Shamlee? And Dairu and Kajlee and her babies? You'll be able to part from this home with the kurvak blooms and the dogs that always watched over you? And your slate? You don't wish to dance the jyapu ever again with baba?' And Bhairavi broke down. She cried loud and unrestrained like a child and Paarvati comforted her like a mother.

A couple of days later when Kuntal walked Paarvati down to her school in the morning, he met Tonkoprasad Rai. Kuntal did all he could to make life go on as it did before, hoping to make Paarvati forget about her calling and return to her old ways and habits, to her life as a normal little girl who feared the dark but loved the stars that dotted the darkness of the sky. He hoped to make Paarvati think of mundane things like beaded necklaces and roasted corn, like other little girls her age thought of. And so he walked her to school every morning, to make her play and talk with her friends there, to keep her away from the banyan-leaf shaped copper sheet. But it was not to be so. Tonkoprasad Rai had, on many earlier occasions, started from home to go to the school like he did as a matter of routine for years, but these days whenever he started for the school, halfway down the valley he forgot where he was heading and wandered away. So that day his son had accompanied him. When Kuntal and he got talking, Kuntal came to know that he and his mother were taking

Tonkoprasad Rai to Kamakhya during the coming ambubasi and that they were looking for people they knew, to go together. Because the journey would be long and arduous, and both his aged parents would need to be looked after. Moreover, Tonkoprasad Rai insisted on taking the black goat that he promised to offer at the shrine of Kamakhya from home itself. The proposition set Kuntal thinking because it suited him too, to have company during this ominous pilgrimage. And Tonkoprasad Rai's son was a knowledgeable young man who could manage difficult situations and had seen the world far and wide, upto the towns of Kathmandu and Pokhara.

'If we really have to take on this pilgrimage,' he tried to convince Bhairavi back at home, 'we should take it now.'

'Why now?' Bhairavi shot back, 'why ever at all?'

'But if it is so destined....' Kuntal was about to speak but Bhairavi interrupted, 'What if it is so destined? Eh? what?' She snapped, 'If it is so destined then it will anyway happen, even if we do not go on this pilgrimage now!'A deep sense of foreboding began to keep Bhairavi irritated and impulsive all the while these days.

'But now we shall have company, Bhairavi, of someone who has travelled and seen around, of someone who knows the ways of the world.' Kuntal explained.

'You and I are company enough, Kuntal,' she replied in a huff.

'But I have never left these valleys, Bhairavi, never. Why don't you see that? Kamarupa is far from here. Way too far. The ambubasi fair it seems is a massive gathering of all sorts of people, lakhs and lakhs of them, from all over the world. We don't know anyone there to seek help from and our languages vary. And most of all, look at the purpose that takes us there. It surely will be fortunate for us to have someone come along with us, someone whom we know and who speaks our tongue. If the pilgrimage is so destined, it will anyway happen even without Tonkoprasad Rai's son accompanying us. But then, look at all the peril we shall come face to face with in that case. Undersatand, Bhairavi, we shall be left to fend for ourselves in an unknown land amoung lakhs and lakhs of unknown people, amidst the disarray of a massive fair, with a child engrossed in a strange calling. So understand, my dearest, for the sake of our love and the child it begot, Bhairavi, understand!'

'Understand what, Kuntal? What peril will befall if we don't take our child to Kamakhya? I am not going, Kuntal, I am not! Nor is anyone from this household. And definitely not my Paarvati! Peril is already upon us. What more of it can befall us?' she said, looking Kuntal straight in the eyes, her own flaring with fear, anger and tears.

'Look, Bhairavi,' Kuntal said, gently kissing those round eyes glistening with tears of anguish, 'Look here. Haven't you told me the other day that Paarvati was considering going on her own to see Thuloaama since you were putting off the visit for long? Haven't you?'

Bhairavi calmed down and nodded.

'Have you seen how intensely she has been expressing the need to go to Kamakhya? Have you noticed the deep and urgent desire in her to go upon her calling?' Bhairavi nodded, still staring into Kuntal's eyes. 'You have, haven't you?' He repeated, 'So then just like she considered going to see Thuloaama on her own because we were delaying the visit, what if even this while she considers going to Kamakhya on her own if we go on delaying and not heeding her need to fulfil her call? What then, Bhairavi?'

Bhairavi lowered her eyes and brought her head to rest on Kuntal's chest. She was exhausted to the bones and sleepless for nights from trying to make herself see what Kuntal was telling her. Or rather, out of trying to refuse to give in to the fact that she had already seen what Kuntal was trying to make her see.

'The Durga temple where Thuloaama stays is still just across the valley. But think of Kamakhya, Bhairavi, you and I cannot think of going to that foreign land by ourselves to look for our little girl if she wanders away to that place all by herself. I think of and panic at such peril, Bhairavi, can you even think of the enormity of such a peril? It is that peril I speak to you of.'

Bhairavi suddenly shut Kuntal's mouth with her palm.

'Enough! Don't speak thus!' she said through sobs.

It pained Kuntal to convince Bhairavi thus, but it had to be done.

Reluctantly, Bhairavi began making arrangements for the journey to the temple of Kamakhya. 'If this pilgrimage really needs to happen, make it happen now when there is an opportunity, Bhairavi,' Kuntal had said.

This once, it didn't occur to Bhairavi to take flowers, incense sticks and home churned buttermilk as an offering to the goddess. For she was taking her only child instead. If the prophesy was to be, then Paarvati would not return home with her. How it pained! But arrangements had to be made and the day of the journey at last dawned.

It would take them four days to reach the Kamakhya temple from Tilibham, if the train from Badrikund station was on time, so said Tonkoprasad Rai's son. The journey was arranged accordingly, for them all to reach the temple in Kamarupa on time for the ambubasi fair. Tonkoprasad Rai and Paarvati, the two for whom the journey was undertaken, carried their own offerings for the goddess from home. Tonkoprasad Rai took a black, bleating goat with him while Paarvati possessively carried her piece of red copper with the engraving of the yoni on it. Paarvati, Bhairavi and Kuntal walked down to the maket place at Tilibham where they joined Tonkoprasad Rai, his wife and son. At the far corner of the street, standing against the wall of a small tea shop, Paarvati saw an old, frail woman who tried not to be seen. She kept herself hidden behind the wall of the tea stall and brought out only her head, leaning sideways, to take a quick, discreet look every now and then at that small group of pilgrims. Strands of hair that peeped out of her headscarf were white like the winter snow on the mountains. She wanted to see them and at the same time, didn't want herself to be seen. She kept standing there and straining her neck to look at them all till Paarvati, Tonkoprasad Rai and the rest boarded the almost empty bus to the sluggish little town of Deohali. Even from the bus, when Paarvati turned around to look out of the window, she saw the old woman still standing and looking at them, especially at her. She had now brought herself out of her hiding and Paarvati could only then see the woman well and fully. Fair but sagging, her skin stood out against the black cotton saree with its red border and the bright yellow misalan that she wound around her gaunt waist to keep her loose, deep green blouse firmly in place. Paarvati felt as if someday in the past she used to fill into that blouse. She didn't recognize the woman, didn't remember ever seeing her. But had anyone else from the group seen the old woman, they would have recognized Kesari Devi.

Inside the bus, the goat was tied around the neck with a short length of synthetic rope and made to sit under Tonkoprasad Rai's seat because he would not let anyone else hold it. As the old, rickety bus rambled down the curvaceous and narrow gravel road to Deohali, it stopped every time someone standing by the wayside raised a hand to board it. And thus, the bus slowly started filling in and by the time it reached the small town of Deohali, its sides were bulging with passengers. People clambered on to the roof as well. Some even clung to the steel ladder fixed at the back of the bus for porters to climb. As more and more passengers got in, Tonkoprasad Rai's goat no more remained the only goat inside the bus. And on top, on the roof of the bus, there were sheep and fowl too.

At Deohali, the bus slowed down but even before it came to a halt, people started disembarking. Because they wanted to be among the first ones to board one of the handful of the mini buses which stood by the side of the road haphazardly and which were rapidly filling up. They rushed to the mini buses to get a seat for themselves and some place for their luggage. Paarvati was slowly helped out of the bus in which they came from the market at Tilibham and she felt relieved to step out of the suffocating crowd into the open air. But before she could stretch her limbs well and fill her lungs with enough of the cool evening breeze, she was hauled into one of the mini buses. And in a few minutes' time, the mini bus with Paarvati, Tonkoprasad Rai and their families sped off to Badrikund Railway Station, throwing her sideways and off balance a number of times during sharp turns. Because the bus had to see that the passengers reached the Badrikund station on time to catch the night train to Kamarupa. Because like Paarvati and Tonkoprasad Rai, for most in that bus it would be a journey of a lifetime. No, not really a journey, it was infact a pilgrimage that had already started with their boarding the mini bus. Because most were travelling to the Kamakhya temple to be a part of the phenomenal ambubasi fair on its sacred grounds.

Swerving and bouncing along the mountainous road, the bus fumed away and reached Badrikund station just some moments before the train dragged itself into the platform along the narrow gauge tracks. And once again all of them, man and goat, were piled into the same compartment and Paarvati's epochal pilgrimage to the shrine of Kamakhya atop the Nilachal hills of Kamarupa began.

Meanwhile, at the shrine of Kamakhya elaborate arrangements began for the ambubasi fair, to celebrate the bleeding of the bloodstone.

END OF CHAPTER 13

CHAPTER 14

KAMAKHYA

Paarvati Devi had at last arrived upon the Nilachal hills at Kamarupa.

It enthralled her as she started to climb the steps that led to the Kamakhya temple. Like all others walking along with them, she too climbed the steps barefooted, into the midst of the saffron multitude of ascetics, saadhvis and mendicants. Suddenly, a loud cursing made by weirdly vibrating the lips and rolling the tongue startled her. When she turned to look at it, her little body cringed in terror. She was aghast to see an ascetic with ash smeared all over his scrawny face and body. He was drinking something from a human skull. 'Come away, child, that's an aghori. He otherwise stays where the dead are cremated.' Kuntal told her as he hurriedly pulled her away. Paarvati turned her head back to look at him and saw an entire bag of other pieces of bones lying next to him. He looked fearful in some strange, unworldly way. Kripababa had already arrived about a fortnight ago and was perched on his seat of matted beard. As they walked up the steps, Paarvati and the others along with Tonkoprasad Rai's black goat passed by the smaller shrines dedicated to the goddesses Chinnamasta, Kali and Tara. Paarvati carried princess Ambaa's last engraving, the image of the yoni upon the banyan-leaf shaped copper sheet, wrapped in a piece of brown paper and buttoned inside a small cloth bag. There was a long string attached to the cloth bag which Paarvati looped around her neck and wore the bag like a large pendant but which she pushed inside her garments. For the first time since she started writing and drawing upon her slate did she come this far from home without bringing it along with her. She didn't tire from the extensive travel and never spoke of feeling hungry or thirsty. She continued to have the same command over her bodily needs into which the aamas had initiated her years ago. Now as she merged with the milling crowd of the ambubasi fair, it astounded her that a fair could ever be this unbelievably awe-inspiring. The crowd, the uniformity of its colour, the religious zeal in the air and the sheer aura of it all were overwhelming. Her little self had never seen anything this vast and all-encompassing ever before. Nor had Bhairavi and Kuntal. The temple's dome itself, as she saw it from below while she walked up the steps, was a magnificent sight. Long strings of radiant yellow and orange marigold hung from it. And yet, the pigeons hovering around it reminded her of the Durga temple back at Tilibham. So did the steps. Only, these were not of cobblestone. Also, the splendour in the whole ambience made her forget to count the steps that took her closer to her destination, to find out whether they equalled those of the temple at Tilibham. There were a few shops along the steps that sold sweetmeats, milk tea and savoury snacks. The rest sold all sorts of bric-a-brac, including objects of adornment for the goddess. The rains were scanty in the past week in and around the Nilachal hills but during the three days of the divine bleeding they would surely fall.

'Look mai!' Paarvati exclaimed, 'the steps, the festoons, the stalls, the pigeons on the dome, aren't they all like the Durga temple at Tilibham during navaratri? Just that, mai, here everything is so expansive!'

'They indeed are!' Kuntal replied.

'And how they all have an uncanny resemblance to the temple she drew on her slate,' Bhairavi thought, 'more so as she added the details in the later days.'

'Only,' Paarvati added after a while, 'Shamlees here are so big and they roam free and close to the temple, see baba? In Tilibham they remained in the backyard of the mata's cottage.' Kuntal nodded. The rams there made Tonkoprasad Rai's black goat appear like a famished, pressed down shadow of one of them during the overhead noon sun. Tonkoprasad Rai never let his goat out of sight even for a moment. When Paarvati saw the ascetics with their limbs knotted and twisted in incredible postures of yoga, her own limbs stiffened. She saw things she never saw before, like the male nudity in its full, with only a smear of ash over it for cover.

Tonkoprasad Rai's son walked ahead of the rest and Kuntal watched as he talked to one of the tea-shop owners. Soon he returned to the rest of the group. 'That man there,' he said, motioning towards the shop owner with his chin, 'knows one of the priests of the temple who runs a dormitory for pilgrims. There'll be room for all six of us there at a nominal price. But we will have to arrange for the meals elsewhere.' Kuntal agreed. He couldn't have made a better arrangement himself, if any at all. 'The goat stays with me,' Tonkoprasad Rai announced.

The next day was the first of the three days of the ambubasi fair in the grounds of the ancient Kamakhya temple. A drizzle had already started and when the moisture laden winds rustled through the trees in the Nilachal hills and grazed past Paarvati, she felt a strange desire in her body to be touched in a way different from how mai and baba did. The doors of the temple remained closed. Outside in the yard, she saw a first-aid centre, police assistance booths and volunteers wearing badges that said, 'We're here to help.' Paarvati was also awed at the sight of the tall, very pink but freckle skinned tourists with hair like strands of jute. Mounibaba too was there, doing just that which he had been doing all these past years, since before the time Paarvati was born. In this entirely new, mystical surrounding as Paarvati was lost in sights and experiences that were overpowering both spiritually and otherwise, Bhairavi hoped for one last miracle to save her from losing her child to the shrine. She hoped, desperately, for Paarvati to forget about her giving up herself at Kamakhya. However, nothing seemed to distract Paarvati so greatly as to make her forget what she arrived there for. Rather, she resumed the rituals of bathing the image of the yoni with a passion like never before. This she no longer did by raising a mug of water above her head and then pouring the water onto the copper sheet as she used to do back at home. Ever since she arrived at the grounds of the Kamakhya, she had been bathing the image of the yoni on her banyan-leaf shaped copper sheet at dawn and at dusk by dipping it in the waters of the pond next to the shrine. Just like Mata Taleju mentioned in her trance. The one she called the Saubhagyakund. Paarvati would dip that last engraving on the copper sheet thrice at dawn and thrice again at dusk. Each time, she held the sheet long enough under water for her to finish the prayers she chanted. These were prayers she had said during her stay at the mata's cottage. Then while she held it up with one hand, with the other she collected some water from the pond and sprinkled it on herself. Once that was done, she let the morning rays of the sun fall on that engraved yoni before going around the temple once, still holding the engraved copper sheet above her head. The cleansing of these three days would be the last and final cleansing of the engraved yoni that had remained buried under the earth for hundreds of years, soiled, stained and unattended for, and collecting in the process any negativity whatsoever of the deep underworld. Paarvati was preparing the sheet of copper for the purpose it was engraved while Bhairavi desperately clung on to hope that was fast slipping away from her.

'Paarvati,' Bhairavi said one evening as they sat listening to hymns sung by a sundry group of pilgrims from lands far and diverse, 'Child, you have followed your calling and reached the shrine of Kamakhya. Now all you need to do is deliver the last engraving where it ought to be. Then we can all return home, can't we? Like you had so much to do here and so you arrived here, you also have so much to do back at home. So shouldn't you return home as well? Why can't we all go back home together?' She paused and wiped a tear before asking, 'Did I tell you something?'

'What?' Paarvati asked, without looking at her mother.

'That even before Kajlee and Dairu were born to Shamlee, she had given birth to one more kid?'

'She did?' now Paarvati turned towards her mother and showed interest, 'where is that kid, mai?' she asked.

'It died, Paarvati and I saw the agony in Shamlee's eyes then. Your grandmother thought it died because of me.'

'Why do you remember and speak of that now, mai, after all these years?' Paarvati asked.

'Because I have no more strength left in me to endure accusations of being the cause for the loss of another child, this time my very own. And this time the spite would be worse because it is your grandmother's own blood, Paarvati, her own son's child.'

The hymn rose to an exalted pitch just before reaching a climax and Bhairavi heard her heart beat loud inside her even above that noise. The pigeons had long fallen silent for the night. They had retired under the many stone crevices of the temple's dome and into the nooks around the base of the temple but sounds of stray hoots of the jungle owl in the hills and the occasional flapping of wings of the night bird reached them every now and then. All around them there were ascetics and saadhvis, hundreds of them. Some slept as they sat, resting their chins on wooden supports like an armrest while some drew passionately from their rolls of cannabis. An aghori was winding his genital around a fibula, much to the bewilderment of onlookers. Yet others were performing bizarre, unheard of feats, causing equal if not more amazement among those present there at that moment. And yet a few, like Tonkoprasad Rai's devi and saadhvi Jayantimai, groped in the shadows of the night to feed the lust of the worldly body. Others were lost in sincere prayers and meditation.

'I am yet to be told that, mai, whether I am to return or not.' Paarvati said thoughtfully, 'But why do you grieve? Even if I don't return, that would not mean the loss of your child. It would only mean that your child shall give up her mortal dwelling to become one with the divine. Your child, mai, shall continue to be with you wherever you are.'

'No, Paarvati, I don't understand such reason! No! I need my child in flesh and blood, to hold and love. I need to see her and take care of her. I do not want her unseen, spiritual presence. I want her physical presence around me, to hear her voice and feel her embrace, to see the light in those dark eyes and wipe the tears that spill out of them. I am human and mortal, Paarvati, so are my needs. I need you the way you are!' Bhairavi's words got choked, 'All of this spiritual reasoning, spiritual calling and spiritual presence, all of this is beyond me! I understand only the simplest truths of life, that we can all return home just the way we arrived here. Together.'

Paarvati sat silent for a long while before saying, 'If it is so destined.'

A streak of lightning tore through the night sky and soon after, it started raining again. The fall of large raindrops on the stone floor of the entire temple yard drowned all other sounds of the night.

The next day was the last day of the divine bleeding. The temple's doors would be thrown open the day after for all those who piously waited to be a part of the festival of fertility and creation, the ambubasi. That would also be the day when Tonkoprasad Rai would make his long pledged offering of the black goat at the altar of the goddess. During the entire stretch of the journey from the market in Tilibham to the town of Deohali and from there to Badrikund railway station then right upto that moment, he never once mentioned the devi for whom, during another ambubasi many years ago, he thought of returning and which led to the offering of the black goat, making him eventually return. But now he had forgotten that devi. More people, more fakirs and more tourists arrived at the temple grounds on that last day of ambubasi. With them arrived more goats and more pigeons. The rains poured all through the day and through the night.

Below, the raging waters of the river Brahmaputra lashed at the sides of the Nilachal hills. A clap of thunder began on the far bank of the river, rolled right across it and hit the hills close to the dormitory where Paarvati was lying with her parents. Bhairavi hadn't slept since she arrived at the Kamakhya. When the thunder drummed right outside, she thought Paarvati would get scared and so quickly put an arm around her. But Paarvati wasn't scared. Not of the thunder, not of the hours to come. She lay calm and seemingly asleep. The goat however did bleat every time a thunder roared through the night. The rains got heavier and with one massive downpour just before dawn, it ceased. It was still dark in the hills but people had already begun to wait outside the closed doors of the temple. For these would open that morning after having remained shut for three days and nights, letting the bloodstone bleed inside.

Somewhere in the plains far below the temple grounds and the ambubasi fair thereon, a cockerel crowed. In her mind, Paarvati saw its silhouette. And in the midst of the jostling crowds in the temple's yard outside, she saw Tonkoprasad Rai and his wife dragging the black goat towards the west of the temple's entrance, to a small shelter with a mud floor. She suddenly remembered aama Ahalya telling her that goats were sacrificed at the Kamakhya temple atop the Nilachal hills. She clutched the copper sheet with the engraving of the yoni close to her bosom and walked through the milling crowd of priests, devotees, ascetics and saadhvis towards the pond where she had been bathing the yoni those past days. Towards the Saubhagyakund. Bhairavi followed her. Even in that wee light, she noticed how Paarvati had grown in the past couple of months. She was rounder of body and her gait, as she walked, was no more that of a little child. Paarvati walked down the steps which led to the pond and raising the image of the yoni engraved on the copper sheet above her head, slowly stepped into the water. The air was cold from the previous night's storm, so was the water. But Paarvati didn't feel it. Bhairavi followed her into the water, nudging through the ascetics, pilgrims and devotees for space. Paarvati continued to walk further and deeper into the water. The waters first came to her knees, then to her waist and when it reached her chin, she lowered her hands with the copper sheet in them to gently dip it into the water. As she was about to dip her head, Bhairavi shouted out, 'Paarvati!' Her cry echoed through the Nilachal hills. Priests and fakirs hurried towards her but Bhairavi stood oblivious to it all. Kuntal pushed through the crowd to reach her side.

'Paarvati!' Bhairavi cried out once more, 'Don't do this! Don't!' She was getting frenetic now. It didn't matter whom she pushed or how her saree got drenched. She just plunged towards her Paarvati. But from a certain point in the pond she couldn't move any farther.

Paarvati only turned and looked once at her mai but said nothing. Bhairavi remained standing shin-deep in the waters, stiffened from numbness in the mind and the cold waters at her feet, waiting for her daughter to return to the banks of the pond. She was told that the Saubhagyakund was the pond of good fortune whose waters never ran dry. Nor did prayers said in these waters go unanswered. For it was the pond where the Gods had themselves bathed. All of a sudden, Goma's voice flashed through Bhairavi's mind. She recollected what Goma had said about this pond washing sins and granting mercy before bestowing wishes. Goma had asked her to pray and seek a child at the altar of Kamakhya long before Paarvati was born but at that time it had gone unheeded in Bhairavi. That day, however, she doled out her heart in seeking her child back. Bhairavi anyway had nothing more to lose. So now standing there in the waters of the Saubhagyakund, Bhairavi joined her hands and cupped them to collect some water from the pond and then holding that water close to her forehead, she said what she had wanted to tell the goddess. From being subdued, fearful and voiceless in the home of Kesari Devi, Bhairavi had now found her voice. But she would use it only for the Goddess to hear. Even if she offended the Goddess by speaking her heart out it no more mattered to her. No greater curse could befall her, she thought, than losing Paarvati. Angst and loneliness even in that multitude made her cry. But she yet vented all of it out on the Goddess at whose threshold she stood. She asked many a question that had never been asked of the Mother Goddess by anyone ever before. But Bhairavi asked these now. That, was she not a goddess? That, was she but a woman just like herself? Bhairavi did not pray. She just spoke to the goddess. In silence. 'Just as you are a mother,' she told the goddess, 'I am one too. Just as you love and want your children, I want mine too. Hear me out, Mata, hear me and answer me.' All around her a buzz began to rise into the morning air above the waters of the Saubhagyakund as people started reciting hymns and prayers. Some recited loudly, others softly. Some understood what they mumbled, others did not. But to them all, it was the devotion they all held at heart that mattered. 'Tell me, weren't I chaste enough for you to dwell in the child born of my womb? Weren't I, Mata? That womb, that was tarnished as barren, why did you fill it, proving all mortal wrong, including me? Why? Was it because you had your own purpose to be served or was it because you pitied and loved me?' The priest standing a little away with three other women told Bhairavi, 'Sister, you can also join us and recite the prayers after me.' But Bhairavi did not hear him. She continued her own conversation in silence with the mother goddess. 'And now that your purpose is about to be served, you want that womb to return home barren once more? Ah! What fairness is this, Mata? Is this how you reign and is this your justice?' Somebody's red hibiscus flower had fallen into the water in her cupped hands but she didn't notice it. 'If you need to cover your nudity, Mata, I have nothing to say. If you need to do so to relieve yourself from pain and shame, I am with you. That's why I have brought my child to you, as you beckoned, bearing that last engraving to where it belongs. To cover your shame and liberate you. But besides that, what difference will it make whether you be worshipped in part or in whole? In yoni alone or in full feminine form? Yes, what difference? My reverence for you shall remain just the same. So shall that of all those who bow before you. And because there is no difference whatsoever in what form you are worshipped, why take away the form of my child? Why, Mata, why?' In one of the temples below, the temple bells clanged loud and long. This Bhairavi heard. She opened her eyes and looked at her hand. The red hibiscus was still there but some of the water had trickled away through her fingers. She closed her eyes once more and continued to speak but in silence, in her mind, 'You have, Mata, the whole wide world filled with your children while I have just one Paarvati. And I wish to go on loving my only child, my Paarvati. And to love that one Paarvati, I seek her from you. Do not take her away from me. Do not, Mata, do not....!' Bhairavi's eyes opened for a split moment but in that moment they saw nothing of the outside world. As if they were deep in the waters of the Saubhagyakund and had opened only to take in some air. That taken, they shut once more and Bhairavi resumed pleading with the mother goddess. Sometimes pleading, sometimes demanding what was rightfully due to her. 'I have the power to neither make a prophesy,' she went on, 'nor to voice an ordain. And yet, I am a mother and by virtue of just that, I have the capability to love. Yes, Mata, I do. And so immensely a mother is capable of love that she can relinquish herself if need be, to nurture that love. So I am capable of that love. And of that alone. Of nothing else am I capable, no other powers do I possess. But that one power I use with all my heart and devotion, Mata, make not the future question you of your intent as a mother, towards another, right upon the grounds of your own shrine. I have not the powers to make a prophesy but in my love for my child, forgive me Mother for my audacity, I believe I have the power to undo that of another. Yes I believe in my love for my child. I do. And also in the trust I have in you Mata. I believe in you. Jai Mata Taleju!' Bhairavi paused. Because sounds of the outside world slowly, feebly, started seeping into her mind and drawing it out of its reverie. 'Now sprinkle the water over your head,' she heard the priest say. Not really realizing what had preceded, she did as was told. And along with the water, the red hibiscus too fell on her head and glided down her body along her front. As it did so, it got stuck at the fold of her saree just above her womb. Bhairavi hadn't noticed it because her eyes now searched the crowd in the Saubhagyakund for Paarvati. Paarvati, however, was easy to find, for there was no one that far and deep in the pond where she was.

Paarvati too had completed her prayers and chants by then. Bhairavi only got to see that she took three dips in the deepest part of the pond, holding the engraving of the yoni upon her head. Then she slowly, cautiously, stepped out of the water, all drenched and her beautiful dark hair sticking to her fair face. Firm buds of breasts forced themselves against her wet garment. Paarvati calmly proceeded towards the temple door, with Bhairavi and Kuntal walking beside her. They stood outside it together, waiting for it to open. The rains had stopped, the divine cleansing of the goddess was complete. The skies were slowly turning clear and blue. The mellow morning sun rose on the Nilachal hills and soon the temple doors opened. But inside the temple it was still dark. It always was, even during the brightest hour of noon. Because sunlight seemed to have devotedly left the insides of the ancient stone walls of the Kamakhya temple unchallenged. Once the doors opened, Paarvati and her parents fell in step with the crowd that jostled to reach the main altar deep in the bowels of the earth under the temple, in what the people of Kamarupa revered as the *garbha-griha*, abode of the womb. Devotees carried bright red, embellished veils of silk and brocade to offer to the Goddess. These they would lay upon her yoni. They also took vermillion to smear upon her yoni. They believed that the goddess would adorn herself that day after days of being in discomfort and isolation. That day would be her Sajaunu. Everything here was just like the way Paarvati had drawn on her slate. The yoni, which had now turned into a stone fissure between two sloping stones that met about ten inches deep into the womb of the earth, was just like the bifurcated 'V' Paarvati drew. So were the three outer chambers of the temple, from west to east. Hails of 'Jai Ma Kamakhya' rang through the moisture laden monsoon air in the Nilachal hills. As they walked past the *pancharatna*, the middle chamber, they saw severed heads of black cattle still warm from lifeblood that flowed through them a mere moment ago, laid in offering in front of an imaginary image of the goddess. This image, however, was not born with the shrine. It was placed in the pancharatna chamber decades later. Bhairavi shuddered seeing these severed heads of cattle. She placed her hands on Paarvati's shoulders from behind thinking the girl might fear the sight of sacrificed heads sitting in little pools of blood. But Paarvati wasn't. The crowd squeezed to a single line and slowly advanced down the steep, narrow stone steps that led to the garbha griha, taking Paarvati, her mai and her baba with it. 'It's a cave!' Kuntal whispered into Bhairavi's ears. She nodded. Whatever the priest chanted inside the garbha griha echoed through the stone walls of the cave, which was a part of the temple. Just like the cave that was a part of the Pashupati temple back in Tilibham. And those who were done paying their obeisance at the bloodstone were returning up those same steep, narrow steps, feeling the sides of the stone wall to find their way up through the dark. They were carrying with great reverence a small piece of the *angodak,* the red cloth with the divine blood on it. Paarvati didn't see anyone bringing back batasha with them. At last she and her parents too reached the deepest and most sacrosanct part of the temple, where Dakshyayani's yoni, turned into stone as in death but yet bleeding as in life, lay calmly wedged into the floor of the cave. The hour of the final words of the prophesy stared them on their faces through the darkness inside the temple. Paarvati tightened her grip over the copper sheet she was holding and Bhairavi tightened her clasp on Paarvati's shoulders. Kuntal put an arm around Bhairavi and held her close. The yoni, now turned into stone, lay further in a depression that could be touched only by kneeling and then stretching forward from the edge of the stone floor of the cave. Paarvati bent down, reached through the layers of red veils and gently placed princess Ambaa's last remaining copper engraving with the image of Dakshyayani's yoni upon the real, stone-hardened one. She inverted the copper sheet so that the image touched the real organ. And equally gently slid her hand away letting the layers of red cloth fall back upon the yoni as they were before.

At that moment all noise within the temple ceased for Paarvati and the only soft whisper that she heard inside her seemed to ring as if in a dream, like a promise fulfilled...

'Some faraway time, on a faraway land,

Unseen from where we now stand

Her yoni etched upon this sheet of copper

Shall Dakshyayani's shame surely cover
Ambaa, dear child, my word I give
This, for you, even in death shall I achieve...'

Back at the palace ruins in Tilibham, another butterfly rose from the rain soaked earth that very moment but this once, it rose from where Poorvimai was cremated. It soared away into the monsoon skies. Like yet another soul liberated.

Outside the temple, a thunder rolled through the Nilachal hills and a large flock of pigeons suddenly took wings, as if startled, and fluttered away from the temple's dome and the ground around it. Blood from Tonkoprasad Rai's goat spluttered through the sacrificial shed. Tonkoprasad Rai's voice rose above the noise of flapping wings as he cried, 'Jai devi! Jai Devi Kamakhya! Jai Mata Taleju!' A misty vision of the nude deity in Thuloaama's pendant flashed through Paarvati's mind. One moment the deity was bloodless and the next, there was blood where her yoni was. Then the vision faded away.

Parvati noticed one more severed head of cattle in the chamber of *pancharatna,* placed in offering to the goddess as she was returning with her mai and baba after finally laying down her sheet of copper where it belonged. The head looked like its life floated out through its open eyes and then because there was no life left to shut those eyes, they remained open. When Paarvati looked at those eyes she recognized them. Those eyes had travelled together with her from the market back home upto Deohali and then again from Deohali right upto the shrine of Kamakhya. As she walked past, she ran her hand lovingly over those eyes. A little of the blood on that head stained her hand but she wiped her hand on her clothes that were still wet.

As they stepped outside the shrine and back onto the yard among the multitude of ascetics, pigeons and revellers of the ambubasi fair, Paarvati felt a trickle of wetness sliding down her inner thigh. It slid further down till it reached her ankle and dropped onto the temple's grounds. Paarvati looked down only to see that it was red.

It was blood.

Scared and dazed that she got, she didn't hear the wails and commotion which rose around the Saubhagyakund at that moment. A child had slipped and fallen into the pond. Police and volunteers had immediately cordoned out the banks, made everyone come out of the pond and stopped more people from stepping into the water to avoid a stampede. Meanwhile, rescuers dived into the waters to search for the child.

'It's a girl!'

'It's a female child!'

That's what people started saying.

But Paarvati heard nothing of it. She saw nothing of it all either. She only saw the tiny drops of blood around her feet as she walked out of the temple with Bhairavi. The sky above turned a clear blue and the air smelt of flowers and insence, like a prayer answered.

The day after, Bhairavi and Kuntal waited at the Kamakhya Junction railway station to board their train back home. Paarvati sat quietly with her head on Bhairavi's lap. She looked pale and she seemed exhausted too. But there was a calm in her eyes. 'Mai,' she asked with a feeble smile, 'Shamlee must be missing us, eh?' She was looking forward to be home with them. Tonkoprasad Rai, his wife and son too sat at the platform with them.

'Might you like some tea?' Tonkoprasad Rai asked his wife dotingly, 'you must be tired.'

END OF CHAPTER 14

CHAPTER 15

YEAR 2121

A hundred and two monsoons had since lashed over the Nilachal hills.

And it was once again ambubasi, of the year 2121. Ascetics, aghoris, devotees, tourists, international media and a whole bevy of curious people thronged outside the doors of the Kamakhya temple which had remained shut for the past three days and three nights. While an ominous silence shrieked through that multitude, scanty clouds of monsoon hovered above. There had been no rain in the past three days and nights on the Nilachal hills. Those three days and nights were the ones that the Tantric lunar almanac had predicted as the days of the ambubasi, the divine bleeding at the shrine of Kamakhya, when rains unfailingly came down to cleanse the celestial yoni of its bleeding. That year, however, there had been no rain. Never had such a looming monsoon occurred since the time the shrine rose, when there was no rain during the sacred cleansing of the bloodstone at Kamakhya. But that year it occurred thus, causing immense dread and premonition among believers, researchers and soothsayers. And so it was that there was an ominous silence that hung over the multitude. Ambubasi that year was a dry one in the courtyard of Kamakhya. It was an omen, of doom perhaps. The skies too were dry. Whatever pathetic cloud hung aimlessly, they bore no rain in them. So the bloodstone too would be dry and bloodless, they said, anticipating catastrophe.

And now after that third and final day of the shutting of the temple doors, people waited outside, curious to see whether the bloodstone had bled that year. To see whether the angodak had turned red. For a hundred and two years ago, the last engraving had been laid to rest where it belonged. People whispered, held their breaths and waited outside to see if a full female form had emerged in place of the yoni as was prophesied. Soon the doors would open to reveal the bloodstone.

'.....blood shall stop flowing...'

What wouldn't yet be revealed was a full female form because no one would think of looking for it deep under the rocky crevices in the waters of the Saubhagyakund. When they would do so, they would see a full female form of an infant. Turned to stone over the years, bored down by water and sucked into the abyss by the hills, unseen on the surface of the pond's bed but stuck in a rock fissure much like that of the stone yoni inside the garbhagriha, like the bloodstone. They would find it lying on its stomach with the head bizarrely bent and resting on a cheek.

Just the way an infant might lie on the ground after a fall.

END OF CHAPTER 15

EPILOGUE

Princess Ambaa and Paarvati's tale is just one of the many tales that surround the many shakti peeths scattered among the deepest of caves under roaring water falls, inside dark, dense forests and high on unreachable peaks on misty mountains around South Asia. Here, every clan, tribe and community has its own intriguing lineage of divinity and royalty, and an equally intriguing story to tell about age-old practices of animal and human sacrifice, about spirits dwelling in their midst, about mysterious beasts making sensous love to their youth and about amazing legends that either bind them together in trust or keep them apart in hostility. But at the end of it all, now as I wrap up and cap my pen, I see that truth and lore have often merged into each other giving new perspective to the original truth, or whatever was known of it in the days of yore. Fable at times took over facts and at other times facts were so fascinating that they have been mistaken for fable. Just so is the tale of BLOODSTONE, Legend of the Last Engraving. So at the end of it all, Creation goes back to where it began.

Be they truth, be they tale

Lores of the ancient past,

Never cease to bewilder...

THE END